D0857532

Cause for Wonder

BOOKS BY WRIGHT MORRIS IN BISON BOOK EDITIONS
Date of first publication at the left

1942   My Uncle Dudley (BB 589)
1945   The Man Who Was There (BB 598)
1948   The Home Place (BB 386)
1949   The World in the Attic (BB 528)
1951   Man and Boy (BB 575)
1952   The Works of Love (BB 558)
1953   The Deep Sleep (BB 586)
1954   The Huge Season (BB 590)
1956   The Field of Vision (BB 577)
1957   Love Among the Cannibals (BB 620)
1958   The Territory Ahead (BB 666)
1960   Ceremony in Lone Tree (BB 560)
1963   Cause for Wonder (BB 656)
1965   One Day (BB 619)
1967   In Orbit (BB 612)

In Preparation

1962   What a Way to Go (BB 636)
1971   Fire Sermon (BB 693)
1972   War Games (BB 657)

Also available from the University of Nebraska Press

Wright Morris: Structures and Artifacts
Photographs 1933–1954

Conversations with Wright Morris (BB 630)
Edited with an introduction by Robert E. Knoll

Cause for Wonder

Wright Morris

UNIVERSITY OF NEBRASKA PRESS

LINCOLN/LONDON

Publishers on the Plains

UNP

Copyright © 1963 by Wright Morris

First Bison Book printing: 1978
Most recent printing indicated by first digit below:
1   2   3   4   5   6   7   8   9   10

Library of Congress Cataloging in Publication Data

Morris, Wright, 1910–
  Cause for wonder.

  ''A Bison book.''
  Reprint of the ed. published by Atheneum, New York.
  I. Title.
[PA3.M8346Cau 1978]   [PS3525.07475]   813'.5'2
ISBN 0–8032–0966–5   77–14594
ISBN 0–8032–5885–2 pbk.

Bison Book edition published by arrangement with the author.

Manufactured in the United States of America

Cause for Wonder

Wright Morris

UNIVERSITY OF NEBRASKA PRESS

LINCOLN/LONDON

First Bison Book printing: 1978
Most recent printing indicated by first digit below:
1   2   3   4   5   6   7   8   9   10

Library of Congress Cataloging in Publication Data

Morris, Wright, 1910–
    Cause for wonder.

    ''A Bison book.''
    Reprint of the ed. published by Atheneum, New York.
    I. Title.
[PA3.M8346Cau 1978] [PS3525.07475] 813'.5'2
ISBN 0–8032–0966–5   77–14594
ISBN 0–8032–5885–2 pbk.

Bison Book edition published by arrangement with the author.

Manufactured in the United States of America

For Leon Howard

Time Present

One

———

What led you, just now, to glance at this page? To make a beginning, right? I've always liked such beginnings as "Once upon a time . . ." Time might well be my subject. But how does one begin with time? If I knew it might help me to get on with it.

Are you sitting or standing? I'm always standing when I start a book. Ready to run if the clerk on duty catches my eye. As a rule I skip the jacket, try the first line or two on for size. A hazardous moment. What if this happened to be it? A beginning. One that might lead to God knows what end. But I'm no booklover. In the line of books I prefer the cardshops the booklover can't stomach. Sick cards, sick jokes, sick women, and a small table of books. So few that I might even read one. If there's a turn in my life it came when the sight of a lot of books depressed me. And libraries. Like a photograph of May Day in Red Square. Too many books can be more depressing than not enough. One human face is the world, but the world has no human face.

From my grandfather I have the name Warren and a bedtime story short enough to remember. It began, "I was born in a log cabin—" and there, as a rule, it ended. He wasn't, but never mind. It's the sentiment that matters. What better place to begin than with your back to a log fire? If my Aunt Winona was right he was born at sea, and toward the end of his life that's where he thought he was. At sea. And so he was. In a sea of grass. Where you begin or you end is pretty much a question of what you think.

To make a beginning was not my grandfather's problem, but it is mine. I came too late for the log cabin. The facts are dull and sworn to. 8 lbs. 7 oz., 127 Elm Street, the county seat of Riley County, Kansas. The house still stands. A swing and basket of ferns ornament the porch. A pair of stilts and a scooter made of one skate wheel lie under the steps. Where I left them. Farther back, in the powdery dust, a wooden runner sled and an Irish Mail. Ah ha, so you missed that! A small-fry velocipede more commonly referred to as a handcar. Yellow wire wheels, red pump handle, steered with the feet. You see that I speak with authority.

All of this I determined by peering through the porch slats, but one vital statistic escaped me. The name. The right sort of name stamped on the seat might have bailed me out. Mayflower, Pilgrim, Prairie Schooner, or the like. But not Rosebud. That story has been told. Nothing is worse than a story that's been told.

The summer day I stopped to determine what the name might actually be, the lady of the house, a pastor's widow, watched me through a slit in the curtains of her bedroom. Or was it mine? By right of priority. In that room, on good authority, I had been born. With my beginning, however, my mother had made an ending. I may have stood there, like a simpleton, staring. The pastor's widow flicked the curtains and a moment later latched the screen to the porch.

A few days ago I received a letter. If you're looking for something never overlook the mailbox. This letter was square, with a heavy black border. The stamp was foreign and showed a goggled, flying skier. I thought of a friend of mine who once collected stamps. I still open letters carefully, as if I had him in mind. This one had been forwarded to me from Quartzite, Arizona. I recognized the hand. My Uncle Fremont Osborn writes a fine Spencerian hand. Never to me, however. Such letters as I get from him come through my aunt, postmarked Boise, Idaho.

That in itself is a story, a beginning, and I let some time pass before opening the letter. My name had first been written with a pen that splattered the ink in an ornamental manner. No hand I recognized. Small, crabbed, and rather hard to read. Nevertheless, I felt that pains had been taken to make it legible. To get it to me. The black border disturbed me. I was looking for a beginning, not an end. Inside I found this card, with the same black border, two short black lines at the center—

ETIENNE DULAC

1887–1962

That was all. As an ending, it was more than enough. I hadn't seen Monsieur Dulac for thirty years: just thirty years. But thought of him I had. Oh yes, and often. For at least twenty years I had thought of him dead. His health had been bad. In some ways he had seemed half dead when I knew him. Or met him. *Know* him I did not. In an effort to know him I had begun something I had never finished. A book. Appropriately titled *Run for Your Life.*

It was typical of Dulac, however, to have lived so much longer than anyone had expected. As it was to send me a notice of his death. A guest in his madhouse. I was no more than that. Near the end of November, with a friend, I went out to his place for the weekend. I was there until the snow melted in March. It melted slowly. I gathered from others that was customary, although Riva is not at all close to the Alps. For several years after the war it was behind the iron curtain. I had a half-baked impulse, at the time, to go. It was about a three-hour drive from Vienna, or a four-hour toonerville trip up the Danube. You get off at Stein, then hike back up the canyon toward Ottenschlag. Schloss Riva is about a good two hours' walk. Or it was. I have sometimes wondered if the place is actually there. I might have dreamed it. Back at the time—the early thirties—I had quite a talent for that sort of thing.

The way you'll turn an imported object over to see the price tag, and who made it, I turned this card to show the backside. In the same crabbed hand a note said: *Services September 19th 4 p.m.* Today is the 15th. The card had probably been airmailed on the 8th or 9th. It seemed a little long to keep a man on ice. Did he expect me to come? I say *he,* not they, since I do know a little about Dulac. An odd one. Today they'd say he was

really far out. *He* would expect you at the services, dead
or not. That well I knew him. It didn't surprise me. Or
that he thought I was fool enough to do it. Fly a third
the way around the world for the services. That was all
in character, very much, the only surprising little item
was that after thirty years he had remembered *me*. I
had made, I thought, very little impression on him. No
question, however, that he made one on me. After thirty
years I can see very clearly his grin-like grimace, or his
grimace-like grin. I never knew which. Bad teeth. Pointed
fur hat, with the dangling tail. A shabby army mackinaw
he had picked up at an army store in the States. Spindly
shanks, wrapped in strips of burlap. In the ankle-deep
snow he looked like some sort of fabled insect. Elbows
sucked in as if breathing gave him pain. As I say, I
spent the winter as his guest—or his captive. Today I'd
say captive. Yes, I think captive is the word. He made,
as we say, attempts on my life. The phrase has an odd
ring now, doesn't it? But that was what they were. Once
on horseback, several times by snow pushed off the roof.
Tons of snow. Buried you—or me preferably—like an
avalanche.

I should add that I was not the first, nor the last, who
came out for a weekend and stayed longer. A chap from
Boston. Parmalee by name. I understand he was deprived of the boots he came out in. He could not walk
to Italy in his half sox. As simple as that. The point is,
you were always off guard because your captivity seemed
imaginary. Or merely silly. Who would believe I was
threatened by snow from the roof? Which is one problem I had with the book. As the days passed I didn't believe it myself. Nor did my public. A patron by the name

of Mr. Seymour Gatz.

In twenty years, however—no, it's now thirty—I've never lost the feeling I should have faced it out. Faced *what* out? I've really no idea. Just a feeling I have— you've had it yourself—that if you stick something out it will prove to be different. Or better yet, *you* will. But I didn't. No, as I remember very clearly I ran for my life. And that's what I called it. *Run for Your Life*. The central problem I had with the plot stems from that. Was I running *for* my life, or was I running away? There are two sides, as we say, to such a question.

Just after the war—this last war—I sent Dulac a book or two to bring him up to date. I thought he might want to run for *his* life. He had been out of this world —or any other—for several years when I met him. At the end of the twenties, he had acquired this castle, not far from Vienna, in what they call the Wachau. Three hours by car, about seven hundred years in time. Moved his wife, kids, and several half-baked friends into it. To beat the game. People thought his intention was to beat the game. That might be a little oversimplified since the move was timed with the loss of his income. He had American stocks. He did, that is, until 1929.

In the fall of '33 a mutual friend took me out for the weekend. All I had was my toothbrush and my razor. Neither proved to be useful. I had a beard and several cavities by spring, when the snow melted. Snowed in? That's how he described it. I was snowed in for the winter. Every weekend, beginning with that one, it snowed. A simple fact. No need to exaggerate. Thinking about Schloss Riva after all these years I can see the problems are still the same. The simple facts. How *not* to exaggerate. There was a time I tried to tell my friends about it, but I gave it up. I began to doubt it myself. A combination loony bin and fairy castle: odd how well they blend together. One of those castles—you don't see them any more—that ornamented fishbowls or glass ball paperweights. When I was a kid, one always set on the sewing machine. When you gave it a shake the castle inside would disappear in a snowstorm. A minute perhaps—it seemed forever—before the storm passed and you could see it. The same with Riva. Both in and out of this world. Silence and snow. In and out of this world.

As I have said, I was not the first guest, nor the last. There may have been dozens. Several were my friends. My Uncle Fremont and his new young bride spent part of their honeymoon at Riva. Mostly in bed. The only place she was able to get warm. A fellow named Spiegel, Sol Spiegel, came along in the spring and we left together. I never mentioned why I asked him to come. That I might need help to get away. He would have thought I was crazy. As wacky as everybody else. It snowed the weekend he came, but it melted fast, and we left before it snowed again. That was that.

Then there was Prutscher. Wolfgang Prutscher. He was the fellow who took me out there. A friend of Dulac, he tutored the boys in English and French. But he spent the summers out there. Not the winter. In the winter the boys were at school in Switzerland. A girl named Kitty—Katherine, that is—went out for a weekend after I left. A girl named Kitty. Note the casual way I mention it. I was the one who introduced her to Wolfgang. A fairly typical hard luck story. But I am not

without my generous sentiments. The first adult sentiment I had (and respected) was the pleasure I felt on
seeing them together. Paolo and Francesca, Abelard
and Héloïse, John Gilbert and Greta Garbo. Wolfgang's
mother, nee Pierotti, was one of those giant blonde Italians that remind you there were giants in the earth. The
Prutscher half gave him the ears and the tubercular
poetic pallor. I like to think I gave him what made him
interesting. The portrait lasted over one weekend—the
Budapest steamer excursion—when a Fräulein Metz
slipped up and told her. She had to be told. She was too
nearsighted to see for herself. Anybody but Katherine
would have loved it, but it was curtains for Wolfgang:
she turned to me. I don't know how we looked as a pair,
but I'm not Abelard.

I took her where she could buy Russ Colombo records and swim in her oatmeal-colored Wellesley tank
suit. She had the figure of a boy who had grown too fast.
I used to wonder how long it would be before she filled
out. I sensed it would not be in time for me. Nor Wolfgang. Little did we know who would be there first. Monsieur Dulac. We thought of him as an *old* man. On
Wolfgang's authority I had it that she came back from
Riva a different woman. That's how we talked in those
days. That's what a man could do for a girl! I thought
it was Wolfgang, he thought it was me, and all of the
time it was Dulac. A *man,* that is. As Katherine would
have been the first to point out.

Katherine came from Buffalo, where I saw the family
name in the paper I picked up the night I spent in the
airport. Furniture. Two full pages of knotty pine. There
was finer grain in her background. She liked Wolfgang,

but she was drawn to what she disliked. Even there I
failed her: she did like me a little. Just before the war I
saw her with her two daughters, described as fillies, on a
sports page of fetes and horses. Long braids they had,
thick glasses, and riding crops. Still a child, the older
one married a painter. Bank on me not to miss it. In the
way we never escape what we have missed, I have never
lost track of Kitty Brownell. I meet people who know
her. I see her daughters in magazines. I am often on the
verge—the verge only—of sending her a mysterious
card at Christmas. I'm still waiting for her to send one
to me. As she never tired of saying, I was just too clean-
cut to bleed.

Then there's one more: Charles Horney. The name
should be familiar. Classmate of mine. One of the mak-
ers—as I've read—of the American mind. An educator.
The celebrated Horney school is off the freeway, just
forty miles east of Los Angeles.

Charles, however, never actually turned up at Riva.
He didn't have to to smell the danger. Anything old depresses him. At the mention of the *past* he runs—runs
for his life. I wrote him some letters from Riva that
more than likely spared him the trouble of coming. His
system was threatened. The American Way of Life.

There are of course other factors. If I recommended
it highly, Charles could not bear to do it. He became a
music lover to get away from books. *My* books. But
that's personal. In his own way, he ran away from Riva
just the way I did. Ran for his life. The one he has managed to make the most of.

These four or five people come to mind when I have
a moment to think about Riva. Quite an assortment,

if you include myself. My Uncle Fremont, inventor of the dustbowl, Charles Horney, inventor of the Present, Sol Spiegel of the Spiegel Salvage Empire, Katherine Brownell, and myself, Warren Howe. If there was one thing we had in common, it was the least common thing about us. Monsieur Etienne Dulac. But I forgot to mention Seymour Gatz. He advanced me the money to write the book. It is, as he rightly says, *our* property. Our tired property. *Run for Your Life* has been on the open market for just twenty-eight years. Just this morning it went off. But I go too fast.

Yesterday, just yesterday morning, I received another notice from Monsieur Dulac. The same notice, but this was sent to Charles Horney, who forwarded it to Spiegel, Spiegel to me. How explain that? Thirty years ago, when I was at Riva, I may have used Horney as a forwarding address. I used anybody who *had* an address, and he had. Recently, Sol Spiegel has been buying his used school furniture. They're quite a pair of hens. When they get together they probably gossip about me.

But why had *he*—why had Monsieur Dulac—taken the trouble to airmail me two of them? The one Spiegel received he opened. On the envelope flap he jotted:

Sorry, Mr. Howe. Need new glasses. Think the old coot would still have that wooden Indian? If you go, make him an offer. Wire me collect.

That wooden Indian, a cigar-store warrior, stood in one of the dark rooms at Riva. Scared the hell out of people. Stood there with his tomahawk upraised. Big fellow with glass eyes, human teeth in his open mouth. I won't get into a description now, but the place had some strange junk in it. A rusted metal plow seat Dulac had found in Kansas. (Before he settled down at Riva he did some traveling.) An early barber chair he'd picked up in Iowa. The plow seat he had hung on the wall, like a trophy, labeled with a tag *Early Bronze Age Armor.* You won't believe it, but that's how it looked. Precisely how it looked. The place was ornamented with stuff like that, some of it with a label, some of it in glass cases. A loony bin? It's one of the touchy points.

Last night I went to bed early. But I didn't sleep. In a small way, a small piece of time seemed to stop. A little corner, say, of the sprawling canvas of my life. One of those fragments you see enlarged in the books that show the artist's technique, his brush strokes, and his talent. I saw before me an evening in my boyhood when I went ice skating on a pond in Kansas City. Not my town. I had just been there a few days. The ice froze while I was there, and I wanted to skate. I had a pair of the sort we called tube skates, racers, which I'd bought in a secondhand store in Chicago. Too big, but I looked forward to growing into them. This has not changed. I still look forward to growing into something. With these skates I took a streetcar and went out to a pond where kids were skating. They had a log fire burning. The ice was like glass. There were stars in the sky.

So what happened? I got cold feet. Otherwise absolutely nothing happened. I did not see a pretty girl, meet a new friend, feel the pangs of love, loneliness, or remorse, or suffer too much from the cold on my cracked front tooth. I skated with my customary self-esteem, got cold feet, departed. So why should I think of it so many years later? But that's just the point. I didn't. It was not

later. Not that particular piece of time. It was right
there, cold and sparkling, in bed with me. To be reasonably accurate, *I* had changed, but that night had not.
The fire still crackled, the ice creaked where I passed
over it like a bat's wing, my breath smoked white, my
nose ran, my toes were stiff in wet socks. So what is it
we mean by *now* and *then*. By present and past? I don't
know, understand. I'm just asking. This fellow Dulac,
dead now, seems as clear to me now as he did at the
time, maybe a bit clearer, as if I'd wiped him off with
my sleeve. He had soft baby hair. An unimportant detail, but that was what he had. Usually whisked up to a
point, like Baby Snooks, by the way he wiped off his
hat. I remember as if it was this morning where he
liked to take his sun bath. Unobserved, he thought.
Where the winter sun warmed the outer court. He would
lie there like an animal, sunning. He would open up his
mackinaw, tied with string, so that the sun would warm
his chest. White as a woman, hairless, with the nipples
like pink buttons. From where I spied on him his torso
looked like a mask. The nipples were eyes, the round
little belly button a mouth. I see now that I always
thought of him, or saw him, as something other than he
was. An insect, say, or a mask. When he was on horseback, he seemed part of the horse. You see what I
mean? It is hard not to exaggerate.

One day I came upon him barefoot beneath one of
the trees in the orchard. In the snow, that is. Barefoot
in several inches of snow. We were having a sort of
warm spell, an early false spring. He stood beneath this
tree using a stick to knock off a few withered apples.
Crazy about withered apples. Carried them in his pock-

ets and ate them like nuts. It was a scene painted by
Breughel, and when I look at Breughel, I think of
Schloss Riva. A landscape with figures. None of them
peering out. Would you say they were *in* time, or out of
it? A clever fellow, that Breughel. One of the few who
could make time stop.

My friend Seymour Gatz likes to say, "Old sport, I
got news for you." Although he seldom has. The news
is never for me. This morning, however, Drusie called
me to say, "Hold on a minute, will you?" I held on
about ten, and then the voice of Gatz said, "That was
Vienna, old sport. I got news for you." I should tell you
he does not refer to many clients as *old sport*. "You
know Ehrlich, old sport?" We all knew Franz Ehrlich
as the man who had put two hundred grand into a sce-
nario entitled *No Place to Hide,* just a few weeks before
the new shelter program. It looked great at the time.
"Ehrlich wants it, old sport."

"Wants what? A better place to hide?"

"He wants our property, old sport. He wants you to
fly over, show him around."

"He wants *Run for Your Life?*"

"Not exactly, old sport. Just the property. He's got no
place to hide. He thinks that might be it."

"He won't like it. There's no plumbing."

"You hear me, old sport? He *wants* it. He'll pay
twenty-five grand for it. All he wants to know is that
the place is *there*. It's the real estate he wants."

"It's there, all right, but he isn't. I just got word that
he died."

"He who?"

"Dulac. The madman who owns it."

"Ehrlich don't want *him,* old sport. If he did it would be extra. Just the real estate."

"There's been a war, but it was there when I last saw it. It's a lot to move—even for the Russians."

"He's dead, old sport? We'll do *Run for Your Life* next. When the property is old enough, old sport, it's new." At that point Drusie interrupted to say, "Honey, long distance calling." "That's him!" cried Gatz. "I'll call you back. I'll tell him if you're free you'll fly over this weekend. He'll pay the fare. Free weekend in the Wiener Wald, old sport. What the hell!"

I didn't believe a word of that, but anything long distance—or even short distance—throws me into a panic. I'll agree to anything if I can't reverse the charges. "I'll call you right back, old sport!" Gatz said, but it was some time.

My apartment overlooks the sea and the new raw hole in my neighbors' yard. Nice people. Keep their TV low and their bedroom shutters drawn. I often window-sit their children while their mother does a little shopping. She is worried, as she might be, about that hole. In my time the kids crawled into iceboxes; now it's holes. Sign of the times. Part of the nationwide movement to find a way out. This morning the swimming pool contractor came to fill this one with concrete. But it's not for swimming. Nor for tanning. The contractor refers to it as a shelter. Just a shelter. The word fallout depresses him. All of the holes he has built in the past were holes to fall *in*. This one is where my neighbor will retire when the warning sounds—with her loved ones. Her husband may not make it, since he works four miles away. *I* just might, she has hinted, if the traffic snarl holds hubby up. She has room for four, including a poodle and a cat named Butch.

Is this part of the story? It's part of mine. I was still sitting there, an hour later, when the phone rang again, and it was Gatz. "It's settled, old sport. If it's there, he'll buy it. He'll pick you up Saturday morning in Vienna. I got the check here now. You like to stop by and pick it up?"

That's where I am now. The West Coast office of Seymour Gatz. TV scripts are piled around the walls like sandbags and the current is off in the water cooler. Not the sort of place where the East Coast talent feels at home. The window overlooks the noonday smog on the Sunset Strip. Just up the street Thunderbirds stand in line for lunch at Scandia. I see a lightly basted arm on a polished initialed door. Tan appears to be slipping. Pale or consumptive ivory may be coming in. For those naturally ill or undernourished, things may be looking up.

It is now ten past twelve, on Tuesday, the 15th of September. I read that on the calendar clock that sits on the desk. A man sits behind it—to use the term loosely —a telephone to his ear, a rapt expression on his face. Did I say he was *here?* The rapt expression is proof that he is not. No, Gatz is not here. He is *there*. What enchants him is that he is now in New York. Another time and country.

This is west Los Angeles. The phone cradled in the

folds of his neck means that the air he breathes is not in this office. It is the pure carbon-monoxide gas over Madison and 48th Street. A call to New York for Gatz is less a matter of business than metabolism, both of which are good. Sometimes he passes me the phone not to hear what is said but the sound of the traffic, taxi horns, and the drills tearing down or putting up something. Music to his ears! It is salvage that speaks to Gatz. It is why he has a controlling interest in me. "Old sport," he likes to say, "you're not with it." By which he means I'm ready for salvage. By which he means I drive a '57 Studie, when it chooses to run.

Gatz began to call me Old Sport in college after reading a book by F. Scott Fitzgerald. Sometime later I began to call him Gatz-A & Gatz-B. Gatz-A lives in the here and now, he drives a Mercedes coupe, and he is very much with it. Gatz-B lives where the inessential present melts away to the essential myth, the fresh green breast of the world that enchanted Dutch sailors' eyes. His taste for salvage is his instinct for survival. If a first-rate mind is one that can hold opposing ideas and still function, Seymour Gatz has a first-rate mind, and I do not. To see Gatz, you must stand back. The close-up tells you nothing. He is huge, seal-shaped, and known as Kewpy to his tax-deductible clients. Loyal, affectionate, and brutal, I know him well. I have never seen him without his clothes, nor do I know what he thinks. I like him, and he likes me. Proof—he says—that I have talent, but no taste.

There are two watersheds to the continent of Gatz. One flows eastward to the sea via Tinpan Alley; the other, loaded with paydirt, flows westward to the Sunset

Strip. From one he pans gold, from the other sentiment. He has an instinct for the sure thing about to fold. When we eat in a place I notice it is often for the last time. He will take a quick look around for anything that might be salvaged: a piano, a piano player, a hatcheck girl who wants the chance to make good. Gatz will see that she gets it. He will be around to salvage what is left.

His office, however, is not the sort of place you feel at home. No chairs to put your feet on, no key to the men's room with a tag for mailing, TV scripts instead of carpets from wall to wall. Some of them are mine. The small painting above his desk, a Dubuffet, like the man behind it, is an original. He will give it away to ease the blow on his income tax. There is a stain on the wall where he rests his head, as he does now, when he tilts his chair back. Just to the left of the stain is a cork dartboard, most of the target chewed away, all that remains of the Gatz-B past of Gatz. Several slips of paper are now pinned there by featherless darts. In the old days we used to play. They are now used to pin down urgent messages. From where I sit I can see one that reads CALL HOWE. Which he did. "Old sport," he asked me, "how you like it? Two fares one way. One fare two ways?" When I didn't reply he said, "Take along a little friend. Make it a long weekend!"

That made me smile. The weekend I had spent at Riva had lasted about four months. What if this one proved longer? A friend, preferably not so little, might have his or her points. Charles Horney, for instance, might be curious to see if there was any truth in the letters I wrote him. So would I. They cost me a lot of money to mail. Not always my money, since Charles always enclosed a dollar for stamps. If not Horney, perhaps my Uncle Fremont Osborn. Through a fluke he had actually been there. He might currently be looking for a place to hide.

As a last resort there was Spiegel. He might want to buy more than the wooden Indian. He didn't like to fly, but he would if it was deductible.

"Glad I'm sewed up for the weekend," said Gatz. "Know what scares me? A place to hide. What if I liked it?"

Drusie interrupted him to say that New York was on the line. The mouthpiece to his lips, Gatz settled back, inhaling deeply.

"Make it two one-way," I said to Drusie, and took from the jigger on her desk one of the quill toothpicks that finished, as she said, what the tooth brush left undone.

Two

My uncle, Fremont Osborn, came too late for God and too early for the Farm Security Administration. They might have fruitlessly advised him that where he planted wheat in Texas it seldom rained. Not that it would have helped. He was not a man to take advice. He was a farmer, but he never noticed, with his eyes on the horizon, the color of the sky. Fremont Osborn was born a few miles west of the line that divides the long grass from the short grass country—or it did, that is, until he came along. For thirty years the line has been concealed by drifting sand. With a small assist from me, Fremont Osborn invented what we now refer to as the dustbowl, staking out his claim near Hereford in the panhandle of Texas. Virgin soil. Never turned by a plow. In the winter of 1923 he turned up fifteen hundred acres of it. That winter it rained. He had to go to Tulsa to get help to harvest the crop. In the winter that followed the soil began to blow. Even the Indians had a word for it—wrong side up.

When I showed up, five years later, it had not rained for seven years, and there were large raw blowouts on his land that looked like shell holes from a plane. He cursed the wind for that, pulling off his mitten to shake his chapped clenched fist at it, his mouth almost closed, the roots of his teeth caked with dirt. But what he didn't eat or swallow blew away. As you may remember reading, some of it darkened the sun over New York. He was a pioneer, my uncle, one of that fearless breed of land pirates who took possession of, and broke, as they say, the plains. He was now living in Quartzite, Arizona, at the La Golondrina tourist court. A handyman. That he had always been. I see him now, something more than lifesize, the crack of dawn like a bow between his legs, crossing the yard toward his tractor with a milk can in each hand. Full of milk? No, kerosene. He was about to break the soil with a gangplow on a new piece of un-broken land.

I haven't set eyes on him for thirty years, but I hear about him at Christmas. My Aunt Winona encloses one of his letters with her Christmas card. She's in her sev-enties, he is now eighty-one. For approximately seventy years he has shocked and pleased her with his agnostic opinions. Her faith remains unshaken. His opinions un-changed. The last letter from Quartzite was dated No-vember, '61.

NONA DEAR:

Took a run up to Oakland a few weeks ago, looked in on Myron's family. His big-ankled Frau

tells me she contacts his spirit daily. Know what
he told her? That I come just to borrow money.
Can you beat that? She comes down to these parts
now and then to attend a big spiritualist conclave.
She really thinks she communicates with all her
loved ones' spirits, whatever that is.

Seems now that Violet's got a little money she
feels it burning a hole in her pocket. Al still looks
good. Tells me he hasn't changed a bit, in spite of
thirty-four years with that woman. You speak of
Donna. I recall her as a very sweet kid. Damsite
more sense than her mother. I got so interested in
your letter I came near forgetting the afternoon
dance. Still like to swing the girls, some of 'em
half my age. Old Abe Lincoln, God bless him,
said, "God surely must have loved the common
people he made so many of them." And so it is
with the ladies. Which reminds me:

> King David and King Solomon
> Led merry merry lives
> With many, many lady friends
> And many many wives.
>
> But when old age crept up on them
> With many many qualms
> King Solomon wrote the proverbs
> And King David wrote the psalms.

I suppose I'll carry on till I'm carried off, but
I better get this over to the P.O. first.

LOVE

FREMONT

When I was in college, a sophomore, my Uncle Fremont appeared on the campus and asked the first student he met to be directed to his nephew, Warren Howe. They used the campus, in those days, for movies, and my uncle resembled one of the extras. He wore stirrup boots, a string tie, and a suit like those of Alfalfa Bill Murray. That afternoon I was in a seminar devoted to the poetry of Keats. We sat in a room with the windows open, and through one of them I saw my uncle approaching. His hands were free, but he walked, or rather cantered, as if he held a milk pail in each hand. His escort trotted at his side. Shown to the room, he took an empty seat as if it had been for him the class had been waiting. He sat attentive, squint-eyed, with his broad-brimmed hat in his lap. Perhaps I had never looked at him before. A plainsman, a seaman's colorless eyes in his weathered face. In the dim light of the room he seemed to grin with his customary squint. His hat removed, he appeared to be freshly scalped. About him, however, was the perceptible aura of something unique, an uncaged but exotic bird, or more accurately, a hawk or falcon perched without its hood. Serenely detached. Disturbingly self-sufficient.

What did I *feel?* I hardly knew, never before having felt anything like it. Pride in my kin. An unheard-of sentiment. He listened attentively to the teacher read aloud passages from "Endymion," and when he had finished courteously asked if he might have the name of the poet. With a borrowed pencil he jotted it down on the back of a card he took from his pocket. On the front of it was a snapshot. Of whom? My uncle, Fremont Osborn. Bound together with a piece of elastic, he

had perhaps two, or three dozen of them. He asked Percy's permission, as the class broke up, if he might offer the cards to some of the young ladies, who might in turn pass them on to a possibly interested party. Interested in what? In holy matrimony with my Uncle Fremont. His name, age, and Texas address were stamped on the card. I was the last to leave the room, too late, happily, to receive one of the pictures of my Uncle Fremont, his hat off, his brow scalped, his seaman's eyes fastened on the horizon. Together we walked silently to the station, where I saw him off. Five weeks later he wrote me he had found the woman he wanted, a Pasadena widow of comfortable means. I never met her. A few weeks in the dustbowl changed her mind. He had more cards printed, and sent me a packet of them. Two years later, back in Kansas, he found the ideal mate he wanted, and it was with her he came to Europe and Schloss Riva on his honeymoon. A Gladys Bekin. The honeymoon ended the spring they returned to Texas. A soft woman? Let me tell you what it was like.

The town of Hereford is in the panhandle, about forty miles west of Amarillo. Quite a big town now, but thirty years ago you went in by bus, only cattle trains stopped. I remember two, maybe three buildings, set on the plain as if the water had receded. Nothing else. A dead sea, a luminous sky. I was born on the plains myself, but it is *this* plain I remember. Empty. Offering no place to hide. Only now, of course, would I put it like that.

I came in at dusk, and a clerk in the store came out and pointed in a westerly direction. No road. A few wagon tracks in the grass. Off there—he said, wagging his finger—about two hours' walk was my uncle. I should follow the fence on my left, keep my eyes on the tracks. As soon as the plain was dark I would see the lights. Of his house? No, of the sweeping beam of his tractor. They would come and go, of course, as he circled his section of land. Twenty-three hundred and forty acres the day I arrived.

On the clerk's suggestion I left with him the brown fiber suitcase I was carrying. It was heavy. I had before me a twelve-mile walk. I got off about a quarter mile when he whistled me back to deliver a letter. One for Fremont Osborn. I had written it a week before, myself. It contained the happy news that I was coming, and hour of my arrival.

About ten o'clock, and ten miles later, I saw the glow of the lights of the tractor, and maybe forty minutes later the wind blew me the *cough-cough*. A lamp no brighter than a candle marked the house. Sometime around midnight I delivered the letter to a man filling milk cans by the light of a lantern. Preoccupied. Unaware that I was walking up. The man turned out to be my Aunt Agnes, getting ready to take her turn on the tractor. Her husband, Fremont, had just come off it and gone to bed. He would sleep six hours, then take it again at dawn. That is, I would. To do just that was why I had come. We stood there together while she read the letter, announcing in eager terms my arrival, the tractor coughing like a dragon, the lights flickering as the motor idled. Together, silently, we returned to the house. In a dark, windowless room, my uncle raised on his elbow to greet me. Had I no bag? Oh yes, I had left it in town. Without raising his voice he cursed me, fluently, impersonally. Did I realize if I had brought it along, it would not be necessary to drive in and get it? I was slow to realize it, other things being on my mind. In the lantern light I saw my uncle's face, his colorless eyes. Dust caked his lips, dirt caked the roots of his teeth. Rabbit hair from the earmuffs of the cap he wore stuck to his ears. He said he had no time to sit up talking, nor did I since I would take the tractor in the morning. His wife Agnes would show me to my bed, which she did. How did I sleep? I slept fine.

I slept fine the twelve weeks, five days, and nine hours I was there. Every hour counted, I counted every hour. For my sixteen-hour day I received twenty-five dollars a month. And my keep. I've always loved that word *keep*.

In the morning I saw nothing but the food on my plate, the slit of light at the window. It was on the horizon, but it might have been attached to the blind. Dawn. Sunrise would not come for another hour. The wind blowing under the house puffed dust between the floor boards, like smoke. There was never any talk. My uncle would slip off his coveralls, like a flight suit, and eat in his two suits of underwear: one of fine, snug-fitting wool, flecked with gray, like a pigeon; the other of heavy nubby cotton flannel with the elbows patched with quilting, the fly-seat yawning. The outer suit came off in the spring, but the fine inner suit was part of my uncle. In the three months I was there it came off just once. I saw him, like a plucked chicken, standing in a small washbasin of water while my Aunt Agnes wiped him off with a damp towel. Dust. He was dusted rather

than washed. I learned to leave a film of it on my face
and wrists to prevent chapping and windburn. Under
the suit of underwear I seldom took off my skin was
talcum'd like a baby. The layers of wool filtered out the
coarse stuff, left a powdery ash.

Where did it come from? The prevailing wind was
reasonably clean until it reached the rise where my uncle and I were making history. From the blowouts dust
blew off like smoke from a grass fire. Some of the natives thought it was. They reported the matter in Hereford. No matter from what angle the wind blew, it blew
the dust in my face as I plowed around the section.
Sometimes I had to stop the tractor till the air cleared.
One day I crawled beneath it and bawled. At the mercy
of the elements, the element I feared the most was my
Uncle Fremont. What God was he fighting? In his opinion all Gods were dead. What did he want of a flunky
like me?

In that respect he resembled Monsieur Etienne Dulac,
of Schloss Riva, who liked to put his guests, me in particular, to the test. To prove what? God only knows. In
my case it merely proved that the flesh was weak. A
great believer in progress, and one of the soldiers in
Colonel Ingersoll's agnostic army, it had not occurred
to me that my Uncle Fremont had something in common with the Meister of Riva. Temperament? Something more than temperament. They had disliked each
other on sight—less than sight. A Texas Yankee in King
Arthur's court, my Uncle had hardly arrived at Riva—
he handed me the two bags he was carrying—when he
stopped to inspect the medieval machine we used to
raise buckets of rocks from the deep dry moat. A primi-

tive winch. You can see them in the drawings of Bosch.
At the sight of this object he almost died laughing. Was
I crazy *too*, he wanted to know. He decided to extend
his visit at Riva until he had introduced certain im-
provements in the way we pumped water, raised rocks,
sawed wood, and cleaned snow from the roofs. He had
seen idle men in the streets of Muhldorf: he would put
them to work. If the idea was to rehabilitate Riva, then
get on with it. He was not able to get on with it, himself,
due to something unforeseen the following morning.
Snow fell on him. A ton or more of it from the roof.
It didn't kill him, but it did leave him impressed. I tried
to explain that it was not unusual, that it happened frequently. Just a week or two before it had fallen on me.
The slam of a door might set it off—among other things.
Allowing for a day and a half to recover, my uncle and
his bride cut their visit from the week they planned, to
the weekend. I rode down with them as far as Stein, and
walked back. He advised me to leave before—as he said
—I was nutty as Dulac.

The castle in the Wachau and the shack on the panhandle had certain things in common. A place to hide?
Some might put it like that. I'm thinking of the way one
thing seemed to prevail: the snow and the wind. At Riva
the snow sealed the place off like that castle in the glass
ball. On the panhandle we were sealed off by the wind.
Impersonal, impartial, mindless, inexhaustible prevailing wind. In three months there must have been one
windless day, but what I remember is one windless night.
Like a clap of thunder it woke me up. As if a supporting
hand had been removed from the wall, the house shuddered. Silence? How describe it as louder than noise? I

raised on my elbow in order to breathe. The silence of planetary spaces broken only by the music of the spheres is now an abstraction I find easy to grasp. A lull—that's all it would be—in the prevailing winds.

That morning I heard the crack of dawn like a whip. Just as, less than an hour later, I could peer out and see the wind where there was neither dust, lines of wash, nor even grass to blow. The yard was like a table, with a dull, flat gloss where the shoes buffed it toward the privy. Scoured by the wind, the cracks had been picked clean by the chickens. Out there, as nowhere else, I could see the wind. The five minutes in the morning I lay in a stupor listening to Agnes build the fire, I would face the window, dawn like a slit at the base of a door. In the kitchen Agnes would put fresh cobs on the banked fire. Was it the sparks in the chimney, the crackle in the stove? The cats would hear it, five or six of them. With the first draw of the fire they would start from the grain sheds toward the house, a distance of about one hundred yards. Was that so far? It can be if you crawl. In the dawn light I would see only the white cats, or those that were spotted, moving toward the house like primitive or crippled reptiles. How explain it? The invisible thrust of the wind. The hard peltless yard gave them no hold. Even the chickens, a witless bird, had learned never to leave the shelter of the house at the risk of blowing away, like paper bags. A strip of chicken wire, like a net, had been stretched to the windward of the yard to catch them. They would stick like rags, or wads of cotton, till my aunt would go out and pick them off. The cats and the hens were quick to learn about the wind. That it would prevail. My Aunt Agnes knew, but preferred not to admit it. The last to learn was Fremont Osborn. He hung on for two more wives, and ten more years. When the last of his money was gone with the wind he went back to his homestead on the Pecos—and from there to Quartzite, where he was known as a handyman.

In the early thirties I doubt if the town of Quartzite was on the map. One of those gas pumps where cigarettes, aspirin, coffee, and water were sold. In the late forties the new gold diggers, armed with walkie-talkies and Geiger counters, found deposits of uranium in the nearby hills. The town is now the home, as the sign says, of 38,000 friendly people, all of whom will greet you with *howdy, stranger* at the drop of a hat. Most of the friendly inhabitants still live on wheels. They sit hub to hub, in trailers, on the man-made mesas at the edge of the freeway. In the desert light it is often hard to tell if they are putting up a town, or tearing one down. I came in from the west, past a sign that warned me to keep an eye out for children, and another that advised me it was 2740 miles to New York.

Due to certain accidents of my boyhood I feel that time exists in space, not unlike the graphic charts that hang on the walls of up-to-date schoolrooms. On these charts the past lies below, in marble-like stratifications: this sort of time can be seen better at the Grand Canyon than on the face of a clock. A young man born where the 98th meridian intersects the 42nd parallel might also feel that time, like space, has a point of departure and a direction. I'm sure that Fremont Osborn did. The past lay to the east—from where one had come. The future lay to the west, where one was going. In *my* time, these

directions were reversed. The past—the mythic past—
lay to the west; the beckoning, looming future lay to the
east. A sense of direction does not come easy to Americans.

At the west side of town the trailers merged with what
we describe as mobile homes. My uncle's court, the La
Golondrina, featured a sign on which a bird had been
painted. It set back on what was left of the old gravel
road. It had once been a campground—a sign reading
FREE WATER was still nailed to the trunk of a sycamore.
Parking space was now renting for $20.00 a month
and up.

In the mid-afternoon a light burned at a trailer with
a strip of aluminum awning, a snatch of picket fence
ornamenting the steps of the porch. A placard with the
word OFFICE was wired to the screen, to the right of it a
notice advising late arrivals to ring the bell. Before I
buzzed it a hoarse voice cried, "Yankee, go home!
Yankee, go home!" A molting parrot, chained to a
perch, eyed me from where he dangled head down. Just
beyond him, undisturbed, a woman crouched in an arm-
less rocker. White-haired. She sat leaning forward as if
about to rise. Hard of hearing? Neither the bell nor the
parrot disturbed her. The window toward which she
leaned forward to peer was a TV screen. On it, a man
stood alone, hatless, half bowed as if in prayer. A hushed
voice enjoined quiet. A dignitary visiting a shrine, perhaps? A religious service? My nose pressed to the screen,
I could see that the hatless gentleman held a stick. After
a moment of concentration he made the putt. With her

I watched the ball arc toward the hole—but I did not see it drop. She had leaned forward so that her head blocked my view. A shout from the crowd seemed to lift her, then the fall set her to rocking. In the general excitement the parrot croaked, "Yankee, go home!"

"We're full up!" she said without turning. I watched her adjust one of the knobs for sharpness.

"I'm looking for a Mr. Fremont Osborn," I called. "I understand he lives here."

"Who?" she barked, then, "Oh him." She got up from the rocker to unhook the screen. Without glancing at my face she wagged a finger in the direction of a tree. "He's under it. If he's not there he's fussin' somewhere. You just wait."

To get to the tree I followed the lane used by the trailers. License plates were used to ornament the doors, seal up the cracks. A dog my uncle would have called a little fice trailed along. Several trailers occupied the leaky shade of the tree, but one sat back so that it leaned against it. Both the trailer and the car sat up on blocks. The car, a Ford V-8 coupe, had the weathered coloring of a desert reptile. The hood was honed down to the metal, the upper third of the windshield like frosted glass.

The dust did not blow like that in Quartzite, but during the war, and the late forties, my uncle lived in the car on his homestead along the Pecos. It had become a piece of the landscape, an armor-plated fossil with a single frosted eye. Cans for gas, oil, and water were now in a rack on the running board. A patch of grass, a little larger than a doormat, grew between a frame of white-washed rocks, a slab of petrified wood placed in the exact center, like a petrified eye. My uncle was a great one for natural wonders, excluding man. His temple of worship was the Carlsbad Caverns—caves appealing to him more than canyons—where the architecture was known to be thirty or forty million years old. To free my mind of certain crass superstitions he took me to the bottom of the caverns, where the tourists, holding candles, assembled to sing the hymn "Rock of Ages." This spectacle brought tears of laughter to his eyes. Smaller in scale, but of the same order, were small bits of crystal known as Pecos diamonds, found around the holes of small desert rodents. They were like tiny stubs of pencils, made of rock. Six-sided, sharpened at both ends. To my Uncle Fremont they testified to the subtle craftsmanship of the Devil, gems from his workshop, to stupefy the crude craftsmen of the Lord. If they defied Aunt Winona's explanation, it pleased my uncle to think they defied all others. When I left the dustbowl for college he presented me with a Bull Durham sack of his Pecos diamonds, with which I would stupefy the men of learning as well as those of the Lord. Soon enough I found they were a type of crystal. Did I think, he asked, *that* was an explanation? He wanted miracles, but he wanted his own kind. The Pecos diamonds were pieces of his own miraculous cross.

I stood gazing at the petrified eye he had planted in his small garden. Several leaves of long-stemmed grass sheltered it like lashes.

"That is wood," said the voice. "Would you believe it?"

An old man with a stubble of beard, smiling, removed his glasses to see me better. He held them out before him to see what it was that blocked his view. Dust? They were fly-specked. He drew them back to sigh a breath on each lens, but without moisture. The air was too dry. He returned them, unpolished, to his eyes.

"Is that so?"

"Yes it is. I polished it myself."

Stooped, I could see the sweat-stained crown of his hat. In the band there were several blue-tipped kitchen matches. Another cornered his mouth. He wore hook-and-eye work shoes, with box toes, khaki pants pressed with an iron, galluses that left their shadowy trace on the back of his shirt. A watch weighted the pocket of his shirt, a leather thong looped to the gallus. He removed the match from his mouth, and used the chewed frayed end as a pointer.

"They estimate such wood to be eighty thousand years of age."

"Is that so?"

"Yes, indeedy."

Glancing at him, sidelong, I saw an elderly hired hand, employed. Nothing in the way of a shock of recognition in what I saw, only in what I heard. The voice? No, the speech. The uncultivated cultivation. I had been wrong about the smile. With the match out of his mouth the expression was one made by the weather, the eye-protecting squint lifting the corners of the mouth.

"You want space? I'm afraid we don't have it. Full up. We've been full up for months."

Over the crown of his hat I saw the familiar waste-land of a used-car lot. What he saw seemed to please him. "Full up for months," he repeated. He spoke with pride.

"I wasn't looking for space. I was looking for you."

"For me?" He removed his glasses, put his head forward as he did at dawn, in the flickering lights of the tractor, to shout directions and curses above the cough of the motor. His eyes slits in the mask of dust. In them, however, I saw nothing of the apprehension I would have felt if a stranger had found *me* out. Nothing but puzzlement. "Now why would that be? You from Mrs. Wylie? I'm afraid I've had to give up the haying. I have not recovered from an operation as readily as I had hoped."

"You don't remember me? That's funny. I have your letter here somewhere. You wrote me to ask if I wouldn't come to Hereford and help with the tractor. Good job. Board and twenty-five bucks a month. Well, here I am."

For a moment, blinking, he searched his mind for the letter, unaccustomed to that sort of horseplay.

"I'm sorry—" I interrupted, feeling like a fool, but he put his hand on my sleeve to stop me. As if he might sneeze, he turned away and drew a kerchief from his rear pocket. But he did not sneeze. He blew his nose, daubed at the corners of his eyes. Still faced away he said, "Don't josh me, boy. I just don't see quite as sharp as I once did."

"Neither do I." He took that for granted. The frailty of others never surprised him.

"You got the letter? Winona gave me your address. You move around so much I can't track you."

"I got it." I felt around in my pocket thinking I might show it to him. "It's from Riva. You remember Riva?"

"Let me get a chair—" he said, turning away, and dipped his head as he stepped through the door of his trailer. One he had made? Birds were nesting in the small peep window at the front, unopened. "Here, boy," he said, and reached me a chair with a freshly patched cane bottom. The legs wired. He took a stool from under the sink for himself. "No, no—" he said when I tried to swap with him—"what would Nona think if I sat you on a stool?" The urban softness of my life had always been a subject of amusement. Before I could comment he was back in the trailer. "Grape-ade or root beer. Do I recall you like root beer?"

I had liked root beer until the winter in Hereford when I had to rinse the dust out of my mouth with it. It had always seemed a little gritty to me since. "Make it grape," I replied, and he made it grape, dissolving the mixture from an envelope into a tall glass of water. He stirred it with the handle of a spoon. With a pick he broke a little ice from the cake in his icebox, a cooling sound I hadn't heard for many years.

"I'm thinking of wiring the trailer, Warren. It would help with my reading. Help my eyes." The confession was intended to make me more his equal, as it did. He had never needed glasses to read, nor pain-killers when he went to the dentist.

"You're looking fine," I said, and looked at him. Did he look fine? It had not occurred to me that Fremont Osborn would age like normal people. Die he would have to, but somehow without aging. Was it correct to say that he had? He offered me the grape-ade—having root beer himself—then sat erect on the backless stool. The remnant of color in his eyes matched the faded denim in his shirt. His tucked-up pant leg, the seam sharp, exposed the fold of underwear in his gartered sock. In the creases of his shoes, and his body, there would still be Texas dust.

"I had an operation, Warren. Prostatic. Clean you out with a piece of wire. Very painful. I passed a good deal of pus and blood. It seems to me my recovery is slow."

"These things take time."

"Five hundred dollars. Dr. Goodnight said, if you can't pay it, Osborn, fill these forms out. Dr. Goodnight, I said, if I could not pay for it I would not have the operation. I paid it. I believe he thought me a plain damn fool."

"Things have changed even in my time."

"Warren, what would you say your time was?" He was not ironic, merely curious.

"My time?" I looked around as if I might see it. Cars. Cars flashing by on the thruway. "At least part of it is your time. Between us, you know, we invented the dustbowl. Just last month or so I heard it was still blowing. Like the good old days."

He put a hand to his forehead, the thumb resting on his cheekbone. Between the fingers I could see the pale veined lids of his eyes. Was he recalling? Did it seem near to him or far? He had been in his late forties— about my age—when I went to work for him in Texas. Perhaps that was not his past at all, but my past. To jog his memory I said, "You remember the trip to the Carlsbad Caverns?" He seemed to.

"I hope you've learned to drive a car, Warren, better than you did then." On the way back from Carlsbad, driving at night, I had run over the curbing of a street divider in Roswell, denting both front rims. I remembered, but it was not the sort of thing that popped into my mind.

He had bought a radio the size of a piano that operated on storage batteries. They had run down before I got there. The names of foreign stations were printed on the dial. The battery space was used to store cartons of the Haldeman-Julius Little Blue Books. "The Little Blue Books?" I said. "You still have them?" I carried one on the tractor with me. *How to Improve Your Vocabulary*. I memorized lists of words, one of them being vertiginous. His head was wagging slowly, as if it hurt him. "You don't remember what happened to the Blue Books?"

"I guess Howard took them, Warren. He was a fine boy, Howard."

"Howard?"

"He come from Wichita, Warren. Nephew of Agnes. Came right along when he heard you left us. He was about your size—" he looked at me—"size you were then. But not afraid of work."

"I was probably not enthusiastic about getting up at four-twenty in the morning. But I got up. I wouldn't say I was afraid of it."

"He wore the clothes you left, so he wasn't any bigger. Might have been a little smaller. But he could work."

"How long did Howard stay?"

"Till Agnes died, Warren. Maybe two, three years."

"He must have really liked to work, but I wouldn't go so far as to say he was smart."

"Howard was smart enough to finish his schooling, Warren. He was smart enough to finish what he started."

That I hadn't finished my schooling had been a sore

point with Fremont Osborn. I had left him to go to college, then left college to go to Europe. He shook his head slowly. "Howard was a country boy, Warren. He knew how to work. You had a city boy's ways."

To have survived four months on my uncle's dust farm, sixteen hours a day, thirty days a month, with a rash on my body from the diet of pork and eggs, had been a point of pride with me for more than thirty years. From the seat of the same tractor the past looked a good deal different. The boy who was proving himself to be a man was a beardless kid with soft city boy's ways, subject to a rash from the diet of pork and eggs.

My uncle's head began to wag. "You were a funny kid, Warren. You wouldn't eat. You'd eat one egg and a biscuit and leave your meat. Agnes used to say no wonder you couldn't work since you didn't eat."

The mention of the food brought its taste to my mouth. Pork. Pork fried in its own fat, then stored in an oil barrel at the back of the house till Agnes fished it out to fry with the morning eggs. If I didn't bolt an egg down fast the smell of the pork would make me sick. I let the biscuits dry in my pocket and ate them on the tractor like hardtack. Had I complained? I took it—I thought—like a man. My uncle uncrossed his legs to place his hands on his knees, rocking forward. His silent laughter brought tears to his eyes. "You're old enough to tell nòw, boy, but I don't think Agnes ever got used to it. You wet your bed. Boy your age a little too old for that."

A wheeze escaped him as he thought of it, he slapped a thigh. I let it pass. Better to ignore it than touch on the subject of a boy's wet dreams. My uncle shared the hog we butchered with a family of tenant farmers named Gudgers. The oldest of their nine children was a girl named Georgia. She liked to wrestle with boys. I was known to be a boy and a wrestler. The smell and taste of Georgia had stayed with me like that of the pork. My dreams had been a boy's dreams, up until then, but they began to give me trouble after Georgia. No one had ever told her to stop doing what she found to be fun. My uncle was a great believer in girls and boys, in preference to birds and bees, but his Blue Book library had come a little early for Freud.

To change the topic I said, "You remember the ducks? I was a pretty good shot if it was dark enough."

"You mean geese, Warren?"

I suppose I meant geese. I had shot at them without knowing what they were. Or seeing them. Two hours before dawn we had left the dark house to shoot at what I thought might be cattle rustlers. In the windless pause before my uncle ran forward hooting like an Indian, I prepared myself to shoot it out with Billy the Kid. When he ran forward, hooting, I shot into the sky over his head. A great flapping of wings, but very little honking. I think I managed to fire two or three rounds. Still dark, we came back to the house where Agnes had coffee perking and a fire going. When the sky was light we went out to see if we had bagged any birds. Just shooting blind into the flock we had bagged nine. So we had fresh gamy meat for two weeks and there were scraps of lead shot on my plate in the evening, some of which I kept and used over in my bee-bee gun.

My uncle put a hand to his eyes, then removed it without speaking. What he saw, or remembered, seemed to be of little interest.

"One cannot live in the past, Warren. I'm glad to say I never wanted to."

Did I look at Fremont Osborn as he had looked at the boy who had wet his bed? My legendary uncle, inventor of the dustbowl, the man who sought his new brides with mail-order snapshots—where, if not the past, did he think he was living? Root beer, ice picks, hook-and-eye shoes, the white heel-and-toe worksox with the mottled tops that came in bundles of one and two dozen, tied up in strong twine that I would find around a spool in his kitchen drawer.

"I'm not suggesting living in the past," I said, "but since you brought it up, I'm not sure I wouldn't want to."

"I'm glad your mother isn't here to hear you say that, Warren."

My mother? It took me a moment to remember she was Fremont Osborn's sister. His younger sister, and favorite. I had learned that from Winona. In the four months I had lived with him in Texas he had never once mentioned her name.

"My mother—" I began, but he interrupted.

"If there was one thing she hated it was the past. She hated all of it. If she thought you were fool enough to want to go live there, don't think she would have had you. As it was, it killed her."

The irony of it did not escape him. His head wagged. "What you think the Lord Almighty would make of that?"

I didn't want to open up his favorite topic, the crazy ways of the Lord. "You sure she would feel that way to-day?" The question did not surprise him. No, I had the feeling he had given it some thought.

"You see that, boy?" He pointed a finger where a piece of frazzled rope dangled from a limb. What was left of a swing. The earth beneath it had been scooped to a trough. "She was a crackerjack, I tell you. Why, you should have seen her. I'd tie bottles to swing from a branch of the catalpa. Fifty yards. She'd be the first between us to hit it. We did that on Sundays when father and the girls would be off to church."

The *girls?* He did not classify my mother as one of the girls. A crackerjack. Time had not blurred the image before his eyes. He seemed to see her as he squinted down an invisible barrel. "Look there!" I looked to where telephone wires dipped between the poles. I looked for birds, sparrows. I had managed to hit a sparrow or two myself. "There, there!" he corrected, "the insulators!" and half rose to wag his finger at the glass knobs on the crossbar. Two were gone. In the desert light the two remaining glittered like ice. "Why, boy, you should have seen her. From the seat of the buggy. Never the need to rein in the horses. From the seat of the buggy she would crack them like bottles!" Two, three times he snapped his fingers. I seemed to see them shatter like light bulbs before my eyes. "See the glass in the ditches when the snow melted. Think the line crew thought it was the cold that did it!" One of his brown hands rose from his lap and slapped smartly on his thigh, like a country fiddler. It set the leg to wagging. "Why, boy—" he repeated, but paused there when words failed him. To see what he lacked the words to describe he closed his eyes.

I had been told my mother was something of a beauty,

but not that she had been a rival of Annie Oakley. I tried to see her, as my uncle did, on the lids of his eyes. Was this my mother—my pioneer mother—or Fremont Osborn's dream of a woman, one of the many that escaped him once his wife, Agnes, died. One who could shoot a Winchester, curse God, and skillfully wring the neck of a chicken. My father, however, would not have wooed a woman who was quicker on the trigger than the heartstrings, and found little more to do in the seat of a buggy than load and fire a bolt-action rifle. Not my father. No, nor his son. What past were we reporting on? For my uncle the past ended when my mother stopped shooting at bottles. For my father, with the birth of his son. For me, it did not end at these points, but began.

"What would she shoot at today?" I ventured. "The telephone people might be a little touchy."

He opened his eyes, wide, as if he might see. The windshields of cars flashed on the highway; overhead, somewhere, a plane circled for a landing. He followed its slow wheeling. Did he think my mother would have sniped at planes? "The kids played with dolls and toys, Warren. Not her. She liked the newest and the best. She liked a good saddle. You know what she would be shooting at today? She would be shooting at the moon!"

The thought had just come to him. It left him unsettled, as it did me. In his excitement at my mother's future he stood up, moved his stool, then sat down. What astonished me most? Hearing such a remark from Fremont Osborn, her brother, or the thought of my mother bloatedly encased in a helmeted spacesuit, the world's first female astronaut?

"Your mother, boy, had no truck with the past. She

turned her back on it. That was the trouble with the girls and father. All of them but Grace believed in his religious nonsense. It ruined their lives. Grace scorned it. She wanted to live—" he brought his hand down on his knee—"right here and now."

Did I seem to question that?

"What are you thinking, Warren?" When we sat around the kitchen range in Texas he would sometimes say, "Boy, what are you thinking?" I never seemed to know. "No, no," he would say, "you are thinking of *something*. The mind never thinks of nothing." So I thought of something.

"I was just thinking that I never before heard you mention my mother."

It set him back. He screwed one finger in his ear as if to clear it of the question.

"What's that? No, no. You have forgotten. I have never for one moment forgotten Grace."

"I didn't say forgotten. I said mention. I don't recall your ever mentioning her name."

"You were young, boy. Same age she was. She didn't moon about the past and she wouldn't want you to. You couldn't do more for her than live right here and now— the way she would have." He blew his nose, then pushed up his glasses to dab his eyes. "You're no more a match for her than Will, boy. That's your father. He was smart but he couldn't match her. If she lived his life would have turned out different, I can tell you."

It was known that my father's life turned out badly. How about mine?

"I don't say better, Warren, just different. So would yours."

"If my mother had lived, her life might have been of

interest, but not mine."

"All I know about your life, Warren, is what Winona writes me."

Did that seem to be more than enough? It did. The odd thing about Fremont Osborn was that he believed himself very much like other people. Not quite so stupid, or superstitious, but of the same clay. In what *here and now* did he think he lived? This hired hand with the ballad voice, the careful speech, the buried past, the snapshots for a new mail-order bride, still an active minuteman in Colonel Ingersoll's war to free men of ancient and modern superstitions. A self-made man, a fossil intact as the leaf and the fish found in the rock face, unaware that the land had replaced the sea, and the tree petrified. On what branch of it did he think he belonged? He had washed his own socks, repaired his own heels, paid for and suffered his own operation, and he would die, in due time, his own death. He sat with lean brown hands quiet in his lap, the foot of his crossed leg nodding to a strong pulse. A reasonably fearless man, he feared the phantom past. It was the past, not the freeway, nor hepatitis, nor strontium, nor polio shots, nor fallout that he warned me against. Why? Out of it he had sprung, and my mother, on a spring too fine for rewinding, and in time such distempered metal as myself. My uncle, Fremont Osborn, had been the first of the Osborns to fly in the teeth of custom, to plow up the dust, to buy a car worth more than the shack he lived in, a radio to bring the world to his feet, a library to ventilate superstition—but he was not the first to seek a mail-order bride. The usable past was the here and now. Twenty years after he had put the past behind him he circulated photographs for mail-order brides, none of whom were hog butchers, like Agnes, sharp-shooters like my mother, nor long the wife of Fremont Osborn, man of his time.

What time was *that?* I suddenly remembered why I had come.

"You remember Riva? That old castle you came to?"

He made no sign, then said, "Boy, we seen nothing but old castles. Too many of them."

"I was there. The one near Vienna. I remember you went rabbit hunting."

His hand raised, came down with a slap on his thigh. "Rabbit hunting? You recall it? Ten of us out there all night, not one seen a rabbit. Why, boy, they were all as crazy as that old man. Crazy as a coot."

"He wasn't so old, at the time." My Uncle Fremont had been a good ten years older.

"Looked old to me. Why, he could hardly walk. Think Gladys thought he'd die before we got away from there. One of the things that scared her. Thought she'd freeze to death herself."

"He just died. What I came to ask you is if you'd like to go along to his funeral."

"You in your right mind, Warren? Why'd I do a crazy thing like that?"

"He sent me a notice. Two of them. He wants some-body there. Somebody who knew him." I paused, then added, "Somebody's got to be there."

"I'm glad your mother isn't here to hear you."

"Look—"

"You can't live in the past, boy. Can't even die in it. Take this old fool you mention. If he's dead, he died in the present. Same as you and me will." He grinned, then added, "Besides, Mrs. Wylie's grown accustomed to rely on me, Warren. Something always needs fixin'." He stood up, remembering something. "Shriveled-up little fellow, wasn't he? Way he looked I didn't think he'd last the winter."

On the highway the cars blurred the hills like a flagging windshield wiper. A pneumatic drill tore something down, or put something up. The polished surface of the petrified wood reflected a foreshortened view of Fremont Osborn. Inside his trailer a buzzer sounded like a door alarm.

"That's Mrs. Wylie, Warren. Guess she needs me." He rubbed his hands briskly together, eager to be useful. "I've got a spare cot, Warren, if you'd like to stay over."

"I've got to get back," I replied. "It's a long drive."

"I remember when it took me three days to get to Hereford." He wagged his head. "Don't they plan to get to the moon sooner than that?" The prospect stirred him. He stepped to where he had a better view of the sky. "I'll tell Nona you were here, boy. She's fond of you. Thinks of you as her boy. You can tell her if there was more women like her maybe your Uncle Fremont wouldn't be a bachelor."

He brought his hand down on my shoulder as he had once brought it down on the haunch of a horse. I led off, but his gait took him past me, crunching the raked gravel in the footpath. From the door of her trailer Mrs. Wylie called, with the handle of a spoon pointed out another trailer. Head down from his perch the parrot croaked, "Yankee, go home! Yankee, go home!" until Mrs. Wylie slapped him silent with a folded magazine.

"How is Mr. Castro?" my uncle inquired, and paused to let the bird gnaw on one of his fingers. With his free hand he waved me a good-by. "If you go to that funeral—" he began, but the parrot, Castro, outsquawked him. Mrs. Wylie threatened him with her spoon, but he paid her no heed.

Three

We put everything on tape today, even time. The tape I have in mind is the line that runs down the center of a blacktop highway. If I straddle it, the car seems to be winding it up. At sixty miles an hour time and space seem to wind on the spool beneath me. Or within me, which is more accurate. Dimensions of time: I see it rushing toward me, worming slightly, then I see it un-raveling behind me. A stretch of time? A piece of space? Or one and the same, weaving together. At the wheel of the car, at sunrise, with the dawn light behind me, the road opening out before me, I sense a dimension of time that otherwise escapes me, the spool of tape being myself, Warren P. Howe.

Curious how the time spilling behind me seems to reel in the rear-view mirror. The road itself like water over the dam. Water over the dam. Up ahead time and space seem to lie in wait; at the rear they accumulate.

The humped shadow of the car is like that of a phantom soaring just a few feet above me. How often I have put my head out to look! Nothing there. No, the shadow ahead of me is myself. And yet the whoosh of air at the window is like that of wings. Inside the car, past and future seem to merge; the present is the wavering needle on the dial. I say *seem,* however. Well enough I know that they do not. One or the other spins the spool of my fancy. Now forward, now backward. But seldom at the still point. But the sensation is both heady and edifying and the signs along the highway speak like prophets— what could be truer than to advise me that my life is in my hands? Time. The spool of it that spins under my seat. That reappears in the shuttle-like loom of time in my head. Ridiculous the waste, sad time that ticks on my watch, chimes on the air waves, or lies in ruins in the time-tired remains along the highway. So many objects in the amber of time-past. As the morning shadow creeps back to the car I lose the flavor of this sensation. It goes with the sun. At high noon, my time-in seems time-out. Virtually time-less. The sort of life one sees in the glass eye of a tub at the laundromat. A tumbling, whirling spin of chaos, with a blue rinse. Without direction. Without a fore, say, and an aft. Nevertheless I know that time, whether spun on my spool, or sucked into the shark's mouth of a jet, joins objects and places that seem to lie asunder. My Uncle Fremont, for instance, Charles Horney, and myself. Not to mention that madman, Monsieur Etienne Dulac. If you can die in the present, that is where you have been living. To avoid certain sentiments, it helps to begin at that point.

Charles Horney, for example, would smile to hear my

uncle speak out boldly for the *present,* his hook-and-eye shoes firmly planted in the past. But only his shoes. He would claim to have his eye firmly fixed on the future. A moon-bound spaceman, his target the satellites. Monsieur Dulac, hearing that, would beam with his engaging simpleton smile, the expression of a man baby-sitting children who were not too bright. Charles Horney, knowing what *he* knew, would be unperturbed. And yet we all—with a little squeezing—might have occupied the front seat of my car, the purling whirr of the same spooling time lulling us all to sleep. What time was it? Could any time be said to have stopped? In Monsieur Dulac's case the answer was yes. Dead he was. His time had stopped. But could it be said that he was now out of time's reach? The thought of it would bring the smile— dead or not—that I would find on his lips.

In the early thirties a man with ideas ended up in some wing of the Communist Party, bumming around the world, or running his own school. The old gang were either bums, commies, or educators. In this tableau Charles Horney is the white hope, I'm the bum.

The year I went off bumming to Europe, Charles Horney took a job as Latin tutor, sixty dollars a month and his keep, at the Boles school. The Boles school had been recently founded to meet the need of children who didn't get along with their parents, and parents who didn't get along with each other. The word was Progressive. At Boles the Progress was slow. Charles began as a Latin tutor but in two years he was chief of the staff. Ideas. Ideas he developed to deal with me. What I might call my influence was never stronger than when Charles turned his back on it, and out of his rebellion established the celebrated Horney System. It can be put very simply. The past is useless. That explains why it is past. Anything that has proved itself useful continues to exist in the present. An educated Horney child needs only to know what *that* is. That's all. I repeat, that's all.

I repeat that it was Horney's idea, not mine, to escape from the blight of my influence, and thereby develop one of the seminal minds of our time. That may be a little snide, my own mind not being so seminal. However, the big decision in Horney's life was not thirty years ago, when he resisted my pressure, but his reluctance, five years earlier, to submit to it. What he himself describes as the formative years.

In high school we read the same books, disliked the same movies, flunked the same courses. But it was *my* idea to go to college. So it was his idea *not* to. That cost him a year. The year he worked as clerk in a bank he fell a lap behind. That meant the book up ahead was always one I had read. The course up ahead was one I had taken. The great idea was one I had had. His record in college was better than mine, and lap for lap we had about the same talent—but that first-lap start made the difference. What he saw of me, as a rule, was the back of my head. I thought—as he seemed to—that it was nice to have a pal who knew the college ropes, but it never dawned on me that I blocked his view. But that was not unusual. At the time, nothing whatsoever dawned on me.

Horney's mother was Irish—Brooklyn Irish—with a large bust, a small choir-trained voice, and a talent for playing the piano by ear as she sang hymns. She and Mr. Horney, a streetcar conductor, lived in the kitchen of their seven-room house, the first floor about three feet below the level of the yard. She kept the blind just far enough above the sill so that she could watch the passing feet of the neighbors, or their pets and children, go by without rising from her seat at the table. The upper floors, where I never penetrated, were given over to her older, unmarried daughters, who were the image of Mr. Horney. A stocky silent man, with a scarlet face, Mr. Horney was active as a ward heeler, evenings, and as a motorman on the Irving Park line during the day. Mr. Horney picked up enough money to support the girls nobody would marry, and buy a car that was big enough to take his five daughters for Sunday rides. Charles, his mother, and I would always stay at home, in the kitchen. Mrs. Horney would make us eggnogs or a plate of divinity fudge. Charles was fair, with almost hazel eyes, small, almost effeminate features: one could see very clearly that Hazel Horney had been quite a catch. Mr. Horney liked to say that God had answered his prayers, but the storks had made a bungle of things in the deliveries, bringing him a son that looked like his mother, and girls who looked like him.

Mrs. Horney would have liked to go for rides on Sundays, but she didn't trust me alone with Charles. What told her I would challenge her authority? Our talk was elevated. Gulping eggnog we talked of nothing but books. Mrs. Horney's generous bust made it difficult for her to sit close to the table; she sat back, as if not to intrude, just the toes of her shoes touching the linoleum. I would say she hated me with a pure gem-like flame. I

disturbed her warm kitchen, where clothes were drying, with the windy air of change. Did it blow good or
evil? She was not quite sure. The apple of her eye,
Charles, seemed to take to it. As I sat gulping her eggnog, or beating her fudge, she watched me with the gaze
of a trapped bird. With a moistened finger she would
pick up the crumbs that lodged in the fold of her bust.
"Don't mind Ma," Charles would say, but I did. What
was there in such a nice, well-intentioned boy as I knew
myself to be that disturbed her? I needed eggnog, fudge,
and a woman's loving care in that order. Keeping her
vigil, her legs would fall asleep. Charles would help to
slide her off the seat and move around. What instinct,
sure as a plumbline, tells a woman like Mrs. Horney
that a book you *must* read can do you no harm, but one
read for pleasure can ruin your life? A pact with the
Devil, no less. And that was me.

One of the first things of the past Horney dispensed
with was me. I went along with Latin, history and the
old world, and any need to go there. Growing boys
could do without it. Horney's growing boys did. They
had their hands full discovering hairpins, cigarette light-
ers, Geiger counters, birds and bees, and in their senior
year, boys and girls. That much I agree with. Boys
should discover girls. If I'm a little snide it's because I
did the trial run for these ideas. I was the boy who met
the girls, Horney the birds and the bees. But my dis-
coveries added up to nothing I've been able to sell or
bottle: Horney perceived this. We might call it Horney's
law. Blessed are those who set the example it is useless
for others to follow. That's me. Or I should say, that
was me. It is Charles Horney who now sets the example.

In a recent interview quoted in *Time,* he described himself as one part square-nik, one part Zen-nik, one part Hor-nik. You can't beat that for being in the groove. Horney is no square. If I was half the man I used to be I would ask him how the hell he does it. I can hear his reply, "Do *what,* Warren?" All he was doing was just living. From day to day. That's all Charles Horney wanted to teach, all he wanted to say.

Those metal-lipped whistles with the wooden pea that hang invisibly from the neck of *educators* Charles Horney has managed to do without. He reads his lectures. He is always asked to please raise his voice. These lectures are taped and rerun on FM stations featuring culture. I know the voice. It is one of the few things in my life that has not changed.

Is he of average height? I suppose. I always had the problem of seeing him whole. He has a spare, even angular frame, that is either somewhat small or his head a little large. One impression that persists is that his head is still growing, his body is not. The same holds true of his hands and feet. I always see him standing, one shoulder just a notch higher than the other, hands rather firmly gripping arms on which the sleeves are rolled, lips parted as he listens to Casals play the suites of Bach. He began to buy records when I bought books. When the record finished there would be a pause while Charles removed and sharpened the cactus needle, his pants hanging on his hips as if draped over the back of a chair. This stoop was usually accompanied by several belches, or a long fart. I was first attracted to and impressed by Horney by his assured, casual way of breaking wind in public. I've never lost it. It is one of the ties that bind.

*   *   *

The Horney school occupies two of the buildings
once part of the Valley View Golf Club, an enterprise,
like so many, just one war ahead of its time. You can't
push a pioneer, dozing in his orange groves, into the
nerve-racking world of leisure. You have to wait till he
knows that leisure is killing him. Today a bigger course,
for the new pioneers, looks like a green fire break on the
foothills, and has made Colton a household name in the
leisure world. The Horney campus can be seen, nationwide, when the matches are televised, a somewhat empty
scene since most of the facilities are underground. The
tennis courts and part of the quad are directly above
most of the classrooms. Space-saving, time-saving, and
now it would seem, life-saving. They serve as fallout
shelters for all of the Horney staff and boys. That was
not intended. Horney takes no credit for being a
prophet. As he says, if you live in the present you can't
help but be ahead of your time. Like many innovations
on the Horney campus it was largely donated by enter-
prising innovators. Horney is the laboratory for their
new ideas. As he says, we'll take it, if it works. Among
other dividends Horney alumni are spared the blight of
nostalgia, since even the recent grads seldom recognize
the place. There is no ivy. There is something new in
laundry, lighting, and TV every year.

Boles' great idea was to take the boys back—back to
cows, chickens, horses, Latin cribs, and horse-sense. An
All American idea, loved by parents, hated by the kids.
Horney reversed it. He moves the boys ahead. The cow
is in the powder, the chicken in the deep-freeze, and
climate is in the thermostat. Before he struck a balance

there were educators who wanted Horney jailed, or exported—but that was all theory. In practice the boys had pimples and problems as usual. The cows and chickens were missing but Nature was in the boy. The first full-fledged Horney offspring, now in their twenties, seem to have much in common with boys in general, getting married, writing books, and forming new Young Republican clubs. Horney feels his point will be made only when they have offspring of their own. To live in the present one still has to live in the world. Horney is resigned to the fact that it may take time.

I timed my arrival for the late afternoon. A sign visible from the freeway points to the stone gates where the parents are advised to please respect visiting hours. The gate swings open automatically at a toot of the horn. The surface buildings are faced around a square that served the Boles boys as a corral, and is said to explain the unusually heavy growth of grass. I found several boys tossing around a plastic football. Normal, acne'd, somewhat fat-assed American boys. The Stratford Manor has been refaced to remove the influence of Shakespeare, but the beige stucco was not quite up to the look of tomorrow. I parked where the boys wouldn't wreck the car and walked across the well-manured grass. In the windows of the dormitory a few study lamps were burning. There were no signs.

"Where's Dr. Horney's office?" I asked one of the boys.

"Sir?" he replied. I liked that Sir. *Goodbye, Mr. Chips* almost made me a teacher.

"Doc-tor Hor-ney, fatso!" yelled one a little thinner. "Don't you know who's Doc-tor Hor-ney?"

The fat boy turned and pointed through an archway, where the door stood open. "He's upstairs, sir. Right at the top."

"Where you hear the mewwww-zic!" the other boy added. I could hear music, but it didn't sound like Horney. The front door opened on a large room with several bare tables, modern chrome-legged chairs. From several the backs had been removed. Music, hillbilly rock-and-roll, seemed to materialize in the space around me. Stereo. A speaker in each corner of the room. A boy sorting records turned to see who had entered, turned away without interest. The volume was not high but the persistent beat set up a vibration. Lifting the needle from the record the boy said, "You looking for Sandy, sir?"

"No, Dr. Horney."

"Upstairs, sir." He pointed. With the rock-and-roll suspended I could hear the sound. Unaccompanied cello. A path in the carpet led to the door of Dr. Charles Horney, Hours 3 to 4, 7 to 8. Behind the door a string vibrated as if I had plucked it. A chord sounded, the bow drawn with the rasping hiss of the resin. Had he taken up the cello? In college he had played the clarinet. When I knocked a voice replied, "Come in, come in," as if the rap was not necessary. The plucked string continued to vibrate as I opened the door. Blinds were drawn against the light at one window, a lamp burned at the desk. No books. Unframed water colors, painted by students, were fastened by thumbtacks to the walls of soft, insulating material, with the punctured surface of a dartboard.

Behind me a voice I recognized as that of Charles

said, "Listen to this!" The cello string stopped vibrating, a pause, then a wave materialized in one corner, washed into the room, broke into a foam of surf at my feet. In the air above me the wing-beating swoop and cries of gulls. Another and larger wave approached, crested and broke. I turned to look at Charles, his back to me, his eyes on the turntable, only the movement of the label indicating that the record turned. I realized this was how I often saw him—facing anything but me. Did he know who had entered? We listened to the wet frothy wash of the surf, the cries of the gulls, the pounding of a breaker. He stooped to slip a finger under the needle, revealing that his thin shanks were even leaner, and brought the arm of the instrument back to the first groove of the record. The plucked string of the cello. He lowered the volume a notch and said, "Remember the old 78 Air for the G string? I've still got it. Think you could bear it?"

He took a step to the left, removed one of the smaller albums from the shelf. Air for the G string was the record we played the year I read Schweitzer and Charles played Bach. He was not drawn to the organ, nor was I drawn to Africa. As the needle rasped he said, "I've been expecting you, Warren. How are you?"

I had forgotten how he could disarm me with that *Warren*. A bit of verbal jujitsu.

"I was fine," I said, "until I got the notice. Did you get one?"

He let a moment pass, stooped to toy with the dial. "What makes you think I should get one, Warren?"

"Since I've received two so far, seems to me you might have got one."

"I see you haven't changed much, Warren. Still the same old sense of humor."

"It's Dulac's idea of humor, not mine. I tend to get depressed at funerals." He did not smile. The sound of the cello on the old record seemed to come to us from a distance, down a corridor. "It just might be," I said, "less humor than desperation. Maybe he died alone. Maybe he wants somebody at his funeral."

"Wanted," said Charles, "maybe he *wanted* somebody." The correction was so characteristic, so much like *him,* so much like *us,* we were back at the moment we had parted, more than twenty years ago. My grammar and my sentiments were always in need of correction. For my own good. Always for my own good. "I'm sorry, Warren, but we need not impute the sentiments to him once he is dead."

"And why the hell not? If he died with them, by-god he still has them!" Did it matter to me? I could hear the silence trailing my voice. Almost a shout. We were back—or had we ever left?—the room in which we had parted. He gazed at me with pity, distaste, and embarrassment. He had once thought so well of me. Once, that is. We faced each other for the first time in more than twenty years. His arms were folded, he gripped the wad formed by the roll of his sleeves. He was still—as when I last saw him—the most eligible bachelor in my wife's class. But she had married me.

"I stopped by," I said, calming my voice, "to ask if you might like to fly over with me. Beautiful setting, as you may remember. Right sort of man could make it self-sufficient. Great place for a branch of the Horney school. Castles a drug on the market. Sure you could pick it up for a song."

So *that*—I could see him reflecting—was what it had been like. Friendship with me. A wearisome sequence of romantic sentiments and sarcastic remarks.

"I appreciate your thinking of me, Warren," he said, smoothing out the sleeve he had just crumpled, "but romantic ruins are your line, not mine. Why don't you proposition your friend Spiegel?"

"My *who?*" I barked. By revelation do we mean anything that comes too late? Had I waited for twenty years to learn that Charles Ames Horney, one of our seminal minds, was *jealous* of Sol Spiegel, a Santa Monica junk dealer? Spiegel, a big left tackle, who ran an orange juice stand at the Chicago World's Fair, my boss the summer before I took off for Europe. He had never heard of Europe till I told him I wanted to go there. What for? I told him to come and see for himself. Not once did it cross my mind that he would. But he did.

Just after the war, looking for some secondhand bookcases, I went into this big salvage store in Santa Monica. The man who owned it looked familiar; and he was. Sol Spiegel. "I seen you drive by, Mr. Howe," he said. "I got clientele who knows you. Smart people." He was right. One of his clientele was Seymour Gatz.

"What made you think of Spiegel?"

"He says you're one of his old clients," said Charles. "It's something we have in common. Charter members of old friends of Howe."

"For chrissakes," I said, "you crazy?" But Horney was not crazy. No, I could see that he was plainly in his right mind. Somebody named Spiegel had turned up at Riva—in the place once reserved for Charles Horney.

Somebody named Spiegel had bummed around Italy with me, shared my life. In the palmy days of Fascism we had shared a prison cell together in Grossetto. On its wall would be found the names of Spiegel & Howe, writ in blood. "If I had any idea—"

"I'm sure that you don't, Warren. If I'm sure of one thing, it's that."

As he turned back to the record player I said, "Let me tell you something. In the last two days I've been thinking about you. Thinking about *us*—" He smiled. "You know what I *thought?*" He waited. "That when you dispensed with the past, you dispensed with me. Like that!" I threw my hands up. "That's how it looked to me, and bygod, that's how it really is!"

"I've always found the past unreliable, Warren. It is anything you want to make it."

"Then why the hell live in it," I yelled, "like you're doing now!"

Did he feel that? He had stooped over the turntable to lift the needle. It calls for steady nerves. No tremor visible. He lowered it without a hiss to the groove, and stood pensive, waiting for the opening. Casals. We listened to Bach. After a moment he said, "Records have changed more than we have, Warren." It was said without malice, an impersonal assessment.

"The records have, but not the music." To soften that somewhat I added, "It's still Bach."

"These old 78's are now collector's items." I could believe it. I knew how he had sacrificed to be able to buy them. Bach unaccompanied by anything except the needle rasp. We heard it through. I watched him slip the record back into its case. All this time we had been standing. Turning he said, "Won't you sit down?"

I lowered myself into a chair with a bellows-type cushion: the hiss of escaping air blew the ash from my cigarette. Charles took a seat on the chair behind the desk. Smoke sucked by the fan widened the distance between us. "I once wrote you a long letter, all about a castle run by a madman. Did you happen to keep it?"

"You've kept in touch," he said, as if he hadn't heard me, "all these years?"

He had placed his hands, the palms together, to his lips as if he might whistle. Or pray. Why did it seem familiar? It was the gesture of a teacher we both admired, Jackson Percy. When a pronouncement was forthcoming Percy would place his fingers to his lips, blow on them softly.

"In touch? I sent him *Inside Europe* and a copy of *Time* the year the war started. I never heard if he received it. The first letter I ever got from him was the one you forwarded, an obituary notice."

"Does he—did he—seriously expect you to come?"

I shrugged. We both seemed to be thinking it over. "You certainly left an impression on him, Warren." The moment he put it flatly I doubted it. My head shook. "You don't think so?" No, I didn't think so.

"Don't get me wrong, I very likely tried hard enough to make an impression. But I didn't. Monsieur Dulac was not the impressionable type."

"If he's remembered you for more than thirty years—"

"What he remembers is the same as what I remember. Not the impression I made on him: the one he made on me. So do I. I was extremely impressionable."

Head tilted, Charles looked at me as he habitually

looked at some unbalanced child, needing only a touch
here, or a chip off there, to level him off. "Percy said
you would never change much, Warren. Guess he was
right."

"If Percy said so, it's the gospel. Did he say from
what I would never change?"

Charles fortified himself with a moment of medita-
tion. Eyes closed. The tip of his tongue between his
chapped lips. I once asked Miriam, with Charles in
mind, if a girl found chapped lips something of a problem. She thought I meant hers. She always thought I
meant something of hers.

"You're a romantic, Warren. An old-fashioned romantic. You know what you remember? What never
took place. You write and talk about it in order to believe it yourself."

"That's the word from Percy, the horse's mouth?"

The cloud of smoke level with his head bothered him.
He fanned at it with his hand, then stood up and faced
the window. The view was toward Colton, the campus
where *Incipit Vita Nova* was engraved on the gates. A
simple statement of fact? Was it there I crystallized into
the romantic who wrote and remembered what never
took place? Charles into one of the seminal minds of
our time? Under the ceiling of smog Professor Jackson
Percy went about his business of destroying culture,
exposing the witless to the fallout of a first-rate mind.

"How is Percy?" I asked. I never went back since I
was one of the many who had failed him.

"I've never forgotten what he once said, Warren. He
said you'd either be a bang or a whimper. That was
what he said."

Above the ceiling of smoke I had a clear view of the back of his head. His hair had always had the tendency to stand out from his neck, where it touched his collar; he had the habit of moistening his fingers, then slyly stroking it flat. He did that, then repeated, "A bang, Howe, or a whimper."

I could not remember his ever calling me *Howe*. Was that new, or a defect in my romantic memory? When speaking boy to boy, it was Warren; man to man, it was Howe. I no more doubted Percy had said it than I questioned its accuracy. A whimper? One readily came to mind.

"Speaking of Percy, I've never forgotten what he said to me. He said, 'Howe, why don't you go see Charles? Now that you're both blighted you have something in common.' "

From Charles no comment. Somewhere on the campus below us a boy puffed at a bugle. "But that's a long time ago," I said, "and my memory, as you say, may be defective. Besides, I'm sure his opinion has changed." Had the back of Charles' head aged more than his face? The import of it escaped me. From the desk to the window a pattern had been worn in the rug. He did that often. The view from the window was familiar to him. "Do the good old days seem far away," I said, "when you live right beside them?"

"You think I'm still just a college boy, don't you, Warren?" He pumped the rolled sleeves of his shirt up and down his arms. "You think because I didn't leave and bum around the world I've never seen life, or even left the campus."

"I've not really given it much thought."

"For your information, Warren, it can seem farther back because you can see it. You don't see it through a haze. Through a glow of nostalgia. You see it pretty much as it actually was."

"And how was it?"

He reflected a moment. "It was not as you remember it, I can tell you that."

"I don't remember ever telling you just what I remember."

"You think you're so different from other people, Warren? You're the same, you know. Only more so."

"That's true in one respect. What sticks in a man's craw he eventually throws up."

"The craw," Charles corrected, "does not serve that function."

I waited—as I once had—to hear what purpose the craw served. Charles would know. He had a mind for the facts. The imperceptible parting of our ways occurred when I read him my first poem. My memory is clear. The first line went—

The sun sweats through the fog

Charles tactfully but soberly advised me that the sun did not sweat, being a ball of flaming gas.

"I didn't stop to talk about the good old days," I said, "but the nice brand-new ones. You know what I stopped to do? Take you to Riva. As my guest. Gatz tells me that funeral expenses are deductible."

He turned to peer at me over his hunched shoulder. "If the past is dead," I said, "let's bury it!"

Did I mean what I said? He had often wondered. It was one of the reasons we had stopped talking.

"Warren—" he began.

"All for free. One of these thrilling weekends awarded the housewife with her own phone number. Paris and Vienna. See for yourself if a place like Riva exists or not. Frankly, I'm not sure. Like to have you as a responsible witness. If it's there, I pick up a check for twenty-five grand."

I saw in his eyes that Seymour Gatz had told him things about me he would not admit to himself.

"You are being offered the chance to make up for thirty years of balking. Not only that, see you were right all the time. The past an air-conditioned tomb, open to tourists on weekends. We'll climb the Eiffel tower, take in the Moulin Rouge, pick up a pair of chicks at the Dome, squeeze a lifetime into a nighttime. How does it sound?"

His lips had puckered from the bad taste in his mouth. As if he might spit, he lowered the window he faced and took a breath of cool air. After a moment he said, "Warren, you mind a suggestion?" He seemed to see it before him, in the haze over the valley. The metal dome of the observatory, a drooping flag, and a row of eucalyptus trees located the campus. In the wash to the left, invisible in the smog, the scene of a triumph. The Greek Theater. The graduate exercises in the open air. With a fellow named Lundgren I had the job of putting up the folding chairs for the ceremony, three rows on the stage for the assembly of dignitaries. A chair with a leg screw missing gave us the inspiration. We removed all the screws, slipped kitchen matches into their place. They served their purpose very well until the dignitaries lowered their bottoms. A triumph. Was it my last?

"What's your suggestion?" I said, smiling.

"If you really mean it, Warren, take Spiegel. He lives back there the way you do. He's never forgotten being over there with you. You may laugh, but he's an old-fashioned romantic."

"I wouldn't question that. His favorite jazzman is Guy Lombardo. Plays him on tape. Guy Lombardo and his Royal Canadians."

"Spiegel keeps your cards. He tells me that one day they'll be worth money."

"He told you *that?*" As if it pained him, Charles moved his head. Up and down, as if it had been for sometime in a cast. "That's the funniest goddam thing I ever heard." A simple statement of fact. I believed it. "Where the hell did he get that idea?"

There was a pause while we listened to that kid puff the bugle, then Charles said, "Me. I'm afraid he got it from me."

Stupefied? Yes, I was stupefied. In that condition, as Miriam often saw me, she said I looked like a kid with adenoids. "I remember having told him—" Charles paused, he put his hands to his lips and blew on them, softly—"I remember having told him that if you could tell the difference between what happened, and what you wanted to happen, you would write a great book."

"That's still quite a difference."

Charles smiled. "Spiegel has the faith, more faith than either of us. He made me a standing offer to buy any of your letters I am willing to sell."

Let me admit that statement moved me more than it embarrassed me. "I may be the romantic," I said, a little hoarsely, "but I'll be goddamned if I could imagine *that*. That's all beyond me." I found a piece of crumpled

Kleenex, blew my nose.

"You made an impression on people, Warren. Percy, Spiegel, Gatz—" then he added, "and me." I was about to comment on that but he said, "In spite of what you say you also made one on this fellow Dulac."

"You think I should go back?"

"Have you ever really got away, Warren?"

A question. One put to me, as well as himself. He turned to a corner of the room with several metal files, drew out a drawer, dipped his hand into a folder. Clipped together, he pulled out several postcards. On one I could see a sepia view of the Prater, the giant Ferris wheel dwarfing the trees. Turning it he read, " 'September 28th, 1933.' That's twenty-nine years ago next week."

"Beautiful day. I remember it. A Rhine maiden named Gerta had me on her hook. The *schöne blaue Donau* lightly tinted with non-Aryan blood."

"Here's another," he said, holding it up. The surface had been roughened with an erasure. The name Charles Horney had been carefully printed over it. But it was the missing name that I saw the most clearly. Katherine Brownell. She had planned to come to Riva on one of those weekends that it had snowed. Was it the snow or me that kept her away? I had my pride. The card I intended for her was sent to Charles.

"How come the stamp is on it?" I said, since *that* had been the reason I had mailed him the card. He wanted the stamps. "I spent half the day finding that one, and it turns out you didn't even want it. What the hell?" Charles wet his lips, as if trying to remember. "Tell me, didn't you *want* those stamps?"

He kept his eyes on the card he was holding.

"Did you or didn't you?"

"It was Percy who collected them, Warren. I said I'd save mine for him."

"You mean to tell me you sent me money so I would hunt up stamps for Percy?" He did not reply. "Maybe what pleased you was the idea of sending me money, seeing me hoofing it around the countryside for stamps."

"I didn't want to hurt your feelings."

"*My* feelings? Are you crazy? *Whose* feelings were you buying?"

"You were always selling something, Warren. You liked people to buy what you were selling. College, castles, love, marriage; the least I could buy was a few stamps."

The kid with the bugle gave it a blast right below the window. As if at a signal, Charles looked at his watch. From the drawer of his desk he removed some sheet music, an object that looked like an Irish shillelagh. Loosening the clasps with care, he removed his clarinet.

"If you hadn't been so busy selling something, Warren, you might have asked yourself what it was I wanted."

"So what the hell was it you wanted, if it wasn't stamps?"

He toyed with the keys of the clarinet. In college he had been torn between the examples of Woody Herman and Pablo Casals. The sight of the reed led him to put his tongue to his dry lips.

"So what was it you wanted?" I felt certain I had him cornered.

"Just a postcard, Warren—saying how much you

missed me." He paused, then added. "I had the money, you know. I really wanted to come."

Beneath the window some kid thumped on a drum. A sensation, common to me, of once more being back where I had come in, led me to wheel and peer around slowly, as if for familiar things.

"You're welcome to the cards." He pushed them toward me. "Perhaps Mr. Spiegel would be interested." Turning away he added, "You'll have to excuse me, Warren. Band practice coming up."

He opened the door, then followed me into the hall. Bells were ringing in the rooms below, and in the hall behind us doors slammed. A tall sallow boy wrapped in a tuba blocked the door like some sick monster.

"Don't tell Spiegel I mentioned him, Warren. He's really very shy. Like a big kid. He'd like it better if he thought it was your idea." He waved his clarinet toward winded members of the cross-country track team, loping across what had once been a nine-hole golf course. They disappeared into the scrub where golf balls were still to be found. I felt sure of that, having lost a few there myself.

Four

A sign that once read, IF IT'S FOR SALE, I'LL BUY IT, visible to the westbound Santa Monica traffic, following the war had been painted over to read simply SPIEGEL'S SALVAGE. It currently serves as a testing sample for the paint Spiegel sells at sacrifice prices. It has withstood many years of Santa Monica sunshine, and little rain. A brick building, open at the front, with ornamental concrete urns at the corners, Spiegel first opened in the wing on the east, but soon expanded to the corner. A lunch counter named *Sam's* hung on until Spiegel was the last cash client, buying coffee in the Dixie cups he would bring back to his office to drink. What was left of *Sam's,* he salvaged, eating up the food he found in the icebox, then selling what remained, shelves, stove, and accessories, over the counter. A nice piece of drugstore marble, he's not so sure he wants to sell it. He likes to sit there on the hot afternoons and drink one of his bottled cokes.

Sol Spiegel is wide, thick, and inclined to give a fore-shortened impression, being several inches taller than he looks. No one would think of calling him fat. A lock of hair, fanned out evenly like the teeth of a bamboo rake, screens the sunken basin of his head. The face is flat, lopsided from the wing dip of his mouth, pegged in place by the dowel of a dead cigar. I have always been too early, or too late, to find it lit. He lives in the store from nine to nine, then goes home to a château with a stucco tower, a sunken pink tile tub in the bathroom, to sleep alone in a bed that once belonged to Marion Davies, shave in a mirror that once reflected Gloria Swanson. "Trouble with me, Mr. Howe," he likes to say, "I'm a hard man to please."

I met Spiegel, as I have said, selling orange juice at the Chicago World's Fair. IIe had the California stand in the pavilion of States. Spiegel had never been to California but if he sold enough orange juice he hoped to go. The big thing about *frozen* orange juice at the time was its laxative properties. A very big thing. After tossing off a couple of two-ounce glasses the customer usually glanced around for the exit. The facilities were overtaxed with the orange juice enthusiasts. California people. All thirsty and far from home. Spiegel's favorite song at the time went like this—

> *Orange juice sorry you made me cry . . .*

He read it somewhere. The last idle reading he did. In the past twenty years he has confined himself to the Sears & Roebuck catalogues. The good old days, only. He considers '27 the last great year.

A realist, Spiegel admits to a core of sentiment. "So

you collect dolls and I collect old records, what the hell."
A metal file of old records, a come-on, specially priced
at five for a dollar, sets at the door where Spiegel can
keep an eye on it from the chair that once belonged to
Wallace Beery. There is usually an empty chair at Spiegel's side. He will ask you to take it, then say, "Know
who sat there last? Clara Bow. You're bottom to bottom, Mr. Howe. How you like that?"

Clients new to salvage are apt to think these celebri-
ties are Spiegel's companions, inclined to stop by in their
idle hours and chat a bit. He refers to them as Wally,
Marilyn, Dick—and if you look a little vague— "That's
Dick Powell, Mr. Howe. Sold him a mirror." Two or
three times a year Spiegel calls me to say he has a fresh
batch of old records. I get an early choice. We play them
on a machine that once belonged to Zasu Pitts. As I
thumb through the records Spiegel reminds me what he
would do if he had my talent. He would write a book to
end all books on Hollywood. *Behind the Silver Screen.*
Something like that. It is Spiegel who sees them when
they shouldn't be seen. Often enough, it is Spiegel who
saw them last. The door locked, or the door left open,
the water or the life blood flowing between the tiles. The
last word. When I want it, I shall come to Spiegel for
it.

Spiegel can be charitable toward my talent, since he
has so many others. He knows the market. He knows
the fallout. He knows why Chinese food will not stay
with you. Why you should own and not rent, why Japa-
nese cameras take bent pictures, and why some people
are duped into buying imported French wine. Spiegel
doesn't *like* wine, but if he did it would cost him ninety

cents a gallon, delivered, squeezed out of grapes that
were bigger and juicier than those grown in France. Just
the way Frenchmen born over here got bigger. Spiegel's
interest in wine dates from the day he saw four or five
bottles in my trash barrel, which he paused to check
over and salvage as an example of human folly. Mine.
Human folly is Spiegel's stock in trade.

Had I forgotten he shared my past? That on the Isle
of Capri, in the frigid month of March, we cuddled like
lovers in one sleeping bag, sharing alike the fleas, lice,
and two memorable cases of hives. I had not forgotten,
but it seemed another country, where the wench was
dead. Those characters had died; others had taken their
places. With Sol Spiegel I now shared an impersonal,
salvageable past. One on wax, and in the pages of Sears
& Roebuck catalogues. Rudy Vallee and Guy Lombardo,
the Mills Brothers crooning "Hold That Tiger," five-cent
beer, ten-cent cigarettes, and cars with bodies that would
never rust. Two sat, museum pieces, in the open yard at
the back of his shop. A Reo Flying Cloud, a Dodge
touring he drove on the 4th of July. This past did not
include a five-cent cigar since Spiegel, at the time I met
him, was already smoking factory seconds, sold on the
market three for fifty cents. Currently he smoked Church-
ills, airmailed from Havana until the mess with Fidel
Castro. He kept them in a safe with a White Rock maiden
painted on the door.

A few weeks ago Spiegel made local headlines with
his Headquarters for Survival Department, created to
help local citizens help themselves. To his usual supply
of salvage canned goods, a large proportion of it without
labels, he added cases of surplus Army water, jam, and

dehydrated TV dinners. His limited supply, as he said, sold out within a week. As he informed the inquiring reporter, interest in survival was great. His display window, once the lunchroom, currently features two dummies wearing masks, with plastic hoods designed to shed the fallout, heavy rubber boots designed to shed water in case it rains. Two hundred forty sets of these outfits had also been sold. As Spiegel says, "What the hell? If it doesn't fallout it'll probably flood; if it doesn't flood we'll have a goddam fire. Be prepared." He had a point there, since only Spiegel proved to have rubber buckets and fire-fighting equipment when we had the big blaze. Only Spiegel had the rafts and the boots when we had the flood. A sign at the door IF YOU DON'T SEE IT, ASK FOR IT, has been changed to read, IF YOU DON'T SEE IT, FORGET IT. Sound advice.

A skillful blending of old, almost new, and new, the prices subject to change without notice, makes it possible for Spiegel to buy mail order, from Sears, and sell with a modest ten-percent markup. Often to me. "Mr. Howe, I went out on a limb to buy it. That's what you pay me for, the insurance. I'm out on the limb." It doesn't bother Spiegel if you tell him that's some limb.

From three blocks east I could see him gently cuffing the parking meter where he keeps, contrary to the law, his Volkswagen truck. On the window behind him a banner read HEADQUARTERS FOR SURVIVAL, with his weekly special, a yellow fallout slicker, attractively draped on a buxom corset model. The light on his corner held me up until he saw me, flagged me over to the curb. Strange how different he looked to me, knowing he thought my early correspondence worth buying. Sal-

vage. In a class with Kid Ory and the Three Black
Crows.

"I got that table for you, Mr. Howe. All it needs is
legs."

"Legs?"

"You wanted a big table, right? Well, I got it for you.
Mahogany door from a Bel Air mansion. All you need
is the legs."

"That's why you flagged me down?"

His head shook. "Nope, Mr. Howe. Just thought I'd
tell you before I lose it. Man in this morning who said
he'd take it. Legs or no legs." Spiegel paused to flex his
knees, hoist his pants as if rising from a stool. "Mr.
Seymour Gatz called, Mr. Howe. Wants you to call him
right back."

One of Spiegel's valued clients, Gatz was always *Seymour* Gatz to Spiegel. A subtle man, I had not fully
fathomed his intentions. Irony? Was he gently twisting
the great man's leg?

"Wonder why he called *you?*"

"Just scrapin' the top of the barrel, Mr. Howe. When
they don't know who to call, they call Spiegel. Charges
prepaid."

I took a seat in the chair that Spiegel assured me had
been the joy and comfort of Jimmy Durante, a sad man.
A TV that was new, relatively speaking, the sound
switched off or out of commission, flickered like the
screen of a silent movie seen through the doors of a
lobby. The cabinet, once part of a bedroom wall, featured drawstring curtains to veil off the screen.

"Some picture, eh, Mr. Howe? Late Mr. Anson had
it wired up to the hi-fi sound, but somebody beat me to

it. Like a good buy?" He gave me a sidelong appraising glance, to see if I was hooked. Spiegel's formula for success is elementary but basic: no one in his or her right mind can resist somebody else's junk. Not at Spiegel's prices. "Feel free to use the phone, Mr. Howe. Mr. Seymour Gatz's number is there on the pad."

Spiegel's private office is fenced off from the clutter behind a heavy oak railing once used in movie court scenes. In the pigeonholes of his rolltop desk are postcards to Spiegel from celebrated people, all of whom are his clients, if not his customers. His phone, part of the numerals bright where he dipped the rubber of his pencil to dial it, sat on an early edition of a Sears & Roebuck catalogue. Spiegel collects them. He is conversant with everything in them. The things of *this* world—if not the other—are at his fingertips. A memo pad with the legend *From the Desk of Leonardo da Vinci* featured several of Spiegel's Rorschach-type doodles and the number of Gatz. I dialed it, got a busy signal.

"Ask him if he wants to dump his Bentley," Spiegel called. With Gatz, whom he resembles backside, Spiegel has a craving for limousines. A craving only. Gatz buys. Spiegel craves. Above his desk, eye level, was a placard about the size of Dulac's funeral notice. I had seen it before, but this time it held my eye.

JESUS SAVES

GREEN STAMPS

It occurred to me—gazing at the card—that Monsieur Dulac had been something of a prophet. One of the first of the sicknik humorists. Far out.

"Like that?" said Spiegel. "Friend of mine the distributor. Have him mail you one."

It crossed my mind that perhaps Monsieur Dulac had done just that. *Mailed me one.* A macabre example of his humor.

ETIENNE DULAC

1887–1962

A joke? One couldn't put it past him. He had probably been dead for a quarter of a century, having left instructions to mail these cards on the appropriate anniversary. Crazy? I'm simply telling you what crossed my mind.

One of the "show" pieces at Riva was a mural in the room that served as a museum. Full of the junk that amused him. Some of it shipped in by his nutty friends. This mural was the *trompe l'oeil* sort of thing, meant to suggest a view from the window. In many ways it did, since the artist had painted what he saw out the actual window behind him. A summer view of the slope below Riva, the canyon, the village of Muhldorf, the mountains beyond. Peace and plenty. Peasants in the fields, fruit hanging on the trees, billowy clouds in the sky. From the door, as I say, it looked pretty good. Through the top, left center of the painting a stovepipe entered the room, or left it, the brass pipe collar ornamented with gold to resemble the sun. From it rays of light lit up the scene. When you move a little closer you notice that a stuffed bird is perched in one of the trees, and that real, paper flowers bloom in the fields. In one corner of the painting the boys and girls are making more than hay.

That's just a few touches I happen to remember. It will give you the idea, but a poor one. That stovepipe, for instance, crosses the room suspended on wires from the ceiling, to where it dangles a pot-bellied stove just about big enough for a dollhouse. A small red light bulb glows through the bolt holes in the grate. According to Wolfgang Prutscher, one of Dulac's artist friends who had been invited to spend the winter had painted the summer mural in an effort to warm up the room. In any case, it's there. A strange sight in the wintertime. The stove was sometimes fired on the weekends Madame Dulac would sing for the guests, half concealed by the piano at the dark end of the room. She had been a diva before she married Dulac. Her friend and teacher, Dr. Horst-Schlesing, would be seated at the piano, the split tails of his coat lapping the floor. A player piano. Madame Dulac had an extremely powerful voice. The end of the number was usually signaled by a sound like a blind flapping at the window, the music roll spinning loose on the bar. At this sound Monsieur Dulac, Dr. Schlesing, Wolfgang Prutscher, and myself—along with other guests—would rise and applaud.

Does it sound a little mad? It didn't trouble me much at the time. For one thing I was cold. There was good reason to clap our hands. The old man at the piano, Dr. Horst-Schlesing, wore a pair of clamp-on ear muffs, knitted gloves with the fingers snipped off so he could sound a few chords. Beside the piano, as if seated, would be the massive head of Madame Dulac, the broad flat face with its crown of titian hair. Prutscher advised me that the voice was not bad. Madame had other problems. One could never be sure if she was standing, or sitting down. An inch or two less than five feet tall, she had the figure of an eggcup. All torso. Head and shoulders like something emerging out of marble. Two sons. I understand she died the year after I left.

"Spiegel, you remember Riva?"

"Riva who, Mr. Howe? What'd she star in?" Spiegel's field of reference is wide, but it's on wax or celluloid.

"Schloss Riva. You know, the place you came to. The castle in Austria."

"The loony bin? Think I'd forget it? I can give you the inventory. He had some nice stuff. Know what I could use? That old barber chair."

One of the objects in Dulac's museum was this barber chair. Turn of the century model, with the pump on the side. Heavy nickel-plate head and foot rest. But it was no simple barber chair. On the leather head rest a cap had been placed, slantwise, and Dulac had chalked in a crude face on the pad. On the foot rest a pair of laced oxfords had been placed, strings tied in a bow. It may be hard to visualize, but that was all it needed to turn that chair into a mechanical monster.

"You might sort of snoop around, Mr. Howe. If it's so much junk, might take it off their hands."

I lifted a laundry flatiron Spiegel was repairing to look at the magazine it set on. *Popular Mechanics*. The illustration on the cover showed an artist's conception of the building of the Panama Canal. October, 1911. The year that I was born. What had life been like? I opened it to face a half-page ad that assured me

TRAINED MEN WIN

Did you ever watch a young man who has had

Navy training? Notice how well he stands, how firm his step, how straight he looks you in the eye. Write for the Making of Man-O-Warsman today! You'll forget it if you wait till tomorrow.

Had *I* waited till tomorrow? Something had delayed my writing. Instead I had written for a ten-day free trial on a silver watch with a snap-lid case. It had not come. A square card marked the place which I opened to see the drawing of two faces on the silver screen. The caption read

SILENT FILMS PROFANITY SHOCKS
LIP READERS

Deaf persons who welcomed the spread of motion pictures have discovered that the actors in certain silent dramas are freely using unprintable language when they act their parts. To those who read lips with facility these dramas have come as a shock. In at least two major cities a protest has been made.

"How you like that?" said Spiegel. "Nice clean copy. Hard to find one that early." He took it out of my hand, flipped the pages loosely. "Listen to this: '$795 cash buys material to build modern seven-room house, blueprints included.' How you like that?" He toyed with the card that served as a marker, tucked it out of sight. "Listen to this: 'Empire all steel range, $18.20. Solid oak bookcase $11.40.' Like me to order you one?" Casually, for Spiegel, he tossed the magazine out of my reach. I eyed it a moment, then got up and reached for it. "Sorry," said Spiegel, leaning toward me, "it's a great little item but I already sold it. Mr. Lloyd. Matter of fact, he lives out your way. Asked me to keep it on the desk so nobody'd handle it. Know how people are. Took me years to trap an old girl who used her fingernails like a razor." He reached for the magazine to show me, but I leaned away.

"My nails are all chewed off," I said, and showed him. "All I want to do is *look* at it."

On Spiegel's somewhat concave brow I noticed the film of moisture. So did he. "Mr. Howe," he said, using a paper napkin, "Mr. Lloyd's got an item in there he wants private. Why he wanted me to find this issue for him. You know what I mean?"

I flipped the pages to the marker. A squarish card with a heavy black border, the name of Etienne Dulac at the center of it. My first thought was, it was mine.

"You mind my asking where you got this?"

"I got it in the mail, Mr. Howe. Monday. Envelope right there in the drawer. My name on it. I kept waiting for you to bring it up first, you know what I mean?" He jerked open the drawer of the desk; there in the clutter was the envelope. S. Spiegel, 1811 Ashland Ave., Chicago. His home at the time.

"See where it was sent. Mother got it." He clapped his hand on the phone and pushed it over toward me. "Why don't you call Seymour Gatz, Mr. Howe? Maybe that's it. Maybe he's got one." To help things along he dialed the number for me, held the phone to my ear. The voice of Drusie, then of Gatz, seemed to speak to me from the TV screen.

"Old sport," he said, as if he saw me, "where the hell you been?"

"Trying to round up some pallbearers."

"I got one for you, old sport. LeRoy Spiers. Peace-Comes-to-Positano Spiers, you remember? He says he'll buy it if Ehrlich don't want it. Another twenty grand."

"This is Dulac's funeral, not mine." I could hear Gatz rapping sharply on wood. "If the place is there, it's the place to hide from the likes of Spiers."

"The word's got around, old sport, thanks to a little shouting on my part. Spiers will pay forty. I'm applying the squeeze to Ehrlich for fifty. By the time you get to Vienna, may be seventy-five." I glanced up to see that Spiegel had cocked his head for an earful. Like a deaf mute he gazed at the silent screen; the lips moved, but what he read did not shock him. "You there, old sport?" cried Gatz. "If I don't see you, call me collect from Vienna. How you like that for a title? *Call me from Vienna.* Make a good movie. While you're there you might talk it over." The voice of Drusie interrupted. "See you Monday, old sport," and the line buzzed.

"Heard you mention pallbearers, Mr. Howe—anybody I know?" I lit a cigarette while he read my face for the obituary.

"You read the notice before I did. Is Dulac somebody you knew?"

"You know the truth, Mr. Howe? Honest to God's truth? When I look at the obits I don't see the names—I see the address. I don't see what's gone, I see what's left over! Now how you like that?"

"There may be a lot left over at Riva, if the place is still there."

"Don't you worry about that, Mr. Howe. It'll be there. Boys who put it up had that in mind, don't you think so?" He clapped a heavy hand on my shoulder. "Couldn't help but overhear what Seymour Gatz was shouting. Don't he believe in the service? Think his voice has to carry? You remember what I said at the time, Mr. Howe?" I didn't. Neither then nor later had Spiegel been silent. "I said, pal, this is one for Cecil B. deMilley. This is one for Howe and deMilley. That's what I said. I said if Lon Chaney was in it I'd go see it myself."

"That's good, since I'm offering you the chance."

He waited, his blank gaze on the flickering screen. "Know what I say to Mr. Horney, Mr. Howe? You're a way ahead of me, but I like it."

"Spiegel, you remember all the juice we poured at the Fair?"

"You kidding, Mr. Howe? I remember it was mighty laxative."

"When I wrote you to come to Riva, it never crossed my mind you would. Why the hell did you?"

"Mr. Howe, I'll tell you something. If it hadn't been for you I'd still be pouring orange juice. You opened my eyes." He blinked to reassure me. "Don't ask me what I see, but it could be a lot worse."

I turned from the page warning the innocent public of the shocking profanity in silent films, to gaze at the movie, a Western, on the silent TV. The jerky movements of the heroine allowed little opportunity for lip reading. But I knew. Oh yes, I *knew* what was being said. Was that because I recognized the characters? My pioneer mother, dressed like Barbara Worth, her wide-brimmed hat pushed back from her forehead so she could sight down the barrel of the rifle she held. Beside her my Uncle Fremont, in his cap with the ear muffs, smiling as he passed out the snapshots of himself to young ladies seriously interested in matrimony. Silent characters. Would it shock me, too, if I could read their lips? What they were *really* saying at the moment the reins fell slack in the buggy, and my mother turned from cracking insulators to more fundamental things? To those who read lips with facility, the danger is always great. Silent or talky. The unprintable language of men and women who act out their parts. My mother, in the silent past, in the clear and present danger on a train trestle, her lips speaking the vivid language of Pearl White. Charles Horney, in vibrant, living color, starring in the Ford hour of tomorrow. The characters of these dramas seemed to gaze out at me, as I gazed in. Whose lips, in this drama, were being read? Mine or theirs? How determine one's proper time and place? On this point both the silent and unprintable language were not too clear. The props were different, but the actors interchangeable.

"You ever do any lip reading, Spiegel?"

"You kidding, Mr. Howe? What I hear is bad enough."

Pushing up from the chair that had comforted bottoms more familiar than my own, I held aloft an empty bottle of Lucky Lager. "Here's to Spiegel and Howe, pallbearers."

"You're not kidding, Mr. Howe?"

"It's deductible."

"Mr. Howe, who was it said the only exercise he got was at his friends' funerals? That's me. Know what I'd tell him? He's goin' to get more exercise when he comes to mine!" Aloft, tapping my bottle, Spiegel held a dented beer can.

"I'll have you back by Monday. You and the Indian."

"Tell you what I'll do, Mr. Howe." He picked up from his desk the copy of *Popular Mechanics*. "You have it back on Monday and I'll loan it to you. Piece in there on how to turn a dime into a gold piece." He winked. "What it doesn't tell you is how to lay hands on the dime."

Time Past

One

———

The stewardess out of Salzburg, Fräulein Pauli, her breath scented with American mouthwash, leaned over the crumpled heap of Spiegel to tap her pencil on the window.

"The Dan-yoop," she said to Howe, "the *schöne blaue* Dan-yoop."

Through a veil of rippled cirrus Howe could see it like one of the canals of Mars. Blue? As blue as the Missouri at Omaha, loaded with topsoil. The slanting morning light, however, gave strips of it the sheen of ice.

"It's been thirty years," said Howe.

"Ah so—" Fräulein Pauli gazed at him without interest, a dental hygiene student curious what she might see when he opened his mouth.

Without opening his eyes Spiegel said, "Where we at? Know what I was dreaming? This old bag came in and bought me out of canned water. One who never comes but what she swipes something. Usually olives. Nuts about olives."

"Fasten your belts, please," Fräulein Pauli said, and moved down the aisle. The debris of centuries, ruined castles and cloisters, peasants and houses like wood-carvings, the scars of peace and war, of indifference and recovery, were not visible as they descended. Spiegel belched, making his own pressure adjustments. A young man with a pocket radio switched on the news.

"Know what it's like?" said Spiegel. "Crawling up the incline just before you do the shoot-the-chutes on the coaster. Ocean Park. Then down you go. Feel it in the loins."

As they approached the door Fräulein Pauli signaled to Howe. A telegram.

> BULL MARKET. FLYING IN WITH
> HOT PROSPECT. KEEP COOL.
>   GATZ

"The deal off, Howe?" *Howe?* Like old times. Were they back in the past? Before Howe could comment they were out on the ramp, a light drizzle falling on the upturned faces. A young man in a soiled drayman's hat stood forward chanting, "Herr Howey, *bitte?* Herr Howey?"

"He don't mean you, does he?" asked Spiegel. He did. He was there with the car Howe had arranged for. A light blue sedan. An Opel. Spiegel loved it. "Remember the Essex coach, Howe? Some lemon. What I liked was the velour upholstery. Goddam car wouldn't run, but it was a great place to sit, read the Sunday paper."

The young man was explaining how to drive the car.

"Ask him which side of the road to stay on," said Spiegel. "Some places the right side is the wrong side. Know what I mean? No wonder they stir up a goddam war."

Howe asked the young man the shortest way to Stein. Stein, on the Danube. Just up the river from Kulm.

"You sure you know where this place is, Howe? There's been a war, you know. You sure of the country? Lines on the map don't mean a goddam thing."

Did it ever stop drizzling? It had drizzled the fall Howe had lived in Vienna. Drizzle and sleet when Fräulein Greta Junger took him to the Wiener Wald. A blonde lady gymnast instructor aus Salzburg, Greta Junger thought culture was a splendid thing. One exchanged it like stamps, or coins, at the Wiener Bankverein. In her briefcase with the poems of Goethe she had the goat's cheese and dates she lived on. While she read aloud from Goethe the seeds appeared at the corners of her mouth. The strong taste of the cheese remained on her lips. In the spring, her corset unlaced, her long flaxen hair wind-blown, she gamboled like a heifer in a nudist camp near Klosterneuberg. But not with Howe. A Finn from Helsinki had been more to her taste.

"The university?" Howe asked the young man. "Is it far? How does one get to it?"

Was it Howe's schoolboy German—or merely a puzzling question? Perhaps the university was no longer an ornament. In one of its chill rooms Howe and Prutscher had hidden from the home-grown storm troopers, the firing in the corridor. It had been comical—almost: like Herr Dollfuss himself. Howe had written an *amusing* account of it to Horney, enclosing several stamps.

"Florianigasse?" Howe inquired. "I want to get to Florianigasse."

That made sense. The young man would point it out as they drove him back to the city. Spiegel drove. He was quick to get the feel of the car. He compared it with the Volvo and the Corvair. He showed a liking for the horn. In a street where the gas pump resembled an object belonging to a foreign movie, Howe signed the papers, and received instructions along with a map. Florianigasse, luckily, was nearby, and more or less on his way. A one-way street, he was advised to please enter it the right way.

"How you like that?" said Spiegel. "You can fly around the world, get into a car, and drive off with it, but back in Santa Monica I can't get the bastards to charge my gas!" Off they went. "Opel—" said Spiegel, moistening his lips, "once knew a girl by that name."

"The top—" said Spiegel. "This what you call the top?"

Nothing, almost nothing, blocked the view through the windshield. This seemed to be the top of Florianigasse. Howe ran down the window as if the glass obstructed what he expected to see. A building on the corner. A building with five high-ceilinged floors. Cars now sat in rows on the vacant lot, most of them drizzle-dampened Volkswagen. Sitting ducks. That was how they looked. A parking attendant in a white jacket waved at them to enter. Behind them, horns tooted.

"This it?" said Spiegel. Howe's head moved slowly

from side to side.

"Something's wrong," he muttered, and peered around for the street sign. One occupied the corner. *The* corner? No, this corner was new. The post was new. The sign reading Florianigasse was new. It was not on this corner a beggar had stood with a child on her haunch, dozing, her feet bare, her hands clasped in an attitude of prayer. Mournfully singing. In the slit between her thumbs passers-by would drop coins. "Something's wacky—" Howe repeated.

"You kidding? Got a friend who talked my ear off about where he was born in Indiana. All I heard was Indiana. Two, three summers ago he drove the wife and kids back there. Know what he found? He couldn't *find* it. Nothing but this freeway. Big six-lane highway where the place had been. Bulldozers come in and just wiped it off the map, like that." Spiegel made a gesture with his hand, the palm down.

"Into thin air," Howe remarked, his head nodding.

"I don't know as the air's so thin." Spiegel took a good sniff of it. "That's gone too, the thin air."

His head at the window, Howe gazed at the sky. In the not-so-thin air a room seemed to materialize. Long and narrow, high-ceilinged, with a casement window at one end. Gray light from the sky seemed to fill the room like water. Anything else? A desk had sat near the window, beside it a marble-topped washstand. The bowl and the pitcher reflected in the tarnished corner of the mirror. In the dark corner near the door a stove of blue and ivory tile, pleasant to look at. Had it ever been fired? Once, in the past, but it had brought little heat and much trouble. Smoke had poured into a similar stove in the apartment upstairs. Since then it had been used as a hanger for the clothes soaked through in the drizzle. The room had the smell of coal oil from the lamp, the charred wick, and drying clothes. Especially, drying socks.

From the ceiling—Howe often gazed there since he lay in bed to keep warm—hung a chandelier, without bulbs, festooned with glass blown in Venice. But no bulbs. It had never been wired for electricity. An ornament, and a reminder, of the house in Buda-Pest where it had come from. There lights had burned, Frau Dorfman assured him, sometimes all night long. In this room there had once been candles, as the wax drippings on the floor attested. But a ladder had been needed to light them, then blow them out. Not to mention, with the war, the inflated prices of candles and wax.

The heat in the room had come from the lamp Frau Dorfman brought in and left when she turned his bed down. Just enough oil in the bowl (a smear of it) to char the wick. Everything in the room, bed and bolster, desk and tarnished mirror, marble-topped washstand and blue tile oven, had been brought up the Danube from Buda—not Pest. Frau Dorfman was always specific on that point. Everything had come from Buda with the exception of herself—she had come from the plain celebrated for the *fata morgana,* the mirage that defied explanation. Frau Dorfman hinted that was also true of the past. Her preferred theory was that events were stored, like films, in space. Come a certain moment, on a certain day, and there one would behold it on the horizon: strange boats at sea, caravans crossing the desert, not to mention an assortment of sights un-

heard of. All stored away—one might say—in the thin
air. Not unlike the place where Howe had stored the
details of the missing room.

"I get it!" said Spiegel, slapping the steering wheel.
"Know what happened, Howe? They bombed it." He
threw up both hands.

Into thin air, literally. Everything in the room into
thin air—excepting Howe. In him the details of the
room were now stored. The sunless light, the window
reflected in the ivory glaze on the pitcher, the figure of
Frau Dorfman leaning out the casement, sniffing the air.
A striding, Dutch Cleanser sort of woman, her skirts
sweeping the floor, her earrings tapping on the taut
drum of her goiter as she talked. Flashing eyes. Howe
had always thought it a poetic conceit. None of this fire
had passed on to her son, who was, as she said, the very
image of his father. In fact, it was his father's clothes
that he wore. He had died leaving them all in more or
less new condition, the only problem being that of the
style. The high *chandelier* style of 1912, and the mid-
depression style of 1933. Hermann Dorfman solved the
problem by frankly admitting to the two worlds, the two
levels of time, wearing a raincoat and rubbers when he
walked in the street, his father's cream-colored spats
when he lived in the apartment. The double life, in fact,
seemed to suit his temperament. The "time" down in the
street gave a certain pathos to the "time" in the apartment, where he sat, with crossed canary legs, wearing
his father's velvet smoking jacket, puffing a cigarette
made of hay stuffed into a paper tube. In what place,
and what time, could Hermann Dorfman be said to live?
His favorite story, the big event of his life, was the ride

he had taken on the Prater Ferris wheel, where he had
spent twenty minutes in one of the cabs at the very top.
Something had happened. A repair in the motor had to
be made. There at the top of the wheel of life Hermann
Dorfman had been stranded: to be caught out of time,
out of this world, seemed to be his fate. Where was he
now? Had he vanished into thinner air?

"Why don't we *ask* somebody?" said Spiegel. "If you
don't see it, ask for it." He beamed to indicate he meant
to be helpful. "Cop'll pick us up if we park here," he
added.

"Make a right," Howe said, twirling his finger. Did it
seem only yesterday that he had? He would come down
the stairs that were no longer there, carrying the English
bike with its four-speed gear, wearing the lightweight
trench coat in which he had pinned the cotton flannel
bathrobe that cost him thirty schillings. Not bad, except
that the flannel came off in linty wads on the clothes
beneath it. Rained on, it smelled of wet burlap, took
weeks to dry out. The same weather, the same drizzle,
seemed to prevail. A surface splattered with leaves
brightened up the walk along the Ringstrasse.

"Now what?" said Spiegel. Like objects in a game of
skill, cars spun in and out of the traffic circle. On this
corner, *this* corner, an old man sold hot chestnuts that
Howe did not eat, but used as pocket hand warmers.
The smell of chestnuts on his hands in the morning, in
his hair.

"Bear right," he said, pointing, then put out his head
as if he had seen somebody waving. On the second-floor
level the window stood open, a maid shook out a rag.
Behind her would be chairs, too many, a news rack

empty of papers, an ornamental fireplace, half-open
sliding doors, a bulletin board for Members Only, a wall
hung with framed photographs of Klub excursions to
Buda-Pest and the Wiener Wald. In the woods one saw
them strewn about in the leaves like a pack of fagged
hounds. On the boat one saw them gathered at the front,
with Fräulein Helga smiling in the frame of a lifebelt.
In the adjoining room, in the hands of the Czech bloc,
the billiard table smoked in the green shade of the lamp,
the players faceless, around the rim of the table their
chalked fingers and cues. Howe did not play, but he
liked the click of the balls. Behind the half-closed folding doors at the rear Fräulein Klinger, a promising
lieder singer, practiced the scales with Anton Otto
Czerny, near the end of his long career as a child prodigy. Bird-like, subject to spells of giddiness, nausea, and
nosebleeding, Anton needed someone near him, hover-
ing over him, just in case he anticipated a seizure. A
loud thumping chord, followed by silence, sometimes
signaled the end, sometimes the beginning. He had a
certain style.

Seated at the bay window overlooking Schottengasse,
Warren P. Howe, from Girard, Kansas, exchanged cul-
tural conversation with Wolfgang Pius Prutscher, a
scholar from Graz. At that hour of the day the lights
would come on, some of them red and green, in token
of Christmas, not unlike the display in Girard, Kansas,
and other outposts. A student of language, working on
a translation of Carl Sandburg into German, Wolfgang
Prutscher took a lively interest in the strange patois
spoken by Howe, and the meaning of some of the
puzzling argot in the literature. Take, "Hey, straw's

cheaper!" for instance. What in God's name could a scholar make out of that? Not to mention such a baffling utterance as "So's your old man." With Howe's aid he brooded over these matters, but not profitably. The definitions were harder to grasp than the term defined.

"Is it in England they drive on the wrong side?" said Spiegel. "How you expect people to get along together?"

Wolfgang Prutscher had been tall, with a falcon's beak, feverish patches of color high on his cheekbones, the blue-veined wrists of a girl in his patched drafty sleeves. He wore rubbers, ankle-length plus fours, a beret so tight it seemed part of his scalp, at the same time exaggerating the wing-like spread of his ears. Shell-like they were, of a coral color once his thin blood got to circulating. Through them the smoking lamps of the billiard tables seemed visible. Wolfgang tutored, for a fee, in French and German, but took Howe on free in exchange for the information concerning the curious language spoken by Americans. Among his cash clients was Miss Katherine Brownell, from Buffalo, a near-sighted art history major. Almost blind without her glasses, she hated to wear them anywhere but in the halls of museums. Wolfgang had functioned, and in some ways resembled, a seeing-eye dog, of the wolf-hound species. Another friend of Wolfgang was Monsieur Etienne Dulac, whose two sons he tutored. Monsieur Dulac, something of an oddball, lived in a ruined castle just west of Vienna, once a weekend hunting lodge for the sporting friends of Franz Joseph. Prutscher had referred to Dulac as a bit Dada, by which Howe had thought he meant dotty, or something of a dodo, since the word *Dada* had meant nothing to him at the time. A

Frenchman, Monsieur Dulac had spent most of his life in exile, since he had refused to serve in the army in the First World War. A pacifist? Prutscher implied that the term did not quite cover the ground. Monsieur Dulac was an odd one: he attacked some things, made a fetish of dodging a lot of others. Many more than the draft.

Now that Dulac was in it, the place itself, the castle of Riva, was even stranger. A medieval Schloss, run the way it was run in medieval times. Monsieur Dulac was something of a nut on the subject, and seemed to think the past was where he was living. No plumbing, no lights, no conveniences. A little rough, to put it mildly, in the winter. Madame Dulac spent most of the time in her room, her feet in the fireplace, reading French novels. There was an old friend of the family they called Uncle Rudi. He had once been Madame's voice teacher. There were four or five peasants who kept the place going. There were usually a guest or two on week-ends. Dulac liked young people. Male or female, Prutscher had been advised to bring his friends out.

Was not Howe male and young? Prutscher agreed that he was, but the winter was no time to visit Riva. There was no plumbing. Worse, there was no heat.

Did he think there was *heat* where he was living? Howe replied. A tile oven that he used for cold storage, a block of ice.

Schloss Riva was in the mountains, Wolfgang added. Not the Alps, of course, but the lower Alps. Curious how often it snowed. And once it snowed it was hard to get in. Even harder to get out.

Did Wolfgang Prutscher think that Warren Howe, from the plains of Kansas, was unaccustomed to snow?

Did he know that on the plains it sometimes drifted to *cover* a house. That Howe himself, as a boy, used to carry his sled through the house to an upstairs window, raise it, and then slide down the roof into an orchard where the trees were like bushes. A commonplace. So better not threaten him with *snow*. On the plains of Kansas cattle were found frozen upright in the spring, so lifelike they scared you.

Wolfgang Prutscher found these details very interesting. Frozen upright and lifelike, especially, appealed to him. Even more, he was certain, it would appeal to Dulac, who had a somewhat macabre sense of humor. Howe must remember to tell him about the frozen cattle when they went out in the spring. In the spring Riva was beautiful. Out of this world.

But in the spring, Howe replied, he would probably be back in Girard, Kansas. Was he going to miss something like a real, live castle just because it was cold?

Wolfgang Prutscher had smiled. How well Warren Howe remembered it. A Mona Lisa smile if his lips had not been so chapped. Very well, he had agreed, they would go out. They would go the next weekend, before the snows came. Friday to Monday. A customary stay. And so Wolfgang Prutscher, wearing his rucksack, with his coral ears clamped in a pair of red ear muffs, took Warren Howe to Schloss Riva, back from the Danube in what is called the Wachau. The last Friday in November. Well Howe remembered it. He had jotted off a postcard to Charles Horney, just mentioning Schloss Riva in passing, which he planned to mail when they got off the train at Kulm. During a night of dreams the drizzle at the window had turned to snow.

"Howe—" said Spiegel. Howe glanced up to see that they were at the edge of the city, where the road curved into the leafy Wiener Wald. A man and woman, single file, clopped along in the trail beside the black top. Heavy shoes and rucksacks. The neck of a bottle thrust out the top. Might it be Greta Junger? Her hair was blonde. Her hips were broad.

"If it's a funeral, Mr. Howe—Howe, that is—who you think'll turn up?"

"Relatives, if there are any," he answered.

"What's a castle worth these days? Know a fellow in Beverly Hills who might buy one. Likes archery. Like a damned kid with his bow and arrow. Reminds me of that wooden Indian. If I can make the right deal ship it back air freight. Man in Laguna collects 'em. Indian pennies and cigar-store Indians. How you like that?"

Spiegel didn't want an answer. He gave the horn a toot as they swung wide on a curve, passed several hikers. One resembled Prutscher. Thumbs hooked in the straps of his rucksack, rubbers on his size-eleven shoes. Inseparable. The shoe came off with the rubber. More than noticeable, at the Klub, was the ripe smell of his overheated feet.

"Some class, eh?" said Spiegel. Howe glanced to see who he meant. He gripped the wheel with an erect regal bearing. He meant *them*. The class in which they were traveling. "In case you forgot," he said, "first time out I hoofed it." His head wagged to think about it. "Couldn't hoof it today, Indian or no Indian."

Two

The first time out Howe had also hoofed it. With Prutscher he had walked the six miles up the canyon. In the summer there was sometimes a car that delivered the mail, if there was mail, to Schloss Riva, but in the winter everybody hoofed it. From Vienna to Kulm they had taken the train that crawled along the banks of the Danube, a poky wood-burning local with a funnel stack like the trains in the Civil War pictures. On the curves he could see it chuffing, the logs piled high on the tender. The cars full of blond children seen on German Christmas cards. Apple cheeks and lederhosen on the boys, apple cheeks, long braids, and black stockings on the girls. Books strapped to their backs, bare legs and garters showing when they stooped. One of the apple-cheeked boys sat on a bench facing Howe. He wore heavy shoes, carried his books in a harness, his mittens dangling on strings attached to his cuffs. Chapped hands, palms down on the board seat, propped him up. A clear mountain stream connected his nose and his mouth. He sat without movement, a film of moisture brightening his eyes. He looked familiar to Howe, with his barked knees, his nose chapped where he dragged his mitten across it—but Howe, not Wolfgang, looked strange to him. Or perhaps it was not Howe so much as his shoes. Foreign shoes. He eyed them as if they concealed a cloven hoof. Howe wanted to tell him that where he came from were boys pretty much like he was, their noses even sorer, since they wiped them with stiff leather gloves, or the sleeves of mackinaws. But that might not be the news he wanted to hear. What good was a strange place with familiar people in it? At Kulm an older sister, with braids, dragged him from the bench like a doll, his eyes rolling as he toppled down the aisle. But once outside he ran wildly to a mound frosted with snow, from where, at a safe distance, he could spy on Howe. The locomotive bell clanged. Smoke from the funnel blurred the view. *That* view, but after thirty years Howe saw him better than ever. He would have made a good soldier. He had probably died in the war.

On the trip out—it had taken hours—Prutscher had told him about the country. The part of it they were in was called the Wachau. Very picturesque. Dotted with castles like the Rhine. Here and there the Danube spread as wide as a mountain lake—or the Missouri. The parallel was not exact, but Howe thought he would mention it. Wolfgang should know that there were rivers in America, as well as snow.

On the Danube they saw steamboats with the names of cities on the paddlewheel fenders. One called BUDA-

PEST, with the hyphen where Frau Dorfman would have
put it. Now and then Prutscher would mention, just in
passing, something about the place where they were going. Madame Dulac had been a singer, of great promise,
but there had been the problem of her figure. One could
not get through an opera concealed in the woods, or
astride a horse. The male lead, unless peculiar himself,
must be up when she was down, or down when she was
up. A quite phenomenal voice. The face—and figure—
of a large frog. A human frog. The question Howe had
attempted to phrase, tactfully, Wolfgang had anticipated. What had attracted Monsieur Dulac, a man with
a notable eye for the ladies? Wolfgang had smiled. A
scholar, he had aptly quoted, *de gustibus non est dis-
putandum*. But that was not it. No, that was not it.
Nibbling at the chap on his lower lip he suggested, just
in passing, that Madame's peculiar appearance had been
the real attraction. Not that he was morbid. No, it
wasn't that. But if Howe should see a woman so ugly he
would say, "My God, who would marry a woman like
that!" well, it would be Dulac! He would marry her on
the spot. And more than likely he had. One couldn't put
it past him. No, nothing. Not even that.

He was a nut, then? Howe had asked.

Wolfgang had tossed up his white hands. His narrow
shoulders had hunched up to cup his ears. He looked
bat-like. It might seem strange to Warren Howe, he
said, but perfectly sensible to Etienne Dulac. Howe
should remember, he added, that living too much alone
made people peculiar, which was as true of Girard,
Kansas, as Schloss Riva, in the Wachau.

With that their talk had ended. They sat, mutually

peculiar, with their gaze out the smoke-grimed window, the Danube like a plate of fudge poured out to cool. At Kulm, silently, they left the train and walked through ankle-deep snow to where the road forked up a canyon. Nothing had passed since the snow had fallen. The road —if road it was—had to be taken for granted. Prutscher waited while Howe, crooking his finger, hooked the caked snow from the heels of his oxfords. Out on the river a paddlewheel boat, headed downstream, honked for the bend. Something about it struck Howe as odd. The boat coming toward him was drifting with the current, not fighting it. Where *he* had come from, boats drifted the other way. He had the impression that the stream had reversed itself. An hour's walk up the canyon this would prove to be true of both time and the inhabitants. At Schloss Riva they both perversely flowed in reverse. The time barrier would prove to be the first barrier they passed.

"What if nobody's there but us chickens?" said Spiegel. "You think of that?"

No, Howe had not. The present had a way of dissolving into the past. Up ahead, swimming toward them, was the future, possibly inhabited by nothing but chickens, but Howe seemed to see it through the long, wrong end of the telescope. Up ahead was that canyon, snow mantled, where Wolfgang Prutscher, puffing and wheezing, his cheeks bloodshot, shuffled his rubbers around in search of the trail. A narrow canyon, now and then it opened into pockets where vines were planted. Water purled under the crust of snow. A downward draft of air smelled of logs and smoke from wood fires. About half an hour's walk up this canyon they came to a sledge that blocked the path. If sledge was the word for it. A sort of hammock made of saplings for transporting logs. It consisted of two saplings, peeled of their bark to make runners, drawn into a bow by a length of rope. In the curve of this bow the logs were piled. Freshly sawed, the ends sugared with the sawdust, smelling of sap. The new fall of snow had spread a white pelt across the top.

Howe had stood there gazing at it, amused and puzzled, until Prutscher had beckoned him to the rear. An old man sat there. Or rather he crouched there, napping, on one of the logs. Between his knees, and a crotch of one sapling, he held one end of a pole that served as a rudder. Up the trail behind him one could see where it had dragged. Why had it stopped? The wind had blown the snow a little thin on that point of the trail. More snow had fallen, however, whitening the old man's hat and collecting in his lap. A long-stemmed pipe with a nickel cap dangled from his mouth.

"What's he waiting for—a push?" Howe asked. It seemed a shame to have to wake him. But Wolfgang had stood there shaking his head.

"It's Langsam," he said. "He's waiting for more snow."

Waiting for snow? Howe had snorted. Who did he think he was, Rip Van Winkle? The sky was clear. It might not snow again for a week.

"We're not going to push him?" Howe had asked. Wolfgang had already started up the trail. It hardly seemed a problem of much importance. Whether it snowed or not. So they let him sleep, and as they shuffled past him, Howe had passed the time barrier.

That he realized later. Time had changed right at that point. What he had brought along with him—the time on his watch, the time better described as time-passing —that time, whatever it was, seemed inadequate. As he passed the old man time-present seemed identical with time-past. Cause for wonder—or so it seemed to Howe.

"Now how about that!" said Spiegel. He had stopped the car on the rise out of Stein, where the road forked. Howe thought he meant the river. Where it narrowed between the mountains a steamboat towed a barge of logs. But that was not what Spiegel meant. He gave a toot on the horn to point it out. Up ahead, at the fork in the road, a slab of wood had been sawed to give a rustic effect. On it, freshly painted, were the words SCHLOSS RIVA. An arrow pointed off the highway up the canyon. "Looks like they're expecting somebody," added Spiegel, and let out the clutch. The motor balked. "Bygod," said Spiegel, peering around, "right here's where it happened!"

"What?"

"Had to get off and walk. Steeper than it looks."

"Otherwise it looks familiar?"

Spiegel toyed with the gas pedal. He seemed to be wondering. The tires spun as they leaped off. "I remember getting off the damn bike," he said, and looked around as if he might see it. The deep grass along the stream bed might have concealed it. A thin coat of black top had been applied to the center of the road. "I got off," went on Spiegel, trying to recall it, "but the moment I did it started snowing." He seemed to see it falling. "It ever stop? I got off this damn bike and the next thing it was snowing. I remember that."

In the clearing back from the stream a few gnarled trees sagged with apples, ornamental as lanterns. More apples, rotting, flattened the hay-like grass beneath the trees. One fell from the branch as if the weight of a bee was too much for it. His head out the window, sniffing, Howe heard the muffled thud. Ripe and overripe apples, the color of leaves, bobbed along the stream like notes to water music. Apples to burn. The oversweet scent of apples in the air. As if the landscape had taken its cue from the painting, that dream of peace and plenty, on the wall at Riva, the vines on the terraced slopes sagged with grapes. That much had changed. Riva had not been like that. Etienne Dulac had carried in his pockets withered little apples the size of walnuts, and the same sort of fruit, looking like plums, had been served in a watery compote. Even the cider had the bitter taste of seeds and pits. A cloudy fluid, but hard, inducing a hemlock sort of numbness, Howe had taken a tip from Uncle Rudi and swigged it to promote interior heating. The room in which he slept, or lay entombed, had a sweeping of snow on the floor.

Spiegel stopped the car to fling open a door, flail his arms at a bee. Above and beneath the water music Howe could hear their contented droning. Thicker than flies. A harvest of honey sickened the air. On the surface of the millpond a duck floated in a pool of luminous leaves, serene as a decoy, the feathers touched up with iridescent paint.

Had it been here? Just below this point they had passed the sledge, the time barrier. On this pond there

had been a creaking crust of ice. Two or three barrel
staves that had served briefly as skis. Around the millwheel a spot in the ice had been cleared and a hole
drilled for fishing. Had the fisherman been sucked
through the hole? Or had he fled hearing them approach. The village of Muhldorf filled the mouth of the
canyon like a cork. A gasoline scooter sat between two
of the buildings. In front of the Gasthaus a gas pump.
The smell of gas, manure, rotting apples, and hot roof-
ing tar.

"How about a cold beer?" asked Spiegel. Through
the open door of the Gasthaus they saw clear through it,
like a tunnel, to the light on the grassy slope. A trail
went up it. They saw the legs of a cow at the top. A moment later, at the fork, another rustic sign directed them
upward, the tall road-grass sweeping the car. The air
clouded with a blend of insects, pollen, and dust. Spiegel
sneezed. He leaned over the wheel as if that might help
the car on the rise. Ahead and above them, plowing
heaven, two cream-colored oxen blocked the horizon.
Straw hats with faded strips of ribbon sat between their
great horns. Immobile, they appeared to be immovable.
From the mouth of one, like a soda straw, dipped a long-
stemmed spear of grass. With tails like lions' they
switched at the flies. On the ground at their side, in a
field of stubble, his hat shading his face, the plowman
napped.

"Now how you like that!" observed Spiegel. "How
you like that?"

The whine of the car left oxen and plowman undisturbed. A single freshly plowed furrow, spotted with
birds, pointed up the slope like an arrow to the hulk of

Schloss Riva. Howe leaned forward to stare. A strange sight? What seemed stranger than usual? Not unlike some prehistoric ark, grounded as the flood waters had receded, the lower portions were dirt and rock, as if time had joined them together, but the upper half, the Schloss that arose from the encircling walls as from an orchestra pit, had formerly had a faded coating of white. It now appeared to be gray, like wet cement, thanks to the brilliant white outline of the windows. The bell tower, daubed with white near the top, looked like a rocket prepared for launching.

"Hell of a time to start spiffing the place up," said Spiegel, "don't you think?"

The effect was that of something patched up with adhesive. The painter had leaned from the window to daub as much wall as he could reach. Did that seem odd? Invisible from the slope was the encircling moat, thirty feet deep and sometimes sixty feet wide. There were no ladders at Riva to climb such walls. Not in the past.

"Know what?" said Spiegel. "They're puttin' it on the market. Castles not the problem they used to be. Nice piece of land." He peered around at it. "How much land go along with it? Enough for nine holes?"

He did not smile as he waited for Howe's answer. Nine holes? Just about nine holes. A clubhouse featuring thirty outside rooms. A deep dry moat for the pets and the kiddies to play in. A relaxing weekend nine to ten hours from Times Square. Howe could see the brochure, photographed in color (once they got the rest of it painted), a haven for suburban Yankees in King Arthur's Court.

"Hey!" Spiegel braked the car. "This fellow Ehrlich want an old or a new castle?"

Howe had forgotten about him.

"Better tell 'em to lay off the paint till Ehrlich sees it. Hell, he may want another color." To lose no time, he stepped on the gas. The road curved away, toward the church of Ober Muhldorf where the rabbit-hunting parties gathered, then doubled back, approaching Riva from the east, up a gradual slope. Nothing spectacular. Quite the contrary, from this approach the past seemed absent. A large rundown estate with a seedy orchard. That proved to be the best approach, however, since it left you unprepared for the entrance. The moats, thirty to forty feet deep and wide enough for a four-lane high-way. The bushes that proved to be the tops of trees, the pack of dogs that proved to be a herd of deer. Howe had stumbled on it cold. Shuffling up through the orchard, on the heels of the wheezing Wolfgang, he had plopped down on the wall leading up to the gate. Behind it the earth seemed to fall away. Light from the sky burned on the snow at the bottom. Had the climb made him giddy? They had both been too fagged to appreciate the sensation. But Howe had never fully recovered from the impression: Schloss Riva was *not* truly part of this world. The huge encircling moats cut it off—even as they seemed to attach it—to the normal-appearing, sur-rounding countryside. An illusion. An illusion it was their purpose to maintain. From the *other* side—the view from the canyon—the castle was spectacular but familiar, unreal in fact but immortal in fiction, the castle in the fishbowl, the paperweight, the timeless cliché. But the moats were for real. His tired knees had wobbled. He had felt it in his loins.

"What's the point of that?" Spiegel let the car idle to wag his finger at one corner of the orchard. The Bastille. A square pile of rocks not unlike an American block-house. To repair it—back in Howe's time—a sort of primitive scaffold had been erected. It was still there, with the sagging boards, but the structure itself had been painted white. A fresh, luminous white. A curious effect. It appeared to be a house inside a cage. A captive. Howe stared as if he might see who was living in it.

"That paint?" said Spiegel. "Or whitewash? I could have made him a deal if it's paint."

It had the sheen of paint. Even more, it had the sheen of wet paint. On one of the crossboards a bucket of rocks, attached to a windlass, had also been painted. A pail of snow? That was how it looked.

"Some joke!" said Spiegel, letting out the clutch. Howe's loud guffaw surprised them both. "I miss it?" asked Spiegel. "The joke?"

No, no. Howe wagged his head. It was neither the time nor the place—if one could speak of them sepa-rately—to suggest that Spiegel's remark pretty well summed it up. "Some joke!" Could it all have been *some joke?*

On a horse too small to ride, the exact color of choc-olate sunned in a window, the Sunday that Howe had planned to leave he had gone for a ride. A little ride. Some joke. His feet had dragged a furrow in snow that sparkled like tinsel. The night before snow had fallen. It appeared to be a world on which the snow had fallen for the first time. The horses seemed to wade in a creamy surf. Nothing moved. Indeed, nothing visible was movable. If anyone had asked Howe what the country looked like he could only have squinted his eyes and said *snow,* as if he saw it falling, and was blinded by the glare. Monsieur Dulac, who went before him, was less a rider than a hump on the horse, both horse and rider licked by a flame as if simmering in oil. Howe had let his feet dangle, since it proved tiresome to hold them up. One of the stirrups was of leather, shaped like a boot; the other had been cut from a piece of wood. A little narrow, it gripped Howe's shoe like the milk cans, usually Carnation, worn like horseshoes by small-town boys. He wouldn't have missed it for the world. So he told himself. The movement of the horse produced a turkey-like nodding of his head.

They proceeded single file, downgrade toward Muhl-dorf, but the snow showed little trace of their passage. The horse ahead cast a shimmering mauve shadow, at which Howe stared, as into a pool, seeing no more than its complement when he raised his eyes. The church at Ober Muhldorf, with its onion dome, rippled like a sheet of film about to be consumed by fire. On the tower Howe could see how much new snow had fallen, and beneath it, the clapper rocking, he caught a brief glimpse of the frazzled bellrope, and the bell. The sound he waited for, however, he did not hear. Nor did he ever know if it came, and the horse heard it first. He saw the white cap of snow split like an onion, one half dissolving as it fell, then his head had snapped as if a hand had clapped him on the back. The saddle lifted, as if loosened, and he had grabbed for the pommel. The flying

mane of the horse whipped his face. Was she bucking
or bolting? He fell forward and hugged the neck. Snow
from somewhere lashed his face like sleet. Did he see,
or imagine he saw, the dark lump of an object ahead?
Between his cramped scissored legs he felt the saddle
slipping; he rode like an Indian ducking rifle fire. Was
he on her or beneath her? Was it the mane, or the tail,
in his face? Then, as if propelled from behind, he lofted,
the saddle serving as a projectile, one foot dragging a
stirrup that snagged him, like a claw, as he arose. He lit
on his side, painless, his arms flailing as if dropped into
water, and through the froth that arose he saw the
mounted figure that loomed above him. A flying horse-
man? Snow frosted his beard, whitened his smile.

"O-kay?" the small voice cried. "Yes, yes?"

Howe's head had wagged. He seemed eager to reassure him. His head had wagged but few of his remaining
parts would move. The object that stuck up like a post
beside him was his own leg. The twisted stirrup was
still attached to the horse. The limb it dangled, plainly
his own, had appeared to him as something disembodied
—something he might wear, or dispense with, as he
pleased. In it he felt no more than the gentle numbness
of sleep. Beyond the stirrup, pointing like a crossbow,
he saw the snow-pelted hulk of Riva, and the heads, no
more, of several figures on the ramp. One called. Another waved red-mittened hands. Cushioned in the
snow, feeling no pain, Howe had listened to the wheezing of the horse, his eyes resting on the shabby figure
of Monsieur Dulac. He sat humped, a smoking cigarette
at the spout of his lip. He took no notice of Howe; his
latticed gaze remained on the walls and the towers of

Riva, more than ever like that castle in the glass ball on the sewing machine. No chimney smoked. Nothing betrayed its unreality. Like the man on the horse, or the snow-capped slabs in a graveyard from which the names have been obliterated, Riva marked the place of something less, and something more, than life. With that ice pond in Kansas City it shared a world where the snow never melted, impersonal, impartial, and out of the time he lived in himself. As if Howe had stopped the film at that clip, and called for time-out. Time-out. A time-less flick neither before or behind, neither past nor future, since time itself was absent, perhaps what the present was like if one could ever lay hands on it. The sensation was so strange it might have been due to the circumstance.

Half buried in snow, not more than half *there* in the normal sense of the word, Howe was able to look upon things—his own leg, for example—as if detached from himself. Strange. There it hung, his impersonal personal leg. Perhaps Howe's head, a little loose on his neck, had been set to spinning in the wrong direction—against the common drift of time, perhaps, or jarred off the track. Whatever the reason, or unreason, he was out of it. He saw it all as if he was not even part of it. Off somewhere, as in a ballad, he could hear figures approaching, grunting as they slipped and fell, calling names, gasping like fish. By several of them, in parts, as if he had been quartered for that purpose, he was hauled back up the slope to Riva, into the court from which he had just departed, where, on the landing, they deposited him, with a broom swept him off.

What had it been like? The memory of it was clear

although it was quite unlike a memory, he saw it so
well. One had taken his shoe off—to do that it had been
necessary to cut the laces—and they stood in a circle
gazing at him, at his swelling club-like foot. How did
he look? He rested on the cushion of snow scooped up
by the tail of his coat. He looked—he knew himself that
he looked like a piece of game, freshly bagged. They
would hang him in the crypt until the time came to skin
him, hanging head down. His pelt would decorate one
of the floors, or one of the beds. Other guests would
sleep beneath it, as he had slept. All of this struck him
as amusing, his eyes closed against the blinding light of
the sky. Like tinfoil it crinkled as they lifted him, not
too easily, and carried him up the stairs to his room.
Some joke? Yes, it had been some joke.

Three

Where the road divided to wind up through the orchard another rustic arrow pointed to Riva. No car had used the leaf-strewn lane for some time. In narrow tracks left by a cart the apples had formed in rows, rotting. Under the gnarled trees they rotted in the yellow, unmowed grass. In this orchard, white with snow, Howe had come upon the old man, a peasant, using a stick to knock the last withered apples from an upper limb. A clever monkey? That had been how Monsieur Dulac looked. Small claw-like hands thrust out of the sleeves. Strips of burlap wrapped his spindly shanks.

"Be some joke," said Spiegel, "if nobody turned up!" He harumphed.

"We've turned up," Howe replied.

"Knew you'd say that moment I said it." No car had passed, but the grass had been trampled where there had once been a footpath. Cleat marks showed in the soft parts of the road. "We go right in?" asked Spiegel. Through the archway the ramp seemed to blur with a sprinkler system. But it was grass—long-stemmed spears of grass that grew between the cobbles. A lane a cow might have made went along the low wall. Leaning on the wall was a scythe, both the handle and the long curved blade painted white. Freshly painted. Some of it had rubbed off on the grass. Like the objects used to ornament New England inns and antique shops, it had been placed near the gate for its effect.

"How you like that?" said Spiegel, leaning out of the car. "First he gets the thing painted, then he decides to use it." The painter had taken a halfhearted swipe at a patch of the grass, streaking it with paint. "Probably more of it on him!" Spiegel laughed. He let the car ease forward on the cobbles. Grasshoppers fell on the hood and the windshield. Spiegel would have spoken but his head bobbed twice, tipped back, exploded with a sneeze. A cloud of gnats and pollen arose as the motor died. Riva had the serene peace of a ruin that had returned, tax-free, to nature. Spiegel checked, just in time, an impulse to toot the horn.

"Know what I think? Think we missed it. Think they buried him and cleared out."

That was how it looked. That they had buried him, say, ten years ago and then cleared out. Except for the paint. The white paint like strips of band-aid around the windows. The paint on the scaffold, the paint on the scythe. Anything else? If Howe could believe his eyes, there was paint, white paint, on the scaly legs of the chicken, a molting Plymouth Rock, that scratched in the dirt between the cobblestones. An old hen with a shabby,

plucked bottom, she had not been seriously disturbed by
their arrival. Had she stepped into a can of paint? Or
had she been touched up a bit, like the surroundings?
Spiegel put his head out the window to cluck, but got no
reply.

"What'd I tell you?" he said. Howe had forgotten.
"Didn't I tell you there was nobody here but us
chickens?"

But that was where he was wrong. Somewhere within
the Schloss a door slammed, and after a brief interval
another. Then another, as if they were spaced down a
corridor. It might have been the wind, of course, a draft
blowing down a corridor where the doors, their latches
rusty or broken, stood open. It might have been, but it
was not. Even thirty years had not disturbed the pattern
of that interval in Howe's mind. Wham-wham—WHAM.
Not unlike the interval between the hissing lisp of falling
snow and its POM! Both, in Howe's opinion, originated
in the same source. The zany madcap Eulenspiegel, who
inhabited the ruin like a poltergeist, thieving, hooting,
and straddling the roof like a gargoyle. He was up there
to clean the roofs of snow—which he did. Curious how
often one of the guests was passing just beneath. His
thieving had been strange: the laces from boots, the belt
from pants, the buttons from a coat—these sundry items
reappearing as ornaments on his own strange attire.
Overalls, belted at the waist so he could wear a com-
pass, a hunting knife, buttons as medals, the bib, with
its handless timepiece, stretched over a series of over-
lapping shirts, all open at the throat, from which his
blond head, his apple-cheeked face, burst like a flower.
Time and again Howe had chased him through the halls,

through door after slamming door, to his eyrie in the
bell tower. There he would dance like an Indian on the
trap door that sealed him off. Hooting like a banshee he
would lean far out—Howe had feared he might fall—to
drop gobs of snow, or with his red mittens cupped to his
head howl like a wolf. A madman? Pure and simple.
Howe had almost lost his mind, but never his disquieting sense of affection.

George, he was called. Short for George Washington.
This name he had from Dulac who considered him the
father of his country. A stallion in a nest of mares,
George was the father of his country by default. The
war, the first war, had depleted the village of all the
young men. Howe had always pursued him, down halls
and through doors, on the tacit assumption the pursuit
would never end. If it had, only Howe would have been
hurt. A puppyish Gargantua, perfectly at home in a
medieval world of cops and robbers, the breaking of a
limb, a man buried alive and left to dig himself out,
were boyish pranks that left him sore from laughing. He
meant no harm. People merely proved to be frail. Once
he recovered from laughing he dimly sensed what he
had done. Howe's safety razor—without the blade, of
course—had been returned to him. Leather buttons
snipped from his raincoat he had found, like nuts, in the
toe of one shoe. Had Schloss Riva, the whole seedy ruin,
been left to madcap George to haunt it?

"What's so funny?" asked Spiegel. Had Howe been
smiling?

"You remember George?" Spiegel did not. "He let
the air out of your tires," Howe added. Spiegel remembered. George had been fond of the hissing sound of es-

caping air. If a bicycle showed up at Riva the owner usually had to cart it away, the tires flat, the battery dead, and the horn or the bell missing. George collected them.

"That—" said Spiegel, then seemed at a loss for the word. Did the memory of it seem vivid? Only yesterday, it seemed to Howe, they had clopped across the court, where the snow was melting, to find Spiegel's bike with the tires stiffly flat on the bottom. The tool kit looted. The rubber grips gone from the handlebars. He had had to carry the bike to Muhldorf, oil from the chain streaking his jacket. "That sunuvabitch," he said, with feeling, and looked around as if he might see him.

"If he's the same old George," said Howe, "we're going to need a pump. We got one?"

"You ever pump up a car tire?" Ash from Spiegel's cigar spilled into Howe's lap. Spiegel slapped at it. "He let the air out of these tires—" Spiegel paused to choose his words with care—"he let the air out of *these* tires, and bygod they can sit here till he fills 'em."

That seemed fair and reasonable. They sat quiet, reassured by the stand they had taken, listening to the metal of the hood snap and creak as it cooled. The snow had melted; otherwise little seemed to separate them from the buried past, the threat of madcap George and his tireless, juvenile pranks. They faced the Schloss, an ark-like hulk that sat in the dry moat, a lake from which the water had receded. Unpainted, the surface peeling, the pitched roof tufted with grass and birds' nests, the strips of white around the windows seemed to be part of another design. Superimposed. Not actually part of the Schloss. The same might be said, it occurred to

Howe, of the two men and the car parked on the ramp.

"I get it!" said Spiegel, opening the door. "He's the nut with the paint, eh? How about it?"

That thought had not even crossed Howe's mind, but he was smart enough not to admit it. He smiled. It seemed fairly obvious. If the place fell in George's hands —along with a can of paint—this would be the outcome. It would go on and on, and on—to the bottom of the can. Out of one window the wall had been smeared, on the bottom side; a thin trickle of the paint ornamented the wall like an unframed abstract painting. It was something to look at, but disturbing.

"Guess we might as well case the joint, eh?" said Spiegel, and heaved out of the seat. At the sight of Spiegel the hen, her white legs flying, made off in the weeds. Spiegel shook his head, screwing a finger in one ear, but the trouble was outside, not inside. The smell of motor oil and hot metal did not cut the sweet stench of the apples. Howe had picked up one thinking he might eat it, but changed his mind. He gave it a toss into the outer moat, where it fell without a sound. Rock-strewn, the bottom was lapped with billowy folds of grass. Howe had never seen it free of snow. On many days the sun had burned in a glassy sky, but as if in a painting since the snow never melted. A perceptible settling had been visible, but that was all. The snow had adapted itself, like a quilt, to the shapes beneath. Just as a comforter revealed the shapes in a bed, or the sag where two slept as one, the quilt of snow ended up revealing more than it covered up. Or so Howe felt. Clearly visible were trails that nobody used. Short cuts that would not be apparent in the summertime.

On the slope to the south the field of stubble had been like a mesa dotted with teepees. Undefiled—so his uncle had assured him—by a rabbit track. Across that field, on a night so bright the shadows of the men were ringed with fire, the beaters, ten furrows apart, hooting like crows and flailing their arms, had marched toward the canyon with the game—so to speak—fleeing before them. A moment later there had been the rolling crash of the guns. Echo answered echo. Then an all-clear, or a hunter's horn, to make sure the huntsmen would not shoot the beaters, as they ran into the open to gather their haul of game. Not a hare. Not a goddam *hair,* as Fremont Osborn had said. The following day Howe and Fremont Osborn had examined the trampled snow in the canyon—the tracks of men, an army of men—but not one single paw of a rabbit. But it was rabbits—not hunters—who ravished the small fenced gardens in the spring.

"Hey!" yelled Spiegel. He had walked up the ramp to where it curved and narrowed to the door of the Schloss. He stood there with his hand resting on a huge, spoked wheel, the hub and rim freshly painted. Howe recognized it as the wheel that had once been on the well hoist. He had spun it himself. "If it's for sale, I'll buy it," said Spiegel. He seemed to be calculating the shipping charges. Wired to the spokes was a small sign with a thumb and finger pointing toward the entrance. The huge iron-slabbed door of Riva stood ajar, the bolt drawn. In the peephole a nest had been built between the iron bars. "I remember this bit," said Spiegel, and slapped the wall to the right of the door. A slab of it was polished as if someone had leaned there. "Rope hung here," went on Spiegel. "Big knot on it. Remember the noise it made when I pulled it."

So could Howe. The rope had been attached, on a series of pulleys, to a huge bell that hung in the court. One of the huge bronze gongs worn by Swiss cows. The sound of it meant a guest had arrived, since the natives, like Howe, had learned not to pull it. It signaled, among other things, an avalanche of snow from the roof. Timed —so it always seemed—to fall on the guest as he entered the court and lifted his bright, somewhat feverish face, to the sky. At that moment the snow, with its sibilant whisper, covered him up. The bell was *also* the signal to the rescue squad, sometimes headed by Howe, eager to see who they might find at the bottom of the heap. There had always been the chance it might be Charles Horney, or Katherine Brownell.

No bellrope hung there now. A small bird flicked out of the hole in the wall where it had dangled. Spiegel gave a thrust to the door, put his head in the draft, then slipped by it. Cool. "Ahhhhh," he said, and lifted his arms like a winded chicken, letting the breeze lap the damp parts of his shirt. A corridor, with an uneven stone floor, narrowed to the point where it opened at the rear. In that opening the white limbs of the dead tree were framed. Hay-like patches of grass grew at its base.

Howe's memory of the scene was confused. Had the tree been dead, or just leafless? At its base the huge surreal dog had been chained. A Great Dane, the black and white markings made it difficult to actually see him. Whole, that is. A collection of jigsaw parts. Like so many huge beasts he was under the impression he was a lap dog. Playfully pouncing on Dulac he would bowl him over like a puppy, then hold him flat in the snow while he licked his face. He was kept chained in the court except for the walks he took with Dulac, gamboling like a calf in the snow, terrifying men and dogs alike. Were they expected to believe this monster was a *dog?* They did not. He was merely one of the freaks who inhabited the strange world of Riva. Howe was another. The hatless, pale-faced American. Was he crazy? If not, why had he come from America to Riva? They had also heard of the petrified Indian and one man had actually seen him. He had never returned. No, one look had been enough.

"That goddam dog wouldn't still be around?" asked Spiegel. He delayed entering the hallway. A trough had been worn at the center of the stone floor. Down it, heaped with snow from the inner courts, Howe had trundled heavy wheelbarrows to the ramp. Day after day. Week after week. A routine that seemed as senseless as monkeys working a gold mine. But the rule. The snow had to be carried out. It was Dulac's idea—his mania—that the rocks beneath Riva were full of rooms, the rooms possibly full of God knows what. Bodies, perhaps? So he seemed to hope. Men and women who had sought refuge in the early sieges of Riva, and might be found there, preserved by the chill, in much the same state as they had entered, a perfectly preserved museum of the past. A loony idea, it seemed to Howe, but less loony as the weeks passed. No, it seemed quite likely. It was one of the things he hated to miss. But at the current rate of excavation—a few small buckets of rocks a day—years might pass before anything was known. It was believed, for example, but not proven, that an underground escape passage existed between Riva, on the cliff, and the village of Unter Riva below. This, too, Howe had come to *believe*—to take, that is, for granted —just as he took for granted that on every weekend it would snow.

"You'd have known it before this," Howe replied, since the dog had been sensitive to Spiegel. Several minutes before his actual arrival he had bayed like a hound of the Baskervilles. Every dog in the canyon had taken up the cry.

Nevertheless, Spiegel let Howe lead off, feeling his way along the wall to the door on the left. A log propped it open against the strong draft. This air was warm, however, slightly apple-scented, and carried a few droning bees with it. Howe first rapped on the door, waited a moment, then stepped into the court. A square, stone-floored yard, open on the sky. Howe peered around at it, smiling, never having seen the floor before. There had always remained a coating of ice, or a dusting of snow. A green that was not grass had taken over except where the path crossed to the flight of stairs. This was worn smooth, even polished. Likewise the iron rail that went along the stairs. Who was it that tramped back and forth, up and down? At the top of the stairs, on the landing, a wire dangled where the bell had hung. Panes were broken in the high windows along the wall. Howe stepped in, then stopped when he heard the creak of a door behind him.

"Christ," said Spiegel, but hoarsely, his throat dry. Howe turned to see a young man, hatless, with goggle-type dark glasses, his thumbs hooked in the straps of his rucksack, staring at them. He wore lederhosen. His brow seemed flushed with prickly heat. What he saw before him did not reassure him. He put a dry tongue to his chapped lips, said *"Bitte?"*

"Bitte?" Howe replied, his head nodding.

That seemed to be enough, or more than enough. He was gone from the door; they could hear his shoes clopping on the ramp.

"Think he come for the funeral?" said Spiegel, but he did not move to stop him.

"If he did, he probably thought we were a pair of ghosts."

"Bygod, I can believe it." In the cool hall draft Spiegel was sweating. "Place gives me the creeps," he said, creeping, "don't it you?"

As he clopped away the young man whistled loud but tunelessly. Right where Howe stood was where the snow, with a silken lisp, had fallen on him. Not once but twice. Said to have been caused by a slamming door. Invisible from the court was the pitched shingle roof where George, astride it like a gargoyle, sat with the polished handle of the long wooden scrape in his lap. Audible, however, had been his hooting laugh, and the muffled clapping of his red-mittened hands. Pleased with himself. The thought of it did give Howe a touch of the creeps.

"Let's go," he said, and they went. Nothing fell from the roofs or the sky but the echo of their racket. Under the stairs, going down, the door to the crypt sagged on its hinges. Not lost on Howe was the chill draft of cave-like air. Down there, in a room of stone, so low a dwarf would stoop in it, were columns with the faces of Halloween goblins carved in the stone on their bases. Also a rabbit, all ears, proving that there had once been one. In the sputter of candlelight Howe had seen them through the white smoke of his breath. Rabbit and goblin had kept their dark vigil for nine hundred years. A scholar had spent one summer at Riva to prove this fact. No one knew when the first rocks were piled at Riva, but one could surmise, as Howe often did, that the first man to pile them had been the Adam, the apple-cheeked gargoyle who straddled the roofs. No doubt of that. The line of descent had been direct. Lantern-jawed, ham-handed and thighed, what was once referred to as a cod-piece seemed his most remarkable characteristic. Father of his country? No one would question it.

At the foot of the stairs another two-fingered hand directed their gaze at two broken dormer windows. Two doves perched on the dung-splattered sill. Several of the panes in the leaded window were gone. Behind that window Madame Dulac had lived with her brindle bitch, Dolly, the old dog wrapped in blankets and kept in a wood box near the fire. Almost hairless with mange, hardly able to stand, suffering from asthma and constipation, the old dog's labored snorfeling could be heard when Madame opened her window. Twice daily, Dr. Horst-Schlesing, whose feeble legs were hardly better, would carry the blanket-wrapped old dog into the chapel where a stone had been lifted to expose a piece of earth. Seldom did anything happen. Dolly would sniff, shudder, and whimper. Back in her box near the fire she would do what she could. It was why the room had to be aired of what Madame referred to as *smoke,* at the same time filling her enormous lungs with fresh air. It sometimes led her to try her voice. Untutored in such matters,

Howe was nevertheless impressed. He could honestly say he had never heard its like before. Aroused by guests, by wine, or by her infrequent hot bath at Kulm, Madame would dress in the costume of the barmaid in Puccini's *Girl of the Golden West,* and sing several of the more difficult arias. Her hair down, her head framed in the small dormer window, she resembled a huge Irish policeman known for his female impersonations. Howe never laughed, however. Both the sight and the sound of Madame Dulac were sobering.

The doves perched at her window had splattered the top step of the landing. In the cracks between the stones there were glinting pieces of the broken glass. A broom to sweep the snow from shoes—or from the half-buried guests—still sat where it would be useful in such an emergency. In the splintered handle there were snips of red mitten wool.

The door off the landing was closed, but a sign read *Herein, Bitte.* Howe delayed, however. From the landing he noted the white drip that crossed the court, unevenly, wagged on the stairs. On the landing a gummy white ring indicated where the bucket had set.

"Know what I think—" said Spiegel, but Howe didn't care to. He tried the latch with a swipe of paint on it. As the door creaked inward he stepped into the hall. The draft stirred the pigeon feathers on the wide flight of steps, and the strips of spider web at the window. A slotted window, Howe had never seen it free of snow. These steps led up to Madame Dulac's room, and were always sprinkled with snow and bits of kindling. But Howe did not think of Madame Dulac; peering upward he thought only of Kitty. Had he, at Riva, so often glanced up hoping she might be there? If a guest had arrived, if there were tracks on the ramp, if a sweeping of snowdust whitened the hallway, there was always a chance that Kitty Brownell had taken his dare. But the dare she had taken had been Dulac's. That fact Howe had not grasped till he imagined her there on the landing. Had she really been here? If so, she would be back. He stood silent as if he might hear her voice.

"Know what I think, Howe—" Spiegel repeated, but Howe didn't want to. He turned, facing away, to the steps that led up to the kitchen, the trough beneath the door swept clean by the draft. Howe had often watched Mizi's skirts sweep it like a broom. He had never known what she wore for shoes. A large girl. Larger by the hour, the day, the week. Native soil into which George had sown his seed. In the fifth month of her pregnancy —the month of Howe's arrival—she had the face of a bowl of cream, blue-black hair, a divine amplitude. Suds, like lace, were always drying on her white arms. Cook and servant, never without a tray, a pitcher, or a bucket to sigh over, on the head of Howe, as she poured his soup, she would rest the pillow of her bust. A deep sigh would escape her. If mussed, she would smooth his hair with a stroke of her hand. She sighed like a sleeper, smelled always like a warm bed. Was it a proper custom, five months pregnant, to spread her charms over an imperfect stranger? It depended on the country. At Riva, it was. In the man-depleted hills of Riva, to be a virgin was no virtue. Virtue was to be thick with child, never mind whose.

"Where's everybody?" said Spiegel, and stepped around Howe to push open the door recessed in the

archway. The *Speisesaal*. The only room at Riva, besides
the kitchen, with a stove in it. Long and narrow, with an
exposed timbered ceiling, a bay of windows at the back
overlooking the canyon, it sat barren and empty as a
loft. The table and chairs, the wagon-wheel chandelier
with the bulb in the hub, the dripping candles, the tub-
sized fishbowl that had occupied the bay, the chest with
the Magnavox radio horn, any and everything that could
be moved had been removed. But not quite everything.
A guest book, with ornamental covers, dangled on a
chain from the bolt to the door. Spiegel opened it, said,
"Here's a guy from Cleveland. Harold LaRue. Ever hear
of him?"

Before Howe could speak, a sound, like curtains
blowing, accompanied by a rattle like peas in a gourd,
swept up the stairs and into the hall. The door Howe
stood facing framed the wide figure of a woman. Mizi?
The pounding of his heart seemed to trouble Howe's vision. He saw the woman poorly. Was there any sign that
she saw *him?*

"Bitte, bitte," she said, but that was all, since the
climb had left her breathless. Broad and thick, her gray
hair in braids, she had the erect assured bearing of a
Grey Mother. A smock, of the sort seen on nurses, hung
to within an inch or two of the floor, buttoned at the
throat. On a strap that slanted across her bust, snug at
the crease of her haunch, was a leather pouch. Into it
she dipped her hands, as into clothespins, fingering the
coins. The run had brought a film of sweat to her face
and darkened her dress where the leather bound it. This
did not disturb her. *"Bitte,"* she repeated, *"fünf Schilling,
bitte,"* in the voice of a bus conductor. Toward Howe

she extended the callused palm of her hand.

"What's she want?" asked Spiegel.

"She says she wants five schillings."

"*Fünf Schilling or ein* dollar."

"What the hell for?" said Spiegel.

Did she follow that? "To see the *alte Schloss*," she said, gesturing with one hand, "to see the *alte Schloss Riva, fünf Schilling.*"

Howe could think of nothing to say. Nothing. He dipped a hand into his pocket for the money.

"I don't get it," said Spiegel. "She know where we come from? Ask her if she knows we were invited."

"There are many rooms," she said, "beneath and above. There is a crypt and a chapel. The tour is five schillings." Something in her tone, the way she pawed the coins, indicated she was anxious for the money.

"Sounds like a racket to me," said Spiegel. "Tell her who you are. Where the hell's the funeral?"

"*Fünf Schilling* for *two*," she said. "I do two for *fünf Schilling.*"

"I get it," said Spiegel. "Know what's happened? The old man's croaked and she's taken over. What she's got is a nice little racket."

"You come in cars!" she cried. "You run around in cars! You think an old castle is for you to look at!" She thrust her head toward Spiegel like a nearsighted tourist in a museum. "You want to look for *nothing!* For nothing you want to gawk and look!"

The frontal attack startled Spiegel. He stared at her face, the froth at the corners of her lips. As if he feared she might bite him, he stepped back. Not to lose her advantage, she moved forward. Her finger at his nose she shouted, "Who you think keeps a castle up? Keeps it open! You know what it is like to live in an old castle?"

"Suppose you tell her you lived here," said Spiegel, backing off.

"*Bitte, gnädige Frau*—" said Howe, and extended two one-dollar bills. She clutched them.

"*Zwei Tour*—" she said, and wheeled to lift the guest book, flipping the pages to where she found one empty. "*Bitte,*" she said, and with her thumbnail chipped the wood from the worn point of the pencil. She offered it to Howe, then held the book so that he could sign it. The same with Spiegel. When he had finished she turned the page to glance at what was written.

Sol Spiegel, Hollywood, California, U.S.A.

Did he think it would surprise her? It didn't. As he rocked on his heels, beaming, she ignored him. The names meant nothing. From a fold of her pouch she took several postcards with photo views of Riva. One for each of them.

"A souvenir!" she said. Thinly, she smiled.

"Ask her when the old man died," said Spiegel. "Ask her where they took him."

"*Bitte,*" Howe said, "Herr Etienne Dulac. How long has it been?"

At the mention of Dulac's name she snapped the lid of her pouch.

"*Bitte?*" she echoed, as if she hadn't quite caught it. Perhaps it was Howe's German. "Herr Dulac," he said. "I once knew him. Thirty years ago I lived here." When she stared at him he put up his fingers, counted off the years. "Thirty," he repeated, "almost thirty years ago. I was here. I lived here over the winter."

Did she believe that? Her hand, for the first time, stopped shuffling the coins. As if to seal them, her tongue moistened her lips. Howe was struck again by how little, if anything, he read in eyes. Hers were small, more gray than blue. On the pupil he saw the barred reflection of the window. In the fat lobes of her ears there were small red stones. It seemed an odd touch.

"When I received the word," said Howe, "when I heard that he had died—"

"Died?" she said, sharply. "Who?"

"Monsieur Dulac—"

"Dead!" she croaked. *"Him* dead?" The very thought of it did more than amuse her. *That* was more than news. She half turned away as if to put such nonsense behind her. The movement of her skirt revealed one of her black, hightop shoes. The toe was polished with the sweep of the hem. "Everybody else!" she cried, throwing up both hands, then dipped one back into the pouch. "Everybody else dead, but not *him*." Her head wagging, she clucked her tongue like a hen.

"Monsieur Dulac is *not* dead?"

"Not him!" she pronounced. "What would kill *him?"* She put it as a question. One she had given a good deal of thought. When Howe did not comment she went on. "You do not know him. No, not *him*." She scoffed. "It is someone else you know, not him."

"What's she say?" Spiegel asked.

"She says he's not dead."

"If he's not dead, where the hell is he? Who she think she is?"

Did she follow that? Only too well. Tipped back as if

about to sing an aria, she plucked a feather from the slope of her bust. "I am *Frau* Dulac, *bitte,*" she said, with pointed emphasis on the Frau. The metallic smear on the wings of her nose came from the way she plucked it with her coin-smeared fingers.

After a pause Howe bowed. "Frau Dulac, Herr Spiegel and I were once guests here. I was here for the winter. I am sure that Herr Dulac—"

She stopped him. All of that, her expression assured him, was long, long ago. If indeed it ever was. "You think he will know you?" She smiled. It hardly seemed to matter. "He knows no one," she said. "No one." Did that include Frau Dulac herself?

"Now what?" asked Spiegel.

"She says he no longer recognizes people."

"I can believe it. How the hell he going to recognize people if she won't let 'em see him? She know where we come from?"

"The reason we are here," said Howe, "is that we received a notice—"

Once more she stopped him. *"Ach Gott!"* she cried. "You come? I could not believe anybody would come!"

Howe slipped his hand into the inside pocket where he had the card stored. Her own hand she put firmly on his sleeve. "No, no!" she cried. "Do not show me! I have seen too much already!" She wheeled as if to leave, but the strap of her pouch caught on the door latch. Both were jolted. "No, no!" she repeated. "Do you know what it is like? That simpleton! Who can keep an eye on them? Do you know what it is like to have one who is mad—one who is a dolt?" Howe did not know if he knew or not. His head wagged. "You know what it is like? From five in the morning. I am up at five o'clock every morning. But it is not enough. Who can see in the dark? They do it behind my back, both of them!"

Solid, impassive Frau Dulac seemed on the verge of a nervous breakdown. She swayed to the right, then the left; a hand covered her eyes. It was Spiegel who stepped forward to prop her up. The pouch of coins, slipped from her haunch, swung freely beneath her bust, the flap open. Would there be a scene? Falling pins, hair-pins, distracted her with purely salvage matters. She stooped, indifferent to her span, and picked them up. Still crouched she cried, "You cannot know what it is to live in a madhouse!"

"Frau Dulac—" Howe began, since he could well imagine. But Frau Dulac knew too well that he couldn't. No, it was not at all, not at all as he thought. She paused to pluck from her lips a loose strand of her hair. Spiegel would have commented, but Howe cut him off.

"Frau Dulac," he repeated, "we've come all this way—"

The very thought of it appalled her. Were they madder than the two she had on her hands? So it seemed. Into the bib of her apron she blew her nose. Her broad shoulders heaved, then settled to a quiver. Was she sobbing? No, she was laughing.

"*Him* dead?" she scoffed, the very thought of it buoyed and calmed her. "Not *him!* We are all dead before *him.*" Erect, her pouch swinging, she swept into the hall and flung the door wide. Were they coming? "*Bitte, bitte—*" she said, and gestured with the hand in which the bills were crumpled. Howe bowed in a manner reminiscent of the crane-legged Wolfgang Prutscher, and she went off before them, two cash fares at her heels.

*   *   *

Had she hid him away? From a niche in the dark
stairwell she took the stub of a candle, twisted the wick
with her fingers, then cupped her plump hand over the
sputtering flame. Fat as it was, it seemed transparent. A
chill, damp draft blew at them from the passage they
entered. Quicklime? The smell of it checked Howe's
breathing. "That ain't changed," said Spiegel.

"Bitte?" Frau Dulac replied. She held the candle high
to get a glimpse of Spiegel, his beaming pumpkin face.

"Nothin', ma'am," he said, with a sheepish smile, but
he remembered too late that the floor was uneven. As he
tripped, he cursed. Frau Dulac and her candle had gone
ahead. Light, such as there was, entered the passage
beneath the doors at each end. The one ahead suddenly
opened. Howe stopped, blinded by the glare. Apples and
quicklime scented the air. Frau Dulac, framed in the
doorway, reached to place the stub of her candle in the
window to the left of her head. Spiegel was the first to
stop beneath it, gazing upward. Up and up, the shaft
slanted so that one sighted down a barrel. Was it by design one drew a bead on the roof of the bell tower?
Shingles were missing. The gabled roof leaked the sky,
light splattering on the towheaded wig of a gargoyle.
The yellow thatch of hair grew down around the face.
It appeared to be streaked and spattered with white, like
pigeon dung. Had it been placed there to frighten off
birds? Several had gathered on the roof just above it.
The film of sweat on Howe's forehead suddenly cooled.
He stared as if unable to move his eyes.

It was Frau Dulac who pushed him away. *"Dumm-
kopf!"* she shrieked, putting her head forward as if the

slotted window was a megaphone. The cry startled
Howe, but not the towhead in the tower. Was it alive?
It looked more like a rustic carving. A hand, white as if
gloved, raised as if directing traffic. "Idiot! Braying
ass!" Frau Dulac cried. Like a jack-in-the-box, the towhead disappeared. A moment later it was back. The
white hand held a brush from which the paint was dripping, raised it overhead like a torch, then motioned as if
to hurl it at them. Howe, Spiegel, and Frau Dulac ducked.
A good thing. Like wind-whipped rain they heard the
paint slap on the wall. Familiar as if he had heard it that
morning, Howe listened to the wheezing laugh, the slap
of a hand on one of his thighs. Something like a moan
escaped from Frau Dulac. *"Gott im Himmel!"* she said,
"zwei Kinder!" The way Howe rolled his eyes upward
when a jet cracked the sound barrier, Frau Dulac lifted
her gaze, then let it fall. If there were two children, the
one in the tower seemed to have her number. His wheezy
gurgle continued. They could hear the muffled clap of
his hands. Frau Dulac let him be, her ear to the door
they faced in the hall, eavesdropping. What she heard,
or did not hear, reassured her. Without knocking she
opened it, announced, "Two more gentlemen, *bitte,*"
then stepped out of the doorway to let them in.

Small and dark, luminous with green light, the room
smelled like a greenhouse. Perhaps it was. Jars of water
with plants, growing seeds, crowded the sill of the only
window. Around the walls, on shelves of slats, were
stored potatoes, squash, turnips, and apples. Especially
apples. Blue with smoke, moist as a cave, the air smelled
of stale tobacco and fresh compost. *"Bitte—"* Frau
Dulac said, moving several jars to make room for them,

then stooped to fuss with the figure propped in the bed. For a moment her backside concealed all but the head. Bearded, white-haired, it topped the pillow, a nightcap with ear flaps sat on it slantwise, the expression was that of a tipsy Santa on a greeting card. The grin—or the grimace—painted on the face. With a twist of the apron around her finger Frau Dulac wiped around the grinning mouth, smoothed down a lick of hair, then stepped back to see how he looked. Her second child was no Santa, however; the small body of a child supported the head, the legs were hardly visible in the quilt that covered his knees. In his lap, with apple parings, a soiled tangle of oatmeal-colored wool. He had been knitting: the sleeve of a sweater, the needles dangling, lay like a poultice on his flat chest, held there by one of the small, claw-like hands.

"Yes, yes," he jibbered, the head wagging, "come in, come in. Yes, yes?" The sounds were like those projected by a ventriloquist. Herr Dulac's lips did not perceptibly move; just the dangling tassel of the nightcap, twisting slowly, indicated the tremor in his head.

Any perceptible shock of recognition? Howe stood with the light in his face, smiling. Spiegel flagged his hand at a fly revolving around his head. The man in bed moved the hand from his lap to flick it toward the light, the window corner, from where the smoke in the room seemed to arise. The opening of the door had reversed the draft, sucking a streamer of it out. Up through it, rising in sections, a tall slab-thin man blocked off the window; some of its light, however, glowed in the cup-like wings of his ears. Stooped, he was still taller than Howe. The hand he put forward took no more of Howe's smaller hand than the fingers, gripping them gently, as if pressed to dry in a towel.

"Yes, yes!" Monsieur Dulac jibbered, "Herr Prutscher, from Vienna, yes, yes!"

"My dear Howe," Prutscher said, smiling, "I see Frau Dulac found you out. I hope you had the five schillings."

"Do you remember Sol Spiegel?" Howe said. Wolfgang Prutscher seemed to be wondering. Tufts of hair—like the weeds at Riva—concealed part of the face with which Howe was familiar. Black in his ears and nose. Wiry and white over his eyes. As he gazed at Spiegel he sucked in his cheeks, made a sound like rinsing his mouth. Did he remember? Yes, he remembered. The last of the cigarette smoke escaped from the hairs of his nose.

"My dear Spiegel," he said, taking Spiegel's hand, then drew him a step closer, examining his face like a tray of lost and found articles.

"Howdy," said Spiegel. "How'd you get up here, you walk?"

Herr Prutscher turned to let the light from the window fall on his legs. He wore plus fours, buckled to hang within a few inches of his shoe tops. He also wore rubbers. There were burrs and seed pods in his wool socks.

"What gave me away," he said, "those burrs?" He stooped, in sections, to pluck several off.

"Nope," said Spiegel. "Didn't see any car, so figured you walked."

That had not occurred to Herr Prutscher. He faced the window as he thought about it, the ramp where only one car was parked.

"I can't speak so well for other parts," he observed,

"but there's still nothing wrong with my legs, Howe."

Almost everything was wrong with Wolfgang Prutscher's legs, but never mind. They had to go—as he had said himself—a long way to reach the ground. Stilt-like, no perceptible calf filled the sock stretched as if on a dryer. A gap several inches wide parted his thighs when he stooped. No matter how new or full the plus fours, they draped from his hips as if over a chair back. Nevertheless they were legs. On them, unaided, he had walked from Stein.

As if commenting on the weather out the window, Herr Prutscher said, "A sight, isn't it? I'm afraid he's not been with us for some time, for some time."

In the same tone of voice Howe replied, "Was he ever? I mean, was he ever *really* with us?"

"Eat, eat, eat!" the voice of Frau Dulac chanted the words, the refrain was so familiar. Stooping, she took the apple core from his hand, wiped his mouth. "Eat, eat, eat! Do you do nothing but eat?"

On Monsieur Dulac's face the smile widened. "Eat, eat, eat!" he jibbered, the tassel wagging.

"When," Howe asked, "did *that* happen?"

"Some time ago," Wolfgang replied. "He's seventy-five, you know. That's twenty-five years longer than even he expected. Don't forget a second childhood is the climax of his life."

Howe stood wagging his head. No, he did not mean that. To indicate what he meant he turned to face the subject. Stooped over the bed, Frau Dulac's corset framed her backside like a drying umbrella. "Oh, *that*," said Wolfgang. "Just after the war. The last war." The remark was not intended to be amusing. There had been many wars at Riva. "If he refuses to die," Wolfgang continued, "I'm afraid she has only herself to thank. He was good as dead when she found him. She nursed him back—would one say to life?"

"Not me," said Spiegel.

"She found him *here?*"

"Oh no. Oh no. Nothing was here. The place was looted during the war, you know. Nothing was here but the rocks, the apples—" he peered around, then added —"the rocks, the apples, and George."

"That him with the paint?" asked Spiegel.

Herr Prutscher seemed to catch a whiff of it in the air. Something out the window held his eye and led him to smile. Was it George? On the ramp below, framed in the archway, an elderly man stood gazing at a map. A cane was hooked on his arm. A small rucksack dangled in the weeds at his side. He raised his eyes to glance up at the hulk of Riva, stare with disbelief, then glance back at the map. "If it's not on the map, they don't believe it."

"Who's that?" said Spiegel. "Anybody we know?"

It was not on the map, but the elderly tourist was impressed. He walked through the arch and took several tentative steps on the ramp. A scholar, or perhaps a musician, a tuft of white hair lapped his collar. The apple he had picked up coming through the orchard he polished on his sleeve.

"Don't think I know him," said Howe.

"Frau Dulac—" Wolfgang turned from the window to look for her in the room. She had moved from the bed to the rack of apples along the wall, turning each of them a half turn, like incubating eggs. Spotted or wormy apples she removed, so they would not contaminate the others. *"Bitte?"* she said without pausing. *"Bitte,* Herr Prutscher?"

"I think we may have a cash fare on the ramp," said Wolfgang.

An apple in her hand, she came to look, pushing aside Spiegel, who blocked the way. As if she might pounce on her prey from the window, Frau Dulac gazed without blinking. Without comment she wheeled, her pouch slapping Spiegel as she left the room.

"Know what she'd make?" said Spiegel. "She'd make a good housemother at Auschwitz."

Wolfgang waited for her to turn up on the ramp. In a moment she did, her skirt sweeping the weeds on each side of the narrow path. Too late to run, holding his map, the elderly scholar watched her bear down on him. They heard her voice, watched him dip a hand into his pants.

"I suppose it keeps the place going?" said Howe.

"They keep the place going," Prutscher replied, and turned to glance across the room at Monsieur Dulac. He sat knitting. The long needles seemed to dance in the light. A soiled skein of wool, oatmeal-colored, lay on the floor beside the bed, an occasional tug on the line making it hop as if alive. The impression—was it the hands, the nightcap with its ridiculous dangling tassel? —the impression was that of a monkey clever enough to pass—well, clever enough to pass. A small fox waiting for the appearance of little Red Riding Hood. Was he witless? Had he ever been anything else? It seemed to Howe that he knew nothing, less than nothing, *about* him. What had led him, compelled him, to such a life?

At the foot of the bed, like a piece of armor of some feeble and senile Don Quixote, leaned a crutch-like brace of the type used by paraplegics. A metal leg, with steel loops to insert his arm.

"He's got a bad leg?"

"A stroke," Wolfgang replied. "One leg is paralyzed."

Was it something he heard, or missed, that distracted him? He stopped the needles to listen. "Where is she, yes?"

"She will be back in a moment, in a moment," said Wolfgang.

"Back in a moment?" he echoed. "Yes, yes?"

A nervous movement of his hands spilled the tangle of knitting to the floor. Howe stepped over to recover it. As he stooped he saw the old man's hand, quick as a cobra, dip into the side pocket of Howe's jacket, claw around for an instant, then jerk it out with his pack of cigarettes. Too startled to move, Howe remained crouched. The old man's glee made his eyes bird-like. He tore open the pack, expertly snipped the filter from the cigarette, put the frayed end to his lips, from his own gown pocket produced a match. The tube glowed hot, then turned to ash as he inhaled the drag with a gasp, then let it out to form a cloud around his head. That too was a smoke. He did not disturb it with a wave of the hand.

"Nothing wrong with his reflexes, eh?" said Spiegel. "Didn't he use to roll his own?"

Howe's head wagged. Some young American, before Howe, had taught him how to roll his own, but he had run out of the papers. Howe had mailed him three packs in an envelope. To the dry spout of his lip a piece of paper was now attached. The full pack of cigarettes he had lifted from Howe he clutched in the hand he had dipped into a pocket.

"You can kiss them good-by, eh?" said Spiegel. Prutscher had moved over to flick some ash from his gown. In four or five inhalations he had finished the cigarette. The butt glowed hot as a rivet between his fingers. Bending over him Prutscher said, "He doesn't get a smoke often. She doesn't let him smoke." The old man let him peel the slip of paper from the spout of his lip. Evidence. It did not disturb his grin. "Have one of these," said Wolfgang, offering Howe one from the tin he flipped open. He took one himself, as Spiegel declined. They were lit up, puffing, when Frau Dulac stopped in the door as if she saw a fire.

"Look! Look!" Frau Dulac waved her arms as if to clear the air. "It is bad for him! It is bad for the plants!" She let the door stand ajar to stir up the draft. The sweep of her skirts seemed to help. As the air cleared they could see her plants, the new ones and the old ones, the living ones, the dead ones, and Monsieur Dulac. He too was a plant. One that required more attention than the others. Was he living or dying? One stem had withered but something of a green shoot appeared at the top. Ridiculous. Like a spear of grass through a concrete block. She hurried to him, dusted him off, raised him like an apple that needed turning, sorted the needles from the tangle of wool in his lap. Like chopsticks, she placed them in his hands. On the shelf at his side seeds were drying: melon seeds, squash seeds, the pods splitting. "Eat! Eat!" she said, and dropped several of the seeds into his mouth. Like a chipmunk, expertly, he cracked the pod and shed the hull. Was this with the teeth Howe had feared he might lose before spring? On the shelf with the seeds, held flat by an apple, were several old newspapers and letters, the stamps peeled off.

"Reminds me—" said Spiegel, then paused to check with Howe. "Who the devil sent off them obits?"

Did Prutscher follow that? He was slow in replying. He sipped his cigarette like a drink through a straw. "I'm afraid I was a partner to that, Warren—" Was that all? "We've kept in touch—" Did Wolfgang smile at what he had said, or at the novelty of it? In touch with *what?* The untouchable remnant on the bed? "I took up law, Warren—" Was it the length of the story, or its ir-relevance that stopped him? What did it matter what one took up? Here they were. "As a lawyer," he went on, "I've been useful to him. He never loses touch with what is useful. There have been problems. Property problems. I'm inclined to humor his obsessions—"

"Have I been one?" Howe interrupted.

"Anything that's part of Riva—" Wolfgang put it like a lawyer, glancing about him to determine the bound-aries. His gaze returned to settle on Howe as a willing accomplice. "Wouldn't you say you were, Warren—now that you're here?"

It seemed hard to deny it. For reassurance Howe turned to Spiegel. Giving his head a wag Spiegel said, "He's not exactly what you'd call dead yet, is he?" Frau Dulac's broad bottom concealed the man on the bed. She was tidying him up.

"It doesn't say he's actually dead, you know, Warren. Just the dates, if I remember it correctly."

"What else could the dates possibly mean?" Howe replied.

Prutscher stooped to stub his cigarette. Had his head grown smaller, or his ears larger? It seemed hard to tell. The blades of his shoulders showed up plainly through the fabric of his coat.

"Can we be so sure he is wrong?" Wolfgang let the comment hang in the air. "Sixty-two, wasn't it? Isn't that still four months to go?"

"Look—" Howe began.

"It never once crossed my mind—" Prutscher shook his head—"that anyone would come. Anyone who *knew* him. Another one of his little jokes. Perhaps his last." He smiled.

"Just what made you think *I* knew him?" asked Howe.

Prutscher turned to face the bed, as if he thought Dulac might answer the question. He was knitting again. The tremor of his head seemed to have increased.

"He did," said Wolfgang. He smiled, then added, "He could hardly wait for that book you were writing. It helped to keep him alive."

Howe would have commented on that, but Frau Dulac, as if her name had been called, crossed the room to the window. There she leaned peering out.

"Another guest?" observed Prutscher. "Or a cash fare?"

A high-pitched whine, not unlike the noise of a stalled power mower, came through the window. On the slope below Riva, up the road from Muhldorf, bobbed a bug-like car with its top down. The lights were on.

"Another lady driver," observed Spiegel, dryly.

This lady driver wore a kerchief of fall colors; her

tanned arm rested on the door of the car. A smaller figure sat in the seat at her side, on his head one of those
caps worn by English schoolboys. A blue and white
flight bag occupied the seat between them. On the road
up through the orchard the driver was sensitive to the
ruts full of apples. She tried to avoid them. One wheel
of the car swept the hay-high grass. She raised one hand
against the cloud of insects that arose, fell on them
both. Immediately the car jolted, came to a stop. Motor trouble? They could see her head bobbing. Above
the whine of the motor they could hear her sneeze—
and sneeze. A moment later she drove with one hand, a
tissue held to her nose. As the car bumped through the
archway Howe could see that it was boiling, the steaming spray wetting down the weeds and dust in the road.
Seeing another car ahead of her on the ramp she honked
at it. When it failed to move she thumped it, backed off,
let the motor die. The escaping hiss of steam clouded
the windshield behind which they crouched.

Spiegel's head wagged. "Know what?" he said. "Probably drove all the way in low gear. Safest drivers in the
world."

As if stalled in a traffic jam she tooted the horn. It
sounded damp. Steam rose as if they had parked over a
sewer. Perhaps Frau Dulac thought the machine was on
fire. *"Bitte! Bitte!"* she cried, "A moment, *bitte!"* Her
arms flailed. She wheeled to leave but Herr Prutscher
was the first to the door.

"Let me handle this one, Frau Dulac," he said. As he
turned away he ran his hand through his hair.

"There is a charge for parking!" Frau Dulac cried.
"Do not forget. Two schillings extra for parking!"

"Par-kink! Extra!" the old man barked, as if an alarm had woke him up. The tassel on his nightcap swung around to hang between his eyes.

"No, no, no!" Frau Dulac seemed to recognize the symptoms. She sat herself on the bed, holding down the leg that he had been about to lift and move sidewise, the stiff stilt-thin limb that needed the crutch. He didn't fight it. On his head she adjusted the nightcap, put the tassel to the back. "You're not a baby!" she said. "You hear?" and gripped him by the shoulders as if to shake him. His eyes were closed, but the smile curved his lips. In the spout of the lower lip she saw the fleck of cigarette paper that Wolfgang had overlooked. Stuck there, as it had always been stuck in the past. "Who gave it?" she cried. "Where did you get it?" and gave him a shake that made his head wag, then held him erect while she picked at the paper with her nails. He made no sound. He seemed to be long accustomed to it. Over the broad shoulder that blocked the view he grinned at Howe like a bearded baby, a prematurely aged child with an old man's leering eyes. At Howe, unmistakably, one of them winked.

"Here they come," said Spiegel, "woman and a kid," and while his gaze followed them along the ramp he slipped a fresh cigar out of its wrapper, bit off the tip.

Four

<hr/>

"My dear Howe—" Wolfgang bowed to one side to let the woman enter—"this is Katherine Morley. Kitty Brownell, you remember?"

She took the hand Howe extended, released it, and as she turned away said, "Warren, this is Brian Caffrey, my grandson. Brian, this is Mr. Howe."

The egg-shaped boy stood erect, hands at his side, the large head capped with a blue dink, like a nipple, a strip of elastic holding it flat on his carrot-red hair. "Pleased to meet you, sir," he said, and took a step forward, his thighs rubbing, to offer Howe one of his small, porky hands. He wore a prep school outfit—one he had slept in—with a tie that matched his blue shorts and half-sox, laced oxfords on his kewpie-like feet. Perhaps his shape made his arms appear a bit short. On his girlish thighs his tight kneepants had left a line, like a garter belt. Both sox and shoes appeared to be painted on his small feet. Howe had not seen a more "comical" boy since the oddities in Our Gang comedies: he stared, but he felt no impulse to laugh. The boy returned his gaze, which he considered proper since this was their first meeting. In his pink wind-burned face the green eyes were like gems.

"And this is Monsieur Dulac." Katherine turned him so that he faced the old man on the bed. He had given the nightcap a twist so that the tassel bobbed in his face. Deliberate.

"Pleased to meet you, sir," the boy repeated, and gave a little bow, the knees together. It left his doll-like feet six to eight inches apart. The side view seemed more comical than the front, the head, with its dink, a little larger, one of the figures brought around for trick-or-treat on Halloween. How *he* looked, however, was of no interest; it was how *they* looked that held his attention. Soberly he gazed at the simpleton propped on the bed. Neither a child's wild bug-eyed fascination, nor the cool appraisal of a little monster. He merely looked. What he saw did not disturb him: not one bit.

"My God!" Katherine blurted. "It's like Uncle Anson." She had turned to Dulac without actually seeing him. From the pocket of his shabby gown he clawed a few seeds and nubby bits of lint, tossed it all into his mouth. "Like Uncle Anson, isn't he, darling?" she said, and let her hand rest on the boy's head. That did not disturb him. Nor did he reply. With the nail of his thumb he flicked at a band-aid that had been looped around one of his fingers; the straw seat of the car had left a waffled impression on his fat legs. Howe was struck—the exact word—by the strangeness of this confrontation, a pair of odd ones at the opposite extremes of life. Juvenile and senile—they seemed content to bask in the confrontation.

Moving his dink a bit forward Katherine said, "It's not polite to just stand and stare, darling." It seemed pointless advice. Even the old man sensed that the child was not staring. What *was* he doing? Did Howe sense that this was what they were *all* trying to determine? What *was* he doing? Absorbing or radiating? There was a pause. They could hear the boy's nail flick the edge of the tape. Gently, but forcibly, Katherine turned him by applying pressure to his shoulder, so that his direct, impersonal gaze rested on Spiegel. The big man squirmed, winked, then braced himself and smiled.

"Spiegel," he said, "the name's Spiegel."

"Darling, this is Mr. Spiegel."

"What's this E for?" said Spiegel, wagging a finger at his cap. Howe had not noticed the letter E at the front.

"It's for the birds," said the boy. The phrase set Spiegel back.

"It's for Earlham," said Katherine. The boy let it pass as a point too often made, and of no importance.

"Might I have that band when you're through?" he asked. Spiegel looked puzzled. He turned to Howe. "Cigar band, sir," said the boy. "I collect them."

"Oh," said Spiegel, "sure thing. Let me give it to you now." Katherine protested, but Spiegel insisted. He tried the wet end of the butt, but shifted, in time, to peel it over the ash. "There you are, son. That's an Uppman sixty-center."

"Thank you." The boy tried it on his fat finger.

"Looks fine," said Spiegel.

"Brian," Katherine said, "these gentlemen did not come here to expand your cigar-band collection." Would Howe have questioned it if she had not pointed it out? For what else, indeed, had they come? Spiegel and Howe, Wolfgang Prutscher and Katherine, and this strange disquieting boy. The air of the room, apple-scented, had been variously parceled until the child's arrival; in what way did he now dominate it? Howe had not questioned till that moment that the center of the scene was himself, around which these other centers were arranged, and overlapped. Now he was not. This fat-assed boy, top and bottom heavy, with the hands and feet of a kewpie, neutralized with a glance the lines of force in the room. His center out-centered them all. A prodigal self-sufficiency left him unattached to his surroundings. Was it an accident he resembled an egg?

"Don't be too sure," Howe said, smiling. "It's not so clear at the moment what we *did* come here for."

"Isn't it?" she replied, as if surprised to hear it. "Isn't it the same as always? To get away from something?"

"What did you get away from?" said the boy. "Not me!" He removed the band from his finger to preserve it. He seemed indifferent to the way they were laughing.

"I'll never get away from *you*," Katherine said, and let her free hand drop to rest on his shoulder, or rather the slope that fell away from his head. Her grandson? There had been two daughters. As if he might see some faint resemblance Howe stared at her face. He saw none. The oval of her face (classic, Wolfgang had described it) was no longer seamless. Screws seemed to tighten the skin on her forehead, loosen it at her throat. "Do I look so horrrr-ible?" she asked, and clawed in her

gaping bag for a mirror. A small compact, she flicked
it open and blew the film of dust over Spiegel. He
sneezed. "I'm terply zory," she said, her lips puckered.
Over the mirror she passed the heel of her hand. A
cubist portrait, fish-mouthed, one eye at a time, stared
back at her. Mercifully, her breath filmed it. When the
lips parted in a grimace would Howe see the flaw that
made her more desirable? Once more Wolfgang's opinion, not shared by Howe. The flaw in question a front
tooth the exact color of a moonstone. The nerve dead.
Extraordinary what it had done to her smile. To Wolfgang it had been the flaw necessary to perfection; to
Howe a problem for the dentist. Had either known its
taste?

"Ma'am," said Spiegel, "you say his name's Art?"

"Brian," she replied, "his name is Brian Caffrey."
The boy himself was not disturbed. People were simple.
He accepted the fact that much had to be explained.
The large head, ornamented like a cushion, was full—
Howe gathered—of new, unused material. Under the
dink would be the label that said so.

"Kid's smart," said Spiegel. "What's wrong with Art?
Art's a good name, eh? Monicker like that makes a
good first baseman." The boy gazed at Spiegel without
returning his smile. Nervously Spiegel added, "O-kay,
you don't like first. Make a good right fielder. Caffrey in
right. DiMaggio in left, Mantle in center, Caffrey in
right."

"I don't play outfield," said the boy. "I play soccer."

That seemed even less likely. Spiegel's gaze seemed
to film over as he tried to visualize it.

"All he really plays is chess," said Katherine. "He

plays chess with his father. His grandmother isn't smart enough to play chess with him—or anything else."

"You're not so bad," observed the boy. "You exaggerate."

As if Howe had spoken her name, Katherine glanced at him over the lid of her compact. Exaggerate. Had he forgotten? She had always exaggerated. The heat if it was hot, the cold if it was cold, the imminence of war, the complexities of peace, the latent germs she carried and feared she might give someone. Had that been calculated? It occurred to him that he had never, once, kissed her. She had always been about to come *down* with something, or was not quite up.

At Howe's back there was a clatter as if the wind flapped a shutter. Apples rolled across the floor to thump Howe's feet. *"Ach Gott!"* Frau Dulac cried, and as she stooped to round them up they saw the culprit. Monsieur Dulac, one stilt-stiff leg out of bed, smiled at them. He had used the leg, like a cane, to tip over the chair on which the apples were sitting. Brian stooped to help Frau Dulac pick them up.

To Katherine Howe said, "I guess *he's* not changed either," and nodded his head toward the figure in the corner. How well did she know him?

"Nobody changes," she said, then repeated, "nobo-dy." When he made no comment she turned to see him smiling. "So I exaggerate? If I didn't do you think we would be here?"

"If you don't mind, why are you?"

"O my God," she said, "I'd rather die than explain it." The usual exaggeration? Not quite. Howe gathered she had come to that decision long before she left. In the tone of someone answering a questionnaire, "I'm a grandmother, you know, but I can't say it has helped much. Not with this one. Is there any—" she paused, than added—"help for prodigies?"

One of her blurted comments. She had not meant to be witty, and waited, impatiently, as if for his answer. The question hung in a room that had fallen silent, except for the boy. Buffing an apple expertly on his sleeve, he turned it to the bright spot, bit into it. There seemed to be little novel, to him, in his being the subject of their conversation. Neither novelty nor interest. Without comment Katherine took his apple, examined it for vermin, then reluctantly returned it. "His father does not *believe* in prodigies," she said, stroking his hair as if for reassurance. The boy gulped the apple as Howe used to, gasping, snorfeling. In a cheerful false voice Katherine said, "Last year we went to Disneyland, didn't we, darling? He didn't like it. This year we come to Riva. It's as simple as that."

Using the metal leg of his crutch, Dulac hammered on the foot of the bed. Without comment, Frau Dulac moved in and took it from him. A familiar scene. The child pounding his spoon on the edge of his bowl. Was it the first lust to appear, and the last to die? Attention. To have their attention. The fit of exercise had left him agitated. The tassel that dangled registered the tremor in his head.

"Yes, yes," Wolfgang said, kneeling at his side. "Old friends are here. Friends from America." The attention pleased him, but he did not smile. The feeble, almost simpleton gaze, however, with which he had greeted them when they entered, was now gone. He seemed to focus on the boy's carrot-red hair. Was that for its color? In what dim way did Howe feel it was more complicated? Did the old man feel a center that conflicted with himself? An object—in its own fashion—every bit as strange? He stood, kewpie-like, examining the wormhole at the core of the apple, meditatively flicking the loose edge of his band-aid.

"My God," Katherine blurted, "he's like—" She stopped there, staring into Dulac's corner. What was he like? Howe waited for her to say. What was he like besides himself?

"Yes—" he said.

"One of them," she said softly. "He's like one of them."

"One of what?"

She turned as if she hadn't caught his meaning. "You don't know?" It seemed clear that Howe didn't. "One of *them*," she repeated. "He took them in. The place—" She flung wide her arms—"the place was full of them. When they came for them they took him along. My God, you didn't know?"

As she talked, her eyes stared him full in the face. Did Howe find them strange—or did he look strange himself? "One of *them*—" he repeated.

"Jews! Jews!" she cried. "One of them, O my God! Didn't anybody tell you? The place was full of them!"

No, nobody had told Howe anything. That was not unusual. Like a fool he stood gaping. In the corner behind them the old man chanted, "Choos, choos! All gone. Yes, yes, all gone!" He held out to them the soiled palms of his hands. Katherine put her own hands to her eyes. "O my God," she said.

"Please don't say that so much," said the boy. On that point he was a man among men. He exchanged a shifty glance of shame with Spiegel and Howe.

"If you'll excuse me," said Howe, "I don't think he was. One of them. Not really. I don't mean he wasn't *there*. I mean, I can't see him as one of *them*. I can't see him as the victim of anything—can you?"

Katherine let her hands fall from her face, blinked as if to see the past more clearly. The idea was new to her, but not strange.

"Not *him*," continued Howe. "I can't see it. Weren't we—weren't we all, *his* victims? Isn't that just it? Can you imagine him being victimized?" Howe paused; was it the smallness of the room, or had his voice got loud? He was careful to avoid the eyes of the boy. The idea, the idea of a *victim,* was not one that would appeal to Katherine. "Isn't that really it? I mean, isn't that why we're here right *now?*"

With some effort, Katherine kept her hands away from her ears. Howe's gift—as she used to describe it —for talking himself into a situation pained her even more now than it had in the past.

"It is not why *we* are here—if you don't mind," she replied, "and I do not consider myself one of his victims."

It was not necessary for Howe and Prutscher to exchange a glance. Victims, they were, of the same suspicion, if nothing else. From her bag, her crumpled pack of cigarettes, Katherine pried one loose, put the wrong end in her mouth. Out of long habit the boy said, "That's the wrong end, Katherine."

Clawing for her matches she said, "Don't think I

don't know what you're thinking. But I'm not going to have him calling me *Grandma!* Darling," she went on, veiling him with smoke, "so long as I have you I don't need to worry."

"I do, though," he replied.

"Well, I can't help that." Her voice came to them from a cloud of smoke. It gave them all a moment's peace. They could hear her flick the ash.

"Choos, choos, all gone!" Dulac repeated. Frau Dulac was quick to shut him up. Holding his head like a melon she cleaned around his mouth with a twist of her apron. The maddening tassel she once more placed behind his head.

"What's this about the Jews?" said Spiegel. "Mind my askin'?"

She fanned at the smoke to see him more clearly. "If you don't know, I'm sorry I brought the matter up."

"Sure, sure," said Spiegel. "Me too. All sorry to bring the matter up. But since it's up, eh, just what's it all about?"

"I don't know why *I* should talk," she said. "I suppose I only know what Wolfgang wrote me."

At the sound of his name Wolfgang said, "Yes?" as if he hadn't followed the discussion. He faced the window. At his back, the right hand gripping one wrist, he held a cigarette butt between two fingernails. The smoke dangled like a ribbon from his sleeve.

"They don't seem to know," Katherine began, "about them—"

"Ah so?" Wolfgang said. "That's not unusual. Here there were no more than forty, or fifty. If one thinks how many there were—"

"O my God," Katherine interrupted, "do we have to?"

"Sorry," Wolfgang replied. He raised his hand as if to put the thought behind them. In the voice of a guide he continued, "Let's say fifty. At the most sixty. They began to come at the end of the thirties. One, two at a time. They came and most of them stayed. Turned the place into quite a little city—" he wheeled to gesture at the open window—"some in the fields, some in the orchard, some were busy with the excavations. As you might expect there were quite a few youngsters—" Wolfgang seemed to visualize a halcyon prospect. A medieval city of the sort Dulac had in mind.

"Sounds purty," said Spiegel. He forced the words through his clenched teeth, the cigar in his mouth. "So what happened? Anti-gentilism? They want to throw the boss out?" He nodded his head toward Dulac. The show of attention pleased the old man. "Choos," he echoed, "all gone."

"Fifty of 'em, eh?" said Spiegel. "That's a lot of people, even Jews." He paused to make a face, added, "So what happened?"

"With the war," said Wolfgang, "as you might expect—"

"That how it is?" said Spiegel. "As I might expect? That what we mean, these days, by expectations?"

"Mr. Spiegel," said Katherine, her mouth a blue thin line. "What happened was that Monsieur Dulac went with them. He was one of them. He never once suggested that he was not."

Spiegel had no comment. The color of a bruise, her lips seemed to chap as she was speaking.

"I understand there was a siege," Wolfgang went on as if there had been no interruption. "Several weeks. Just like the old days. Forced them out since they had no water. The Germans wanted to use it as a field head-quarters, rather than blow it up. Monsieur Dulac was carried out on a stretcher, like most of them."

"You hear that!" said Spiegel. He turned to Howe. "You and your place to hide." He paused there, peering around. "Know what it is? Just a big booby trap. Felt it the moment we got in here."

"Poopy trap!" echoed the old man.

"If they took him along," Howe nodded toward Dulac, "how did he get back here?"

Wolfgang answered that with a shift of his eyes. Frau Dulac. A good, responsible hausfrau, she busied her-self sorting the apples. "I don't know the circum-stances—" Wolfgang's detached air made it clear he knew more than he was telling—"but it was Frau Dulac who brought him back."

Hearing her name pronounced she said, "A moment, *bitte!*" But she remained in the corner, fussing over something. Stooped, her broad beam was like the back of an overstuffed chair.

"Tell you one thing," said Spiegel, sizing up her span, "her circumstances were better than *his* were."

Wolfgang did not deny it. "I'm afraid they found the place looted. Nothing much here but George and the pigeons—" He laughed, then said, "That it's still here is thanks to Frau Dulac."

"It is thanks to God!" Frau Dulac interrupted. "Or maybe it is thanks to the Devil. I do not longer know which." Had she followed what they had been saying?

"Who's George?" asked the boy. Wolfgang took a moment to consider.

"George is a sort of handyman—" He smiled.

"Sounds like Father," the boy soberly observed.

"His father," Katherine began, for the benefit of them all, "his father is a painter. He works at home. Anybody who works at home has no real business. Is unemployed. Isn't that so?"

"He's not a handyman," said the boy. "He's not handy."

"Is anyone less handy than you are?" she put her head down to ask him. He turned his head away as if she had offered him a saucer of milk. "When you're handy yourself you can feel free to criticize your father."

No hard feelings. No, just a customary homey exchange. Howe could see the boy went right on thinking from where his grandmother had stopped to talk. She would never catch up. She was always one question behind. From his sweater, stretched tight on his chest, she took the piece of Kleenex she had stored there, dabbed it to her own nose.

"Know what you got?" said Spiegel, almost friendly. "Summer cold. What my mother called it. She didn't believe in this allergy stuff but she knew a runny nose. Let me give you a tip. You got any airsick pills? They help."

Airsick? Howe was thinking that was how she looked. Sallow, the sheen of her hair gave it an artificial brightness, a wig of finely spun wire.

"No! No!" she cried, and grabbed from the boy's hand the apple in which he had left his teeth marks.

Squirrel-like. The taste of it puckered his small, red mouth.

"What the hell?" said Spiegel. "Worm won't hurt him. Most kids got more worms than an apple."

"I'm sure you speak from experience, Mr. Spiegel." Katherine looked around for a place to deposit the apple. Monsieur Dulac, one hand extended, beckoned to her. Was it the apple he wanted? Katherine hesitated. Tipping forward, the old man gripped the quilt thrown over his legs, tossed it aside. Flat as the limbs of a rag doll, his feet in heavy bedsox, his legs were exposed. There seemed no more to him than the bones that joined the separate parts. The left limb he gripped, partially raised, then let it drop like a stilt at the side of the bed. "O my God," Katherine said. Frau Dulac, her hands full of apples, headed for him.

"I think he's getting restless," Wolfgang observed. That seemed obvious. What could one do about it? As she had done more times than she cared to remember, Frau Dulac dropped her apples on the quilt, picked up the leg that did not bend at the knee, returned it to the bed. The moment she released it, he grabbed it, raised it, dropped it on the floor. Did that give him pain? On his face was the smile of a child that had learned to toss things out of its crib.

"A child. He is a child!" Frau Dulac spoke without turning. Mechanically, she lifted the stiff leg, returned it to the bed. One hand, gripping his robe collar, held him back against the pillow. "He will not stop till you leave. He will go on showing off till you leave."

"A wog!" he cried, squirming at her leash, "a wog, a wog, yes, yes?"

A *walk?* Howe took the remark as senile—but not Wolfgang. "If you'll excuse me—" Wolfgang said to Frau Dulac, and put his hand on Dulac's shoulder. She was happy to excuse him. Only too happy. She turned her attention to the apples she had spilled on the quilt. "I think we better indulge him," he added. "He seems restless." He took the metal limb from the foot of the bed. There were clamps that made it possible to strap it to his arm, like a brace. Was there something familiar about the scene? Illustrations, perhaps, for Don Quixote. The strapping of armor on the feeble remains of the knight errant. He had the gauntness. He had always been sufficiently mad. "There we are—" muttered Wolfgang, hoisting him up, and slipped an arm around his waist to lift him. It wasn't hard. The scarecrow seemed to dangle from his supporting arm. "A wog! A leetle wog!" he barked, and thumped the tip of his cane on the floor.

"Is he—are *you* serious?" Katherine said.

"Oh yes." Wolfgang did not smile. "If you don't mind—" he added, glancing round at them. "He still does his walk, weather permitting."

"He does it to show off." Frau Dulac's voice showed some strain, thanks to her stooping. "He does not walk if there are no ladies."

"I'd be glad to leave if it would help." Katherine looked around as if for an exit. Monsieur Dulac, with a metallic clatter, was already there. He seemed to do pretty well. "Wog! Wog!" he yelled, and thumped his cane on the floor.

"Isn't there something," Katherine said, "something else he can wear?" He was draped in the shabby flannel bathrobe. The dragging belt had once had tassels, but they had been worn off. From the nail on the door Wolfgang took a raincoat. Was it perhaps Frau Dulac's? It looped loosely twice around him. One of the pockets proved to hold sprouting potatoes. He was nervous to be off.

"I should've brought some other shoes." Katherine waited for some sympathetic comment, but none came. At the window Frau Dulac waved to someone on the ramp. The pillow she had taken to the window to air she propped her bust on, peering out. A cash fare?

"Bitte!" she cried. "One moment, *bitte!"* and as she turned from the window they made way for her, her pouch of coins slapping Spiegel as she went through the door.

"I understand they've put Riva on the new map," said Wolfgang. He spoke matter-of-factly. "On the weekends she has quite a good thing going. Some of them stay for the night."

Five

Monsieur Dulac's little tour? How many times had
Howe, his feet on the rail of the wood-burning stove by
the name of Blackbird (where did the names of stoves
and sardines come from?), how many times had Howe
felt the draft that swept along the floor like water,
looked up to see, framed in the door, the Bosch-like
figure of the *Meister,* snow to his knees, the fur hat
down on his face, the soggy butt of a smoke glued to his
lip, his small hands dipped in the pockets of a World
War I army mackinaw? An apparition? He often looked
it. A plant wrapped in rags against the winter. In the
folds of his clothes the snow seldom melted. Ice formed
in his sleeves. And what had brought him to the door
of the room? A *wog.* A *leetle wog.* What reason was
there to go walk in a blizzard and leave the comfort of
a banked fire? No reason. Which was why it appealed.
Which was why he had married Signorina Gambetta,
the sideshow diva. Which was why he now, feeble and

half paralyzed, had to go for this walk.

In the past it had been to exercise the huge dog. That was the answer if he was questioned. But that was not *the* answer. No, it was more to exercise the inhabitants below and the guests, to wonder. An important detail. To keep them wondering. The simple folk in the canyon naturally wondered what it was like, up there in the castle, and the guest in the castle naturally wondered what it was like below. Cause for wonder. There had always been plenty of that. The small frail man, the huge dog, the white goblin faces at the windows, and then, without warning, Schloss Riva on its cliff. One had to see it. The letters Howe had written all failed to describe it. Excepting one phrase. It's like a castle in a glass ball, he had said. One of those in which, if shaken, the castle inside would disappear in a snowstorm. As this one did. Time and again before his eyes. Howe's eyes, not Dulac's, since it was Howe the little man gazed at, and if he saw a castle it was on the pupil of Howe's eyes. No question he was clever, if one considered how mad he was.

They went off single file, Howe at the rear. The boy was close on the heels of Dulac, who resembled a maimed, crippled guide to some ruin. The brace strapped to his arm creaked as if it would snap.

"Is that the dungeon?" They all halted on the stairs to see at what it was the boy pointed. All but Dulac; he proceeded as if nothing had been said. Down the stairs, across the court directly in the path of the boy's pointing finger, as if Dulac, not the dungeon, had been the subject of his question. It explained the delay in Wolfgang's reply.

"That's the crypt, Brian. I don't really know if we can boast of a dungeon."

This evasive reply did not lead the boy to ask more questions. He continued down the stairs. From where Howe stood on the landing he resembled an Easter egg, with a cap on. His walk, or rather his stride, that of a small prep school cadet, was purposeful. The impression that his large head was stuffed with new, unused material seemed stronger. Did it imply that Howe's old head was full of shoddy?

At the door to the passage Monsieur Dulac beckoned with his cane. Wolfgang stretched his long stride to draw equal to Katherine, take her arm, and point out the low, sagging beam in the door. The sweep of Monsieur Dulac's fur hat had polished it. Framed in the door, Prutscher gallantly bowing, they made a handsome pair. The envy Howe had felt so long ago in the past had not diminished. No, it seemed a bit stronger. A pair of well-bred wolfhounds, Howe had been the lad who, whistling, walked along between them. Had it been *his* fault? With relief he remembered the problem of money. Neither of them had had it. Katherine Brownell was accustomed to it. Was she also accustomed to the *pair* of them? She turned to look for Howe in the passage. It led him to straighten his back, walk on the balls of his feet. Even in the ugly saddle shoes she had worn to appear an inch shorter, Howe had always been a fraction short of the mark. Her lips were on a level with his ear. A Far Hills version of a wolfhound, Katherine always looked chilled, or coming down with something, in her habitual effort to *look* a little shorter, to shrivel up. In her teens—she had told him the story before she had told him her name—she had been a beanpole among her normal companions.

As they stepped into the light on the ramp they stopped as if at a barrier, huddled blinking. Howe could not see, but he could hear Dulac. "A wog! A wog! Yes, yes?" The carrot-top of the boy seemed to burn like an artificial sunflower. Up ahead on the ramp there seemed to be a squabble: they heard the voice of Frau Dulac. Hooding his face with both hands Howe could see a tall youth with a short blonde woman. He wore blue jeans. A knapsack sagged low on his back. The young woman wore shorts. About her waist, skirting a bell-shaped bottom, the blonde had draped the young man's sweater, the sleeves dangling at her behind. The voice, however, was that of Frau Dulac. Something to do with schillings. More effective than a toll gate she blocked the path. Between the two groups, trailing the boy like a pet, Monsieur Dulac seemed to feel himself trapped. Or was it abandoned? He thumped the leg of his metal limb on the wall. How was it that none of them had noticed the ridiculous nightcap with its dangling tassel? He still wore it. The tassel swung and bobbed like a tangled yo-yo. In the summer heat the whack of his cane was like that of a piece of farm machinery. Perhaps a mowing machine. Putting her hand on Howe's arm for support, Katherine sneezed.

"Gesundheit!" said Spiegel. Too late he realized that did not help his cause any. Wolfgang flicked the kerchief from the pocket of his jacket. Did Frau Dulac think he had waved? She came toward them, her coin pouch flapping, but stopped to turn Dulac so that he faced her. *"Ach Gott!"* she cried, and wiped the nightcap off his

head. Her hand flattened the wispy strands of hair.

"My hat! My hat!" the old man yelled, not to Frau Dulac but to the boy. He took a grip on his sleeve as if to shake him. "My hat!" he yelled. "You hear me?" The boy did not seem to. He gazed at the old man's wild face as if it hung in a cage before him. The claw at his shoulder did not seem to disturb him. "You hear? You hear me?" Dulac shrieked.

"Where is the hat at, sir?" he replied.

"Brian!" cried his grandmother. "Come here, darling!"

"Let me get it!" yelled Howe. "I know the way, let me get it!" and like a fool kid he turned and ran for it. Almost, that is. God knows he knew better than run. At a trot, hearing the voices behind him, the now shrill voice of Katherine, he wondered if it was toward something he was running, or away. Both. In this instance it was both. He went back as he had come, across the inner court, up the flight of outside stairs, then along the landing to the stairwell, dipping into the darkness like a diver. There, unable to see, he stopped. His left hand before him, he went along the wall, the crack below the door like the dawn on the horizon. Was it for a hat he was doing this? No. For what then? It was not for a hat the old man had howled but for attention, to which he was accustomed, and to rid himself of the little monster at his heels. That was what he wanted. To get rid of that kid. Howe could not blame him—vividly he could see them in the light on the ramp, a surreal confrontation, the shrieking old man and the child with the sober, all-absorbing gaze. What was one's impression? That nothing, no nothing was missed. The pile of new, unused

material between those ears soaked up what he saw like
a blotter. To hell with understanding. First one soaked
it up. The understanding would come, if at all, years
later when it dripped, like a bright red fluid, from the
tip of his brush or his pen.

Empty of guests, the room hummed with bees and
flies. In the green light near the window they appeared
to be suspended in a liquid. He wondered why he had
come. Perspiration formed on his hands and face as on
a chill glass.

Below the window the old man barked, "My hat! My
hat!" reminding Howe to peer around for it. Could he
mean the fur one? Not in weather like this. There was
no hat of any sort on the hooks along the wall, but a
hat, a straw hat with a cracked green visor, served as
a container for small potatoes. Howe transferred them,
as if they might be eggs, to the shelf reserved for apples.
He slapped the crown of the hat to free it of dirt. A
flexible panama, of the sort worn by secret agents in the
silent movies, the band was stamped with the initials
C. H-S., in gold. Conrad Horst-Schlesing. Also stamped
in the band was the message

TODD'S HATS
We Top You Off!
Cedar Rapids
Iowa

In Cedar Rapids, among other places, Dr. Horst-
Schlesing and Madame Dulac had given lieder recitals,
for which Dr. Horst-Schlesing had obligingly written the
rave reviews. Howe had seen them. Each piece dated
and lovingly mounted in a photo album. The label of a

Deutsche Grammophon disc of Madame's one record-
ing ornamented the cover. A photograph, a photograph
of flowers in which Madame's massive head seemed to
emerge from a basket, served as a hand-tinted frontis-
piece. That had been taken in Shrevesport. The trium-
phal end of her tour.

Of all that grandeur nothing remained but this soiled
panama, the label in the band appropriate to the empty
crown. It had topped off, for years, the strange head of
Dr. Horst-Schlesing, divided, somewhat unequally, like
two loaves of bread. In this fold a parcel of hairs wired
his ears for sound. The baldness of his dome explained
—in his opinion—why the panama hat left his head
only when lady guests were at the table, or when he es-
corted Madame. A blue serge coat, from Garden City,
Kansas, with the name of the store sewed to the lining,
was all that remained of what had been a two-pants blue
serge suit. It had the sheen of oilcloth on the sleeves,
and where he gripped the lapels, as he stood at the
stove, the imprint of his fingers never left the cloth. The
rippled, permanent wave on his front reinforced the impression of a slightly out-of-focus photograph.

Through the window he had turned to face, Howe
blinked at the light. Below him, featureless, he saw a
blob of faces. As if swelling as they rose he heard the
squabble of voices. What he took for an extravagant
woman's hat was the head of the boy. What was he
thinking, that kid? What impressions had been made on
his new, unused material? Between the soiled panama,
symbol of grandeur faded, and the boy's red-top, symbol of grandeur blooming, Howe sensed a connection as
frail as the web strands at the window, invisible unless

seen in a favorable light. And yet as obvious as the pull
of web on the face. Life fading and life blooming, the
sound tracks confusingly overlapping, the new material
making new music out of the old. Was what he saw on
the ramp below him new music in the making? The first
step being the erasure of the old? The yapping old man,
one hand to his crown, with the other childishly thumping his cane as if he feared that his music would soon
go off; that from the head of the boy a new, disturbing
noise would emerge. The crackling senile yap of Monsieur Dulac like static interference.

"Hat! Hat! Hat!" he shrieked, like a brat with a tan-
trum, the boy standing sober as a judge beside him.
Their roles reversed? So it seemed to Howe. He stood
back from the casement, the shutter framing the view.
Brown and gold, the contours softened by a film of insects as dense, if seen from outer space, as the sea. Like
millions of craft they swam in it, their small outboard
motors droning. Brown and gold, scarlet and yellow,
green the color of muddy water, but Howe would always see it as white. A remarkably unifying stroke of
luck—or was it taste—on the part of nature. After a
season like this to paint it all over white. In the spring to
paint it all in again.

Now that everything was revealed he seemed to see
less than when it had been covered. One day one of
those sleds buried in the snows of Everyman's childhood
would emerge: one that would determine, as the snow
melted, the course of his life. One that would have the
name of Rosebud, or Larkspur, or Mayflower, with a
silly twist of rope, knotted, and curved wooden runners
on which Everyboy dragged the laundry washed by his

mother through the sleet and snow. On such a sled, grasping a rope that had been knotted at one end, the other end fastened to the pommel of the saddle, Howe had been dragged, more dead than alive, through a blizzard to the town of Stein, where a stable attendant had come out with a broom to sweep him off. The broom had not proved enough. A crust of ice had formed in his hair, and extended like a brow over his face. A *living* snowman? No, the more accurate word would be dead. Snow stuffed his sleeves like cotton, freezing some parts, insulating others. He had been left in the stable to thaw with the steaming horse. Out of self-pity, rage, and shame Howe would have stood there and died of pneumonia, but the barman in the Gasthaus had come out for him. With a wooden ladle he had cracked his ice cap, scraped him off. Snow that had turned to ice remained in his hair. In that condition, like a huge, mute pet, Howe had been led inside to the fire, where, as he thawed, he watched the Meister of Riva feed himself. Alone at a table, sipping coffee, his own clothes giving off the stench of wet burlap, he sat reading the month-old French paper that the waiter had brought him. In the room there had been two sounds, the drip from Howe, the old man's rasping snuffle. A habit, a nervous tic, the sound was out of all proportion to its source, the small, ailing man with a nose that seemed transparent as wax. So it appeared when it was cold. White as the wax that dropped on the floor from a candle, a nose that belonged to some highborn, consumptive face. From such a nose came this snuffle that seemed to tear at its lining, and made Howe nervous. The membrane of his own nose would become sore. In the Gasthaus, frozen and thawing, all he could put his mind to was the old man's snuffle, the way his claw-like hand plucked the soft center from the bread, like a bird.

Unchanged, but perhaps shriller, the voice on the ramp cried, "Hat! Hat! My hat!" Howe wheeled to look for it, forgetting that he held one in his hand. Would that be it? He leaned to flag it out the window. Up and down, up and down, pumped the head of Frau Dulac. She spread her arms as if she thought he might toss it to her. They made a curious group: the upturned faces glistened with sweat but seemed empty of meaning; Howe felt himself part of a scene for which the script was missing. Was he about to leap? To call for help?

"You look great!" yelled Spiegel. "Want me to shoot it from here?" He screwed his cap around on his head and took a spread-legged stance, like an old-style camera man. No one seemed to be amused. On Monsieur Dulac's head Frau Dulac had placed a kerchief, as if it might burn.

"My matches?" Katherine called. "Do you see them?" She looked up from the bag in which she was searching. In her left hand she held the crumpled pack of her cigarettes. With an identical gesture the men on the ramp, Wolfgang, Spiegel, and the young man with the blonde, put hands to their pockets, as if the scene was rehearsed. In the window Howe, who had made the same gesture, looked down to see a single pair of eyes fastened on him, the faintest smile in the porky, cherub face. Was it *with* Howe or *at* him? As if to blur the boy's impression, he flagged the hat.

"Coming!" he yelled, a pointless remark, and turning from the window bumped into the table. His eyes closed in pain, he heard the apples rolling about on the floor. He let them roll; as he rubbed his shinbone he was pre-occupied with the sensation that he was losing what he took for granted: his point of view. A confused over-lapping impression of a man at the window, perhaps himself, seen from the angle of the boy on the ramp, had been imposed on the scene he had just that moment viewed from the window. A double-exposure, as Spiegel would have said. A failure to wind the film before taking the next shot. The latest cameras corrected that defect. At that point where Howe's glance intersected that of the boy the scene was open, a point of view did not close it, the apparent overlapping did not blur it, and some-thing faintly suggestive of the scene itself might be said to exist. Inclusive rather than exclusive. An event with-out a beginning, as such, or an ending. Where his glance intercepted the boy's a current from the past spliced to the present; the future would consist of this sound over-lapping sound.

"Hey, Howe!" It was the voice of Spiegel. "You want to bring the kid an' me a coupla apples?"

"Make it three!" That was the young man with the blonde. From the floor, where they were scattered, Howe selected half a dozen that were not so wormy, dumped them into the crown of the soiled panama hat. On his way down the hall he bit into one of them, found it good.

They had moved into the shade of the archway to wait for him: the young man and his blonde, her arms prickly with heat rash, the elderly scholar with his open map, Katherine and the boy, Spiegel and Wolfgang, the old man with the kerchief on his head. He looked, Howe thought, like one of the faithful headed for Mecca. Flies had singled him out but he seemed indifferent to them.

A little wary, as if she had herded them to this spot, and thought they might bolt, Frau Dulac looked on. Perhaps she had her doubts about such imports as Spiegel and Howe. The elderly scholar—whom it was clear she trusted—and the young man and the blonde had been persuaded to join them. At reduced rates. Both tours for the price of one. From Howe she took the hat, distributed the apples, then filled the crown with a handful of leaves before she placed it, like a pith helmet, on the head of Dulac. He did not complain. Howe had turned away to avoid his glance, feeling certain that he knew how he must look. If he did, he no longer cared. A hat to him was a hat. "A wog! A wog!" he barked, as if the movement of his head had started idle machinery to working. Off he hobbled, the boy at his heels. Until water was found to clean it Katherine would not let him bite into the apple that Spiegel had polished on his sleeve. With Howe's matches it went into her bag. From the archway Frau Dulac called advice to her husband: not to rush. When they reached Unter Riva not to drink too much. She herself was not going since who would be there to watch Riva? Besides, she was not one of those who suffered from lack of exercise. Far from it. Her voice trailed off as they went their separate ways. On the rim of the orchard, eying their departure like a troop of crossbowmen, a pair of hikers, man and woman, resembled the bug-like creatures in fables, their spider legs anchored in heavy divers' shoes. Monsieur

Dulac's metal limb, sweeping the grass, made the hiss of a dull scythe blade. A yard or two ahead of him, as if he stirred the air, the seeding heads of the grass would dip as the grasshoppers moved out of the way.

"Know when I last saw the Dodgers?" said Spiegel. "In Brooklyn. Back in the thirties. Know why I never see 'em in the Coliseum? Too far to drive." He let that sink in, then he added, "So I come ten thousand miles, at a cent a mile, to take a goddam wog."

Six

_____

What reminded Howe of the word pallbearer? The way they marched single file. Spiegel's shirt glistened on his shoulders. He used his cap to fan the flies. It made for silence walking like that. Clearly Howe could hear the chuff of Wolfgang's rubbers. Did he think it might rain? Stronger than the smell of rain was that of his feet drying at the Klub. Across thirty years the wet brew of leather, rubber, and sock. To save money both Wolfgang and Howe would wash their shirts and shorts in the Badhaus, then wear these garments home *wet,* under their clothes. But they did not die. No, they had not even been sick. The worst had been that Wolfgang suffered from a chronic case of athlete's foot. Howe had guessed it. It would have been easier to discuss the clap. Now wing-tipped seeds clung to the flaps of his low-drooping plus fours, his hands, with their red palms, carried at the back. Three fingers were coiled; two that

extended periodically twitched. The tips were the color
of iodine. Howe recalled that Wolfgang, unobserved,
stuck toothpicks into his cigarettes, in order to smoke
them right to the tip. He often saw the smoldering end
of the pick. He bought his cigarettes singly, or made
them in a machine that stuffed a moss-like material into
a stiff paper tube. The burning tube made a smell. That
too seemed fresh after thirty years.

"Like old times—?" Wolfgang had turned as if he
felt the focus of Howe's attention. Was that what it was?
They had paused on the trail where a tree scattered
some shade. The blur of heat made it difficult to look
around them. Sweat burned his eyes. It was at this point
—due to its exposure—that Howe had always suffered
the most from the cold. He had sometimes thought his
teeth might chip from chattering. Old times had been so
little like this it made him smile. On this spot, hoarsely
wheezing and winded, Wolfgang and Howe would pause
for a smoke, the blood like scratched patches in Wolfgang's cheeks. After the climb—any climb—his nose
might bleed. A handful of snow pressed to his forehead
did not help. It had been Howe who showed him the
trick he had learned from his Uncle Fremont. A piece of
paper, folded, thrust up sharply between the gum and
the upper lip. The only paper available had been from
a pack of Howe's cigarettes. Like taking snuff, Wolfgang had remarked, but it had stopped his nosebleed.
A small, dark patch of it had dried on his lip. His head
tipped back as if scanning the sky, Wolfgang had mentioned the name of Katherine. The word came out a
little gargled, due to the position of his neck. Howe
had not been sure he had caught it correctly. "Kath-

erine," Wolfgang had repeated, "you love her?" A little strangely, as if forced out of his throat.

Had Howe managed to reply? The word love had always embarrassed him. What did one mean by it? He preferred, at the time, a less committed term such as *like*. But love was what Wolfgang had said, and whatever he meant he meant more than like. No, he meant love. Was it, just by chance, love that Howe had felt? Love in so far as such a ninny as he was might have felt it? But he had been spared an answer. The excitement that Wolfgang had felt had set his heart to pumping, his nose to bleeding. More paper had to be rolled and stuffed up under his lip. Why had Howe failed to commit himself? What had he feared? On this spot they had stood, ankle deep in the snow, the green light of dusk on the face, unhealthily bloodless, that Wolfgang tipped to the sky. His lips were parted. He resembled a soul about to depart this life. Shame. Shame had warmed Howe much better than such love as he felt he might have: shame that as a lover he was so easily eclipsed. That as a lover, indeed, he did not know how love felt. He had *liked* Katherine, and thought it would be nice if she would come and spend a weekend at Riva, preferably in the small, cold cot that served as his bed. That would be nice. If it didn't happen to prove to be a disaster. In either case it would hardly have produced a bleeding of his nose.

Had Wolfgang gone on to *possess* her? Howe turned away from the thought of their coupling. It seemed to have no place—no proper place—in the album shots of *old times*. Such times, indeed, preserved their character by a scrupulous winnowing of all couplings. Strange to think that Monsieur Dulac had eaten of the apple denied to both lover and liker. How else explain why she was here? For what other reason would a woman return to the scene of—well, the scene? Katherine would surprise you. Had she surprised Monsieur Dulac? She had a gift for unpredictable gestures, offhand remarks. Hadn't she once blurted out that she had given serious thought to having herself *fixed,* like a cat? Think of the problems it would solve, she had said. And Howe had. But not her problems. Such a remark would come from a woman who had been, for a weekend, the mistress of Riva, and thirty years later turned up with her egg-shaped prodigy. They made a grotesque trio on the weedy trail. The tall, handsome woman, the egg-shaped boy, the fragile old man with his cricket-like jibber. What did Howe feel? That Dulac would outlast them all. That what there was to die in him was already dead. What remained would continue to lead a life of its own.

Was that the life now being transferred to the boy? The old man's withered hand rested on the boy's head. Through that arm which way did the current flow? How much past did it take to balance how much present and future? How much old material could be swapped for how much new? The boy seemed to be listening: he looked where Dulac pointed his metal limb.

"How do you like it, darling?" his grandmother asked. Not that she cared; but perhaps she sensed Dulac's skillful maneuver. Peace with the enemy by taking sides with him.

"It's not much like you said it would be," he answered.

"Nothing ever is, darling," was her reply.

Through Dulac's hand, as through a cable, Howe sensed the flow of an alternating current. The past into the present, the present into the past. What had died of the past was dead, or more accurately put, was past—but what had persisted was now being taped, in some cryptic manner that would need decoding, in the head of the boy. From the old, the charge was now being passed to the new. *What* charge? That was what one never knew. The new, unused heads, like empty deep-freeze cartons, would not give up their meaning—if it could be said they had one—until thawed. The present would prove to be whatever proved to be unexpendable. Good or bad. If it existed it had proved itself. But was it by accident or design that the old man toyed with the current? Now turning it to flow into the boy, now into himself? Had he sensed that what survived of Monsieur Dulac would prove to be what remained in the head on which he leaned—on such terms that neither of them would understand? In the present, as in the future, the past would lead a life of its own, the predictable elements being those already dead. As a pallbearer, the boy carried the future, or nothing at all.

Turning from the boy and Monsieur Dulac, Katherine sneezed over the young man in the blue jeans. He passed his hand over the dampness on his brown arm. "I'm sorry," Katherine said, "I hope you don't think you might catch my cold. It's just this damned hay fever."

The young man grinned. "Shots help you any?" he said. "They don't me. I get a rash."

"My wife has an asthma—" Skillfully, with clinical indifference, Wolfgang broke the news to the *group*.

"—an asthma," he repeated, "that keeps her in Ventimiglia."

"What a pity!" Katherine said. Her tone was so false even the boy winced to hear it.

"Quite the contrary, my dear. Fortunate for us both." Wolfgang did not smile. Were they silenced by his frankness, or had something in the air made them indifferent to it? A tour of the past. The dead but not gone.

"Ventimiglia?" Howe echoed, to break the silence. "They wouldn't let Spiegel out, or was it in?" He turned to Spiegel.

"That goddam bike," said Spiegel. "Bought it in a hockshop. Nobody told me I had to have papers for it."

"What did you do?" asked the boy.

"Sold it to the bastard for eight dollars more than it cost me!" Spiegel's arms lifted slightly as he crowed.

"The things we remember, yes?" This remark came from the elderly scholar. Reflections on his glasses made it impossible to see his eyes, judge his intentions. Was it, or was it not an anti-Semitic remark? Spiegel hoisted his pants.

Her voice flat, with a dubbed-in sound, Katherine said "Ventimiglia? O my God! This boy sat and stared at me all night. I was wearing garters. I was certain he could see the marks on my legs. I was wearing a raincoat and galoshes, but I felt I had nothing on my body but stockings. Silk stockings and earrings. O my God!"

Howe was reminded of her gift for offhand remarks. Also the way she would stand, her arms sucked in, toying with the beads that kept her hands from dangling. Rather than let her hands *dangle*—she had said—she would cut them off. In the same vein she had cried she would have her teeth *out,* rather than drill them. Had it been her intention to horrify him? She had. Without her glasses she would walk directly toward any face that would smile at her. In the foyer adjoining the ladies' room at the Klub he stood so close to the door he was viewed with suspicion. If he did not stand close she would walk, smiling, toward any smiling man. Howe had thought her an excellent example of everything wrong with progressive education, needing the supervision of a clean-cut Kansas boy like himself.

Hearing a sound behind them, they turned. The old man and the boy had gone ahead on the trail. The bushes just beyond them were the tops of trees. They watched the boy stoop, pick up a rock, and with an awkward girlish motion throw it skyward. A long moment later they heard it fall with a plop.

"Bryyyyy-nnnn!" his grandmother cried, but he had moved out of her orbit. He stooped, found another rock, let it fly. They waited for the sound of its fall but nothing occurred. In the direction of the millpond a dog barked. Howe, too, in the outer court of Riva, had sailed away snowballs that never seemed to land. Over the long, white winter he filled the air with them. In the spring, when the air thawed, he thought they might drop. They hung in his mind like the puffy ornaments on a Christmas tree.

A racket, like the flapping of shutters, led them all to turn and look at Riva. Had it come from the tower? The disturbance had stirred up the pigeons: several hovered above it. A rhythmical thumping sound, like that of a drummer setting the beat for a jazz session, disturbed the pigeons perched on the roof. Their eyes followed the one that rose, flew off. Howe knew the racket so well that he waited for the clatter that had always followed. The ringing of the bell. The clatter was intended to split the frozen pond of the sky, and so it did. Snow often fell from the roofs. In the silence that followed the huge dog bayed. A fiendish, madcap racket, sometimes followed by the wheezing glee of the madman, his head ducked out of sight as if he expected the sky to fall.

This time nothing occurred. Had the mistress of Riva deprived him of his bell? A door slammed as she hurried toward, or away from him. Clearly, as if made by a pet that had been unleashed to gambol in the leaves, Howe heard the crackling behind him, then the boy calling, "Katherine! Katherine, look!"

By the time Howe wheeled he saw nothing but the egg-shaped boy, his arm pointing downward. He stood alone on the trail. From the slope below came the sound of a tumbling boulder, plowing up the leaves. At that point Wolfgang, his rubbers chuffing, blocked the view. The young American, however, had gone before him leaving his rucksack at the feet of the boy. The racket tapered off as Katherine muttered, "O my God," putting both hands to her face.

With Spiegel and the elderly scholar, Howe found himself at the point where Dulac had stood. One patch of the slope, steep as an attic stairway, had been swept clean of leaves. The trail zigzagged back and forth, but Dulac had cut across it like a zipper. Tufts of grass, still green, indicated in what direction he had passed. The stiff leg had plowed a shallow furrow in the soft earth. Thirty yards below, just short of the bottom, he had

been stopped by a coil in the trail; the metal crutch indicated where to look for him in the leaves. One arm
thrust out. A cloud of dust hovered above him, flecked
with bees and flies. The young American was there, mut-
tering, brushing away the leaves that concealed Dulac's
face. What he found would be the parts of a broken
puppet. Mercifully dead. No doubt of that.

As he clopped down the trail, Wolfgang at his heels,
Howe waited for the sense of the tragic to grip him, but
he felt only the lightheaded swoon of a farce. The errant
Knight of Riva, his lance beside him, once more un-
horsed. At a turn of the trail, glancing upward, he
caught a glimpse of Katherine, a suburban Ophelia, her
hand resting on the head of her grandson, a welcome
prop. At her feet, as if collapsed, the blonde crouched
on the rucksack of her companion, her head cradled between her plump bare knees, as if she might be sick. To
one side, at a respectful distance, the elderly scholar
folded his map, preparing himself for what he recognized as an emergency.

Had he slipped, perhaps? Or fainted? Even as Wolfgang prepared to face such a question, Howe knew its
answer. The old man had done neither. He had deliberately taken the plunge. In what way could he leave a
more memorable impression on the boy who had stood
there beside him? On the future, that is. He was now
secure in the boy's past. Senility had not deprived him
of the wisdom of his folly. A dead man, he returned to
life in the boy.

Was he dead, or merely dying? One arm lay slantwise

across his chest. The eyes were sealed, creased, as if he had been felled playing hide and seek. The mouth, however, the lips parted, was set in that smile compounded of a grimace, exposing the abalone-colored teeth. Leaves and twigs tangled in his hair gave him the look of a napping satyr. Gratified. Nor was there any doubt about that. Howe felt that he took on life from the eyes that focused on him. A pulse beat at his throat. Wolfgang fanned a cloud of gnats from his face.

Winded, Spiegel wheezed, "He out cold? Just don't move him. More goddam people killed by them first-aid females than they killed in the war."

"Where's a doc?" The young American looked at Howe. Cascading down the slope he had torn his britches, drawn a fleck of blood.

"There's a doctor in Stein," replied Wolfgang. "I'll go on ahead and call him." He went off with the clopping gait of a spurred milk horse.

"You let him lie here," said Spiegel, "ants are going to eat him." He brushed a few off. "He don't look so bad. Maybe he's just shook up." Spiegel raised his eyes to look up the slope down which he had come. It would have killed Spiegel. At the thought of it he blinked his eyes. "Friend of mine," he said, peeling a cigar, "stepped off the curb and broke his leg in two places. That's how it goes. Then you fall off a cliff and muss up your hair."

"If you'd let me have your coat—" the young man looked at Howe—"I think we can move him."

Howe stripped it off. From the inside pocket he removed the notice with its black border. Monsieur Etienne Dulac, dead. Was he?

"Think we need that coat?" It was Spiegel. He stooped

to lift the limp leg. "What the hell, there's nothin' to him."

"Just in case he might have hemorrhaged," said the young man.

"Hear that?" said Spiegel, chortling. "Not everything the kids learn in the army is baloney."

"I didn't learn that in the army," he replied, "learned it at the Y." On a bed of leaves he spread the coat, folding the sleeves to make a sort of hammock. "You want to take the legs?" he said to Spiegel. Spiegel didn't, but he faced it. Cautiously as if one might kick out at him, he gripped the knees. One leg thrust out stiff, the other dangled limp.

"Just half dead," said Spiegel. "What'd I tell you?"

To the young man Howe said, "Why don't you let me do that? Maybe the young lady needs you." He held the sleeves of the coat in which Dulac was cradled. Back on the trail, still crouched, was his blonde companion. The sun was warm on her hair, her exposed fat knees. Off to one side the elderly scholar held the boy by the wrist, and fanned the air with his map. Katherine Brownell had not moved, one arm dangled her gaping bag. Her unblinking gaze was level on the air high above their heads. Seen from below these figures seemed to symbolize a profound disorder. They appeared unrelated, almost abandoned. Did they await a sign—or merely a delayed suburban bus?

"She'll be o-kay," said the young man, shrugging. "She's got one of these nervous stomachs." Did he have one himself? His voice implied as much, but he had learned to live with it. His blue lips were firm.

"One-two-three—hoist!" said Spiegel, and cupped the

old man's knees like the handles of a wheelbarrow. Off they went. Trailing, his eyes up ahead where Wolfgang filled the door of the Gasthaus, Howe had the impression that this event had been recorded, as those preceding, from a point in time that superseded his own. He was part of the frieze, a provincial scene often painted on pottery, showing the hunters, their game bagged, coming home from the hill. At some future time this scene would unroll as if filmed from the rim trail, where the boy, in silence and wonder, made it his own. A title for it might be, *Monsieur Dulac Goes to His Reward.*

Seven

On a table in the Gasthaus, cleared for that purpose, they stretched him out in the light from the window, a bar rag beneath his head, his wild hair strewn with leaves. Not dead, not even noticeably dying, but with some irregularity in his breathing, the jogging portage seemed to have lulled him to a fitful sleep. His pulse—such as there was—was that of a faulty ignition system. A new set of points—as Spiegel said—would perk him up. Neither the barman, his wife, nor the guest who stood on the porch, peeing, seemed unduly disturbed at the sight or condition of Monsieur Dulac. Quite the contrary. This seemed a familiar turn of events. In the eyes of the barman Howe recognized the ancient and professional dilemma: the man was a nuisance, but he did pay for his drinks. In one form or another a table or a stool was reserved for him.

With the young American, who carried a bottle of beer

for the blonde with the nervous stomach, Howe went back up the canyon trail to where Katherine Brownell stood where they had left her. There had been one change. Her gloved free hand was gripped by the boy. Shock perhaps? Howe thought it might do her some good. The elderly scholar, free of the boy, had turned his attention to the blonde Fräulein, who, with his help, was making her way down the slope. In one hand she gripped a lemon rind he had given her to suck.

"It's all right!" Howe called, to reassure her. "There's no cause for alarm, Katherine!" He put a smile on his face. Against the diffused light of the sky her own was dark. When the boy moved she suddenly gripped him, like a leash. "We've got in touch with a doctor," Howe added. "There's no cause for alarm."

A sound like an uninhibited burp parted her lips. Was she ill? Another nervous stomach? "No cause for *what?*" she cried, then, "Oh my God!" She dropped the boy's hand and put her own to her face. Howe had not expected such emotion. He felt a sudden irritation with the boy who stood there, chewing something, as if unaffected, his fat thighs holding apart his tubular legs.

"Katherine," he said, "he's just shaken up. Come and see for yourself."

"She can't," the boy replied. "That's just the trouble."

"She can't what?" Howe said, moving toward them. The pounding of his heart seemed to blur the figures on the rise.

"See for herself," the boy answered, and poked one of his fat fingers toward his eyes. It pulled Howe up short. Did he mean what he said? The light on the sky made it difficult for him to see. Katherine had placed

one hand on her brow as if alone and faced with the
$64,000 question.

"Look——" Howe called.

"She *can't!*" yelled the boy. "She's lost her contact
lenses!"

What impulse did Howe feel? One to club him. As
simple as that. The head of his grandmother wagged
slowly from side to side, speechless. Both Howe and the
boy were impressed. Scornful but resigned, the boy
added, "She can't even see to look for them. What's
worse, she can't drive. She's blind as a bat!"

They were silent while the blonde, beer foam sudsing
her lip, stopped to look at Howe. "She can't see? That's
awful. Come all this way for the view, and not see it?"
An arm around her waist, the young man led her away.
Over their heads Howe fastened his gaze on the porch
of the Gasthaus, where a large green bug seemed about
to go up the steps. Couldn't he see either? The green
bug proved to be a Volkswagen. The horn tooted as if
the driver felt the Gasthaus blocked his way.

To Katherine Howe called, "That must be the doctor
now!" as if she had waited for that reassurance. Did she
smile? At her side the scholar aimlessly toed a few
leaves. Moving toward her, wheezing, it crossed Howe's
mind that he was back, now, where he started. Her eyes.
The worried seeing-eye pet of Katherine Brownell. She
waited, held in place by the boy, rather than holding
him, in that self-sufficient coma of the true blind. He
felt even the crackling racket he made was not heard by
her. "This way——" he said, taking her arm, relieved to
feel that she did not withdraw it.

"She lost one in the Chevy," said the boy. He spoke

without turning, striding before them. "You know where it turned up? Stephen's shirt pocket. It went to the laundry and came back in it."

"Stephen is his father," said Katherine.

"He's still not adjusted to the fact," said the boy. "I can tell you that."

A soft, velour hat, worn by poets and lovers in the reign of Franz Joseph, concealed the head and face of Dr. Hofer except for the hair that lapped his collar. From the rear he appeared to be wearing a tasseled lampshade. As Howe approached with Katherine Brownell, however, he removed it. Like the head of Spiegel, his dome was veiled by streamers of hair attached to his sideburns, held firmly in place by glasses that concealed a hearing aid. He removed them, using his tie to polish one of the lenses, as he listened to Wolfgang describe what had taken place. Without smiling, or showing disbelief at what he heard, he gazed at the slope below Riva down which Monsieur Dulac had tobogganed. No, it did not surprise him. One gathered that he had often heard worse. "Аннннhhhhh," he said, blowing on his glasses, then went before them into the Gasthaus where Monsieur Dulac lay out on his back, one pantleg rolled on a leg that appeared to be chewed. A damp bar rag had been placed on his brow. The shoe on the chewed leg had been removed. Just before he had toppled over, Monsieur Dulac had clutched at the bank, and one clawlike hand gripped a nosegay of twigs, grass, and leaves. That had been placed, appropriately, on his front. Irregular, fitful little gasps of air that he inhaled with a hiss, exhaled with a puff, indicated that the patient was still breathing. That got a smile from Dr. Hofer. Yes, that was a surprise. He had not expected to find the patient alive.

From the sleeve of his bathrobe Monsieur Dulac's limp arm was not too carefully removed, the shoulder exposed, and a needle inserted into the flesh. There had been many others. Something, no doubt, to do with the heart. A hint of it could be seen fluttering in the rib cage, wanting out. With a piece of cotton moistened at the bar Dr. Hofer cleaned the chewed limb of dirt, sprinkled the wounds with powder, and paused to glance at his watch. One should keep the patient quiet. Quiet, if possible. Unmistakably, as he wiped his hands, Dr. Hofer left the impression that in calling *him* they had made a mistake. An undertaker, perhaps? No, not even that. Neither strictly in this world, nor as yet in the next one, Monsieur Dulac presented something of a problem. Who was there to call? Who *was* there, to call for help? Not Dr. Hofer. He had problems enough as it was.

After repeating there was no cause for alarm—he seemed to mean no matter *what* happened—Dr. Hofer coasted away with the ignition off, an economy measure. He took with him Spiegel, hitching a ride to where the road forked out of Muhldorf, from where he would walk up the slope to Riva and return with Frau Dulac and the car.

Wolfgang Prutscher, with a stein of beer he frequently salted but left untouched, sat on a bench where he could keep an eye on Monsieur Dulac. When one least expected him to, he would come around. Unless someone was there to stop him, he would be off again. It was

Wolfgang's suggestion—while they were waiting for Spiegel—that Howe might show the rest of them the view. That was what they had come for. The view of Riva from the canyon. A pity that Katherine would not be able to see it, but perhaps Howe would be able to describe it. One inclined to doubt what one saw anyway. Wasn't that true? It might be more real, strange as it seemed, just to hear it described.

The elderly scholar said *jawohl* to that. It took him a moment, since his mouth was full of food. He had taken from his pocket a sandwich, part of which he shared with the boy. The crust they fed to the flock of geese eying them through the door. When his eyes were good —quite remarkable, in fact—he had seen all of Europe and not a little of Greece, but it was only now, that his eyes were no good, that he enjoyed what he had seen. Strange, was it not? Unable to look out so well, he looked in. He smiled with affection and some mystification at the red-haired lad beside him, his green eyes disturbingly impersonal. What did he see? One would never know. And perhaps a good thing.

Howe thought Katherine would jeer at Wolfgang's suggestion, but she did not. Perhaps she hadn't heard it. She sat with a glass of mineral water into which she dipped her fingers. Relative blindness, in Howe's opinion, improved her looks. With a few touches, a change in her hair, the profile was that of a renaissance portrait, serene and suggestive as the landscape framing her head.

"Like old times, eh?" he said, taking her arm, but she didn't seem to care in what way he meant it. Perhaps, indeed, it was like old times, if times changed so little. Before they could leave the porch the boy had to chase

away the geese. A big gander, rearing back like a swan
approaching Leda, had to be bypassed with a detour
around a heap of manure. The odor led them all to
walk with lifted heads. Howe was about to comment
that certain things were the same everywhere, in both
Riva and Kansas, when it occurred to him where he
had made that remark before. Right here. Passing the
open stable on his left. In the adjoining house he had
been midwife to a sow named Hilda, baby-sitter and
nursemaid to her farrow of nine suckling pigs.

How had that happened? He could not keep his big
mouth shut. He had let slip—in a loud voice—that in
Kansas pregnant sows were common. As indeed they
were. But not very common to Howe. In the Kuchel
house, where she had been moved to a bed of clean yellow straw in the corner, Howe sat on a milk stool for
three nights, and as many days. On it he slept, there being no other chance to sleep. He was the wise man from
the West: the one who knew about sows. He would su-
perintend this all but miraculous birth. In that dim
room, the air moist as a steambath, dark except where
pink Hilda glowed in her corner, more whale-like than
hog-like, her legs like tapered flippers, Howe dutifully
kept the watch. She whimpered and fretted. She made
little noises in her snout. Her pink ears were like limp
flippers on her huge head. Now she was bored, now she
was anxious. Rolling a bloodshot eye she made it clear
that she suffered; bedside, Howe's sentiments had been
extremely complex. It was no sow he tended. It was
Mother Nature in labor herself. In her sprawling bulk
she occupied about a third of the room inhabited by
five people, most of them obliged, during her crisis, to

remain in bed. Two small boys and a girl, they sat with
eyes like lanterns. Behind Howe was a bench on which
visitors came to sit. They were concerned. Like Hilda,
they had time on their hands. When her time came, happily, Howe was alone. She had made a pitiful effort to
rise, a barefaced appeal for attention, then with a sigh
that seemed small for such an occasion she gave birth.
Nine times. Some said ten, or even twelve, but it was
nine. Howe was there. He suffered, and he knew. It
seemed strange, indeed, to feel, as Howe felt and never
questioned, that a newborn pig was one of the marvels
of this world. And nine times. Hilda outmarveled the
marvelous.

As one of the four men at the bedside Howe tried to
keep order in the food department, all but two of the
nipples being spoken for. What a racket they made. He
may have actually flushed a bit. Pumping machines, one
moment they were sucking, the next, milk dripping on
their chins, they were sleeping. Nor was the worst over.
Not by any means. A mother as vast as Hilda had no
idea of her dimensions, or what havoc she could make if
she moved. And a woman, a mother, she had to move.
At such a crisis Howe, with one of the others, would
risk a limb to sweep the litter to safety, while others persuaded Hilda to stand quiet, or lie back down. Morning
brought spectators, but no relief. It was assumed that
the family was safest in Howe's hands. A stool was
placed at her head, where he could stroke her ears when
she seemed disturbed, or lean on one knee to arrange
the litter at the pumps. What were his sentiments? Pride
and anxiety. Very much the same as those of Hilda, herself.

In the long day in which he often dozed off a moment, like the farrow, he became impressed with some of Hilda's details. In particular her vastness—to be balanced on such small feet. Not much larger, were they, than a good-sized knife handle, a place they one day might turn up. Hilda's great pink snout could puff a blast that spread straw chaff like a blast of water, or sniff, eyes lidded, as if inhaling the fragrance of rose water. From her huge body a basking warmth, less odorous than that radiated by overheated females, kept Howe warmer than he had been for months. One of the few radiantly warm periods of his life. He grew to like her. To say more than that would be indelicate. He seriously considered, in the light of his rank, asking for custody of one of the farrow—the smallest, as it happened, the least to be missed. A screw-tailed little squealer with a gem-like cloven hoof. But that was a passing infatuation, soon gone as the little monster fattened.

The good Hilda embodied the basic virtues. Her resemblance to Mizi was striking. Both confined their remarks to sighs, their influence to bulk and pneumatic pressure. When her work was done Hilda was moved from the moist room, with its steamed windows, to her cold straw pen in the stable. Not that she seemed to care. On his freezing walk with Dulac, Howe would sometimes see her, or part of her, glowing like a carefully banked mound of coals.

"I think I like it better this way," Katherine said. How did she mean that? To let Howe lead her? That had been true, he remembered, when they danced. She

wore no glasses, and was—as she loved to point out—
at his mercy. But not entirely, since he looked to her
like everybody else. "What are you thinking?" she asked,
nudging his arm. That too had not changed, he was
thinking. When she could not see what was on his mind,
she had to hear about it.

"I was thinking," he said, rapidly thinking, "what the
professors will think when they turn up your lenses.
Tiddlywinks in their sifter. What would they guess? A
race of nearsighted midgets, who stone-ground their own
lenses?"

"You haven't changed. Not one bit."

The sound he made surprised them both. Wide-eyed,
she stared at him. Without the lenses, her eyes had lost
their luster.

"You *have* changed—?" she asked. Did her voice
seem plaintive?

He shook his head, her eyes following the motion.
"No, it just sounded familiar. That's what my old
friends have been saying."

"You're fortunate to have so many," she replied.

At the edge of the millpond the boy gazed skyward,
his head leaning for support on the front of the scholar.
Howe had once stood in the same position. Had he had
such a face? Was the wonder in the boy or in what he
saw? The elderly scholar, a finger to his lips, cautioned
them not to disturb the boy's attention: he, himself, did
not breathe, fearing to jar the lens or one leg of the tri-
pod. Howe seemed to hear the ticking of the time-
exposure. The boy did not blink.

"And to think I'm missing it," Katherine said. The
irony was not lost on the boy, but he ignored it.

"You want me or Mr. Howe to describe it?" Into the pocket of his pants, man-fashion, he tried to insert his fat hand but it would not go.

"I'll get your impression later, dear, won't I? Why don't we let Mr. Howe describe it for us both?"

"You haven't changed much either," Howe observed, and moved so that he stood behind them. Was it the bank of the pond that trembled, or his legs? For a moment he saw nothing but the sky. It was customary for Monsieur Dulac to walk his guests, through the knee-deep snow, to where the ice could be heard creaking on the pond. There he would stop—the sound of it pleased him—and turn to glance, little more, over his shoulder. They were in, so it seemed, the trough of a foaming wave. Up there, up there on its crest, was the last of the winter light. The effect was due in part to the shimmering light, in part to the onlooker. His state of mind, if he had one: the film on his eye. A cresting, permanently captive wave such as one saw in Hokusai, with Riva no larger than a buoy gilded with light. The moat wall seemed to lap it, fall away. The Gods lived there, if anybody. That seemed obvious. The Gods, Warren Howe, and Monsieur Etienne Dulac.

"It's like the castle in a glass ball—" Howe smiled, pleased to wiggle out of that one.

"What glass ball?" the boy turned on him.

"They used to come with sewing machines," said Howe. "It snowed when you shook them. They were kept on hand for boys to play with when they had measles."

"It's all right to talk to *me* as a child," said Katherine, "but not to Brian, is it, darling?"

"I've never had *anything*. What're measles like?"

"They're better than school, if that's your choice."

"If Mr. Howe won't tell me what it's like, suppose you tell me." Katherine drew him to her, turning him, once more, to face the cliff. A swarm of gnats hovered like specks before their eyes. The weeds and tufts of grass along the moat wall, growing out of the cracks, gave Riva the look of something left by nature, rather than made by man. Like a photograph enlarged too many times, it looked slightly porous, an illusion constructed out of particles of light. Was it actually up there, or on Howe's eyeballs? Some of it seemed to flake off when he blinked. "You know something," she said, as the boy might have said it, "I never really believed it. Any of it. And so I come back and I can't even see it. What a goddam joke!"

At the goddam Howe flinched slightly, just like old times. The way she swore had always been at odds with the way she looked. The image of Riva quivered a moment as if it felt itself threatened.

"You still don't like girls that swear, do you? That's too bad. Neither does Brian. He would like both his grandmother and father to be more respectable."

"I've never said *that!*" said the boy.

"As a matter of fact," put in Howe, "neither have I. I like a girl to be thoroughly unrespectable—but preferably one who doesn't swear."

"I failed you on two counts then, didn't I, dear?"

She had tipped her head so that her chin protruded. Once that had been attractive. Howe turned away from the touch of a gobbler in the profile. Soon now would she cackle like an old hen?

"Failed me?" he echoed, as if the idea was novel.

"I was certainly too respectable to make your winter in Europe more romantically rewarding. Mean of me, wasn't it? I knew perfectly well there wasn't anybody else."

Howe was too respectable, there in public, to question that. Sensing trouble, the hand on his shoulder tapping out a message, the boy suddenly wheeled, as if pushed, and ran toward the loving pair standing near the millwheel. The blonde had tucked a flower into her hair, her head dreamily inclined on the young man's shoulder. The hand he looped at her waist she gripped like a buckle. Howe saw them double, once on the bank, where her short fat legs appeared to be in the water, once on the rippled surface of the pond. Nothing seemed to be lacking from the tableau but a pail of milk.

"You think I don't know what you're thinking?" That she *always* knew, but had she ever told him? "You're thinking what a lucky thing it was it *did* snow!"

"O my God!" he said, no irony intended. Simply O my God. She had thrust her head forward as if to smell what she could not see. Very much like old times he noticed the pink wings of her nose, the chronic sniffling. "You forget it was *your* idea," he said. "You didn't want me to catch your goddam cold!"

A mistake. Never mind how true it was. Her weight tipped away from his supporting arm, but she gripped it like a porch railing.

"A cold!" she cried, her voice hoarse. "You were afraid to catch a cold? It wasn't even worth a measly little cold?"

Howe said nothing. Nothing.

"O my God! What a lover! Did I pick myself a bold lover!"

Although hustling away, the elderly scholar wheeled to see if she might have swooned. One might have thought Howe had struck her. Such was the scene. To calm her, to support her, he had to grip her forearms. Her dangling, gaping bag swung between his legs. So there they were standing, or reeling—the slope of the bank put her above him—when Wolfgang appeared at the door of the Gasthaus, calling her name. What could he think but that Howe—what *could* he think?

"Yes, yes—!" Katherine replied, then snuffled. Howe released her arms so she could blow her nose.

"He's come around," called Wolfgang. "He's waiting!" He gave no indication what he was thinking. Between his bowed legs Howe caught sight of a car winding up the road.

"Coming!" he replied. "We're coming." Wolfgang was kind enough to turn and walk inside. The hand Howe put out to Katherine's arm she did not shrug away.

"My God!" she said. "What does it matter? Did we come here to live it all over? That poor old man is dying, and we—we . . ."

"We haven't changed much," said Howe, "have we? The bold lover and his sniffling beloved had some good fights. That's about all."

"That's *not* about all. Not for me." She started away but Howe held her.

"Not for you?"

"Do you suppose I came back to the scene of a head cold?" When she turned to leave, he let her go. In the

long-legged gait he remembered—but he remembered
too late she was blind—she took three strides, tripped,
threw her bag into the air as she fell. On her knees, ignoring Howe's assistance, she crawled around in the
grass feeling for objects that had spilled from her bag.
Brian panted up to help her, his feet muddy to the
ankles from wading. The situation, Howe gathered, was
not so unusual. How often did she fall?

"You know what?" the boy said. "You can see money
better when it's not so light."

"That's true of almost everything, darling," she replied. Bent over, her skirt happily concealing the grass
stains on her knees, Katherine returned the found items
to her bag. The fall had attractively loosened her hair,
brought color to her face. Dialogue with this boy, Howe
gathered, served her as the echo chamber in which she
found items once thought to be lost. The fall had brought
her back—or was it forward?—to where they stood in
the dusk below Riva, the light from the sky rather good
now for searching for coins. Standing erect, flushed, she
said, "Do I look a sight?"

She did, indeed, but a good one. Falling, she had
sucked in her lower lip, and smeared it with a grin of
lipstick. In the filmed eye of her compact she saw it.
"Just be glad it's not on you!" she said.

Did they shuffle, Howe wondered, between the past
and the present so easily? All of them? Bold lovers one
moment, old fakers the next? In which world did they
live? In what place did they hope to hide? The toot of a
horn led them to turn as Spiegel, in the Opel, bounced
into the courtyard. An aging rooster soared into unaccustomed flight. On the porch of the inn Wolfgang was

speaking but he could not be heard above the roar of the motor. On Spiegel's broad head, like Barney Old-field, his cap had been reversed. Frau Dulac filled the space beside him, a shawl around her broad shoulders, a settled, resigned expression on her face. Howe had the feeling she could *will* the car to stop. The tangle of knitting and wool she forked on the needles, then backed from the car in the manner of a seasoned, com-muting housewife. Knowing what she would find, she entered the Gasthaus and found it.

His head out the window, beaming, Spiegel called, "Taxi, anyone?"

Wolfgang peered at the car. "It looks a little small for us all, doesn't it?"

"Seats five!" Spiegel barked. "If you don't mind who you sit on."

"I'm sure that Katherine doesn't—" Wolfgang paused, then added, "She used to sit on you, didn't she, Warren?"

Did Katherine hear that? She did; from his arm she removed her hand. "I beg your pardon—" she began, but unable to see them, it seemed impossible to say who she meant to question.

"That's how we used to taxi, isn't it, Warren? You re-member that night we went to the Prater?"

Did Howe remember? It seemed that ticklish wisps of her brown hair blew across his face. The lobe of her ear had smelled of the cologne Wolfgang had had the taste and nerve to buy her, so near to Howe's lips he might have nipped it, but he did not. It had been a long ride, permanently pressing the lap of his pants.

"Kid here can ride in the trunk, eh?" said Spiegel. He gave the boy a wink and puffed smoke in his face.

"There's no need to disturb anyone," said Katherine. "We have a perfectly good car of our own."

"A lot of good that does us," said the boy. "We got a car, but who's going to drive it?" Had she forgotten? "You know what? When we got a new car we couldn't find it in the parking lot. They were all alike."

"That was *not* your grandmother's fault. I could see well enough to see there was no difference."

"Why don't I go and get it?" asked Howe. "Spiegel can drop me. It will only take a moment."

"Might I make a suggestion?" Wolfgang smiled as he bowed. "If you haven't a lap to offer the lady, might I offer her mine?"

What had brought it on? Katherine could hear, but not see, what a spectacle he made on the rim of the porch, his courtly bow emphasizing the gap between his legs. Lap? He had none. It would be like sitting her on the shafts of a stretcher. If Howe had little else to offer, at least he had a lap.

"Look—" Howe began, but Katherine happily spared him what might have followed. Would they have dueled? Heaving rocks at each other from twenty yards?

"I'm very much obliged to you *both,*" she said, "but I have to think of Brian. You'd rather grandmother sat on *your* lap, wouldn't you, darling?"

Turning his head slowly, like a panning camera, the boy took in the situation. Howe saw himself, somewhat underprinted, loose among the snapshots of his mind. Part of the jigsaw scene he would one day assemble. They waited for him to take them all off the hook. He said not a word.

"How's the old man?" asked Spiegel, scratching a

match on the doorpost. Had they forgotten him once
more? Wolfgang wheeled to peer through the door where
the light fell on a chair near the window. There he sat.
Frau Dulac was cleaning him off. An eye unaccustomed
to his appearance might have thought she picked lint
from an old throw rug. Where damage could be observed she clucked her tongue. Dulac's stiff leg was
propped, like a gun barrel, on the frame of his crutch.
His wild hair had been combed. The air of a man about
to be sprayed with a barber's scented water, then fanned
and powdered, was unmistakable. He was accustomed
to service, be it good or bad. Frau Dulac, without turning, muttered something to Wolfgang.

"He wants us to be his guests, his guests for dinner."
Wolfgang turned to see if there were any objections.

"That's very kind of him," said Katherine, "but—"
She pushed back her coat sleeve to glance at her watch.
Howe could read it, but she could not.

"It's ten past five," Howe put in. "We've got to think
about getting back."

"That's been thought of," said Wolfgang. "Frau Dulac assured me that's been thought of. There's no problem if the gentlemen will double up."

"Double up in *what?*" Spiegel queried, accustomed to
a four-poster bed to himself.

"I'm afraid it's out of the question—" Out of habit,
Katherine held her watch to her ear.

"I'm afraid it is," said Wolfgang, "for you to leave.
Either Warren or myself would have to drive. If you
have come this far to bury him . . ."

"I did not come to bury him!" cried Katherine.

"That's right," Howe said. "The lady came to praise

him, not to bury him."

"I hate you all!" she cried, stepping away from Howe.

"That simplifies the sleeping arrangements," said Wolfgang. Unable to see the face of Wolfgang, Katherine seemed to question what she had heard. Sleeping arrangements? Could it be Wolfgang talking like that? "Besides," he went on, "I'm not so sure we have a choice. We're his guests. I'm sure you remember what it was like."

"You kidding—?" Spiegel would have gone on, but there he paused, his mouth cigar-corked, to look at the pair who stood in the door. Monsieur Dulac, his face bloodless, propped between Frau Dulac and his crutch, gazed about him like a man accustomed to returning from the dead.

"The poy, yes, yes?" he jibbered. "The poy, yes?"

The boy was right there before him, his hair flaming.

"The kid's right here," said Spiegel, and plopped a hand on his shoulder. The old man squinted his eyes. Perhaps the light seemed strong. One could not tell if he smiled or winced. Apropos of nothing, nothing visible, he extended his free hand before him, the palm up, the clawed fingers coiled. Was it for rain? Was it the gesture of a beggar? Strange indeed was it how clearly Howe could hear, if not see, the bird that hovered in the air before him, flapping its wings.

The knees of Katherine Brownell, a tall, bony woman, thrust out of the tweed skirt she was wearing to serve as posts on which to rest her bag. Leaning forward, as if she could see, in the pose of the chronic back-seat driver, her right hand gathered the folds of her skirt beneath her thighs. Howe, and then Prutscher, had proposed to walk, to make it more comfortable for the others, but Katherine would not think of it—no, they should all either walk or ride. So room for them all had been found inside. Monsieur Dulac, to accommodate the leg that would not go elsewhere, sat between Spiegel and Frau Dulac, his metal crutch in their laps. The boy—weighing more, it seemed to Howe, than his grandmother—sat on Howe's lap.

On the road to Muhldorf they passed the elderly scholar, who waved to them with his guide book, marked with his finger. They did not see more of the young American and the blonde. But they were no sooner settled, no sooner resigned, than Monsieur Dulac thumped on the door with the tip of his crutch. What did he want? "Stop! Stop!" he barked, and when the car stopped with a jolt he wanted out. Was he carsick? They had stopped before a building with a cave-like stable on one side. Dark. The smell of fermenting manure on the draft. Dimly, as in the background of a painting that needed cleaning, Howe could make out the forms, creamy and glowing, of two huge beasts. Oxen? They might have been carved out of marble. Between them, a pair of eyes only, peering owl-like, a creature possibly ancestral to man. A beard blackened his face. Lank hair thatched his eyes. One hand gripped a comb with which he stroked a creamy flank. Sounds came from him, a speech for oxen. As he moved one shoe came out of the manure with a suck.

Pitched high, like a child, they heard the voice of Dulac give orders to the man behind the oxen. His head pumped. He raised, then let fall, a ham-like hand. Was it the pale, smoking light in the village? In the dark frame of the stable, the only sound that of the suck and the whisking comb, the creamy, steaming monsters were not oxen but mythic beasts. As if nailed to Howe's lap, the boy stared. The prickle they felt at the roots of their hair they both shared, without time's intervention, with the first man who had put such beasts in a marble frieze. One great pair of eyes fixed Spiegel with a marble gaze.

"Fellow over in Chino—" Spiegel paused to take a breath, hunch his shoulders—"would give me a thousand bucks a head for the pair. Nuts about oxen. Till the hoof-and-mouth boys caught up with him, used to bring 'em up from Mexico."

Hobbling, one foot smeared with dung, Dulac came back to the car, climbed in. A moment passed while he maneuvered, panting, his inflexible leg. Would it kill him? He took the air in rasping gasps. In his wheezing exasperation there was everything but self-pity. An animal fighting a leash, or a' trap on a maimed limb. It came slow to Howe, as always, that Dulac had skillfully used them to transact a little business, the walk to Muhldorf being a little too far.

To no one in particular Wolfgang said, "It is better to humor him, like the weather."

"But the weather varies, doesn't it?" asked Howe. There seemed to be some doubt of the matter. Wolfgang made no comment. Spiegel let out the clutch. In the rear-view mirror Howe looked for someone with whom to share the sentiment. He could see only Katherine, her head bobbing, the lids mercifully closed on eyes that no longer saw anything.

"She's asleep," said the boy, matter-of-factly. "If she can't drive she falls asleep."

Eight

The Gasthaus at Stein, the garden hung with grapes, lines of drying wash, and a wide panoramic view of the Danube, had prepared a table for Monsieur Dulac and his guests. It sat at the rear, in an arbor where birds rustled in the vines, the bench serving as a foxhole for a lean orange striped cat. Pitchers of new wine, faintly rose in color, were covered with napkins to keep off flies too smart for the lumpy strips of flypaper that dangled from the vines. Seen from the bar, where they had stopped for a drink, the strips glistened prettily and looked highly ornamental. Festive, Katherine would have said, if she could see them, but of course she could not.

Pried out of the car seat, where his sore limbs had stiffened, Monsieur Dulac insisted on escorting Katherine, whom he seemed to be aware of for the first time. Wolfgang and Frau Dulac had walked ahead to the garden, from where they had to be called back, since Monsieur Dulac, with Katherine and Spiegel, had stopped at the bar. Had it been some time since the barman had seen him? So it seemed. A big thick fellow whose head had been selected to fit the small opening of his collar, the barman's sleeves were rolled to the elbow on hairless arms, dumpling-colored. He seemed pleased to see Monsieur Dulac, but on the cool side with Frau Dulac, who tossed off in one gulp her glass of new wine. And how was the weather at Riva? *Gut.* And how were things at Riva? *Gut.* Frau Dulac gave him these answers, dipping one hand into her pouch of coins, since Monsieur Dulac had never been one to stand and talk. But if Monsieur Dulac said little, when was it he had ever said much? *Wie geht's? Was gibt's Neues?* And that was that. Unless he was buying something when he might want to know how much. He was still the same. Down to the way he tossed off a schnapps. The barman proposed a toast to his health, which they drank in three flavors, beer for Spiegel, schnapps for Dulac, new wine for the rest of them. For Brian Coca-Cola in the bottle was available.

The times had changed, the barman admitted, and flagged his bar rag toward the garden, where the cars of several nations were parked. Tourists. There were even two from America. Ladies, traveling alone. One hardly knew what to make of it. There were even more tourists, according to his father, than in the great days of Franz Joseph when the hills rang with the pop of guns and the sound of horns. Buggies were parked under trees near the river, waltzes were played. The train from Vienna brought out hikers who slept in the woods. And

not always alone, he added with a wink. Not always
alone.

Frau Dulac, her tongue loosened by the wine, said
that it was in the past *they* should have come to Riva,
when both the castle and Monsieur Dulac were in their
prime. One could not order these things, of course, but
that was when they should have come. Not when the
place was a ruin and the master of the house didn't
recognize people, and the mistress was unable, for
countless reasons, to supply them with food. Did they
know what it was like in the past? Wolfgang would have
replied but she stopped him. How would *he* know, being
still relatively young himself? There was a *Glasgemälde*,
a painting on glass, of which she had a picture and
would show them, of Schloss Riva in 1789. *Fabelhaft.*
The orchard had been larger, the trees younger, the
fields fuller, the skies higher, and on the broad slope
under Riva the peasants danced. One could see them!
The monastery was full of men for the love of God. Of
all that she had just one picture, the original to be seen
in the museum in Vienna, but of Monsieur Dulac,
thanks to Frau Dulac's presence of mind in a crisis, she
had proof that things were not always as one saw them
now. A ruined castle, an old man—Frau Dulac broke
off to signal the barman. No more schnapps for Monsieur. No, enough was enough.

Little enough Frau Dulac cared if he had an extra
schnapps or two, but did they know that he wet his bed
at night? That in the morning his clothes would have
to be changed? Like a baby, and at her age she was
simply too old for a baby. She needed help. From where
was it to come? Frau Dulac broke off, as if waiting for

volunteers. Had she been in the sun? Her throat and forehead were flushed. She had had just time to change her dress and put a gemmed comb in her hair, hinting at the sort of woman she had once been herself. A sad moment, felt by them all, embarrassing, touching, all too human. Unaccountably, in the voice of a choirboy, Monsieur Dulac chirped, "My wife, my wife, yes, yes, yes, my wife?"

Was he proposing a toast? He had lifted his glass in her direction, smiling. The syrupy schnapps brightened his lips, darkened his teeth. Before they had fathomed his intentions Frau Dulac took the glass from his hand, tossed it off.

"He is sleepy," she said, and with a twist of her fingers squeezed the remnant of syrup from his lips. "Eat and sleep, sleep and eat, eat and sleep."

"Perhaps we should get started, then—" suggested Wolfgang, and nobody objected. No, they were all starved. Howe was actually a little weak. The wine on his empty stomach had a pronounced effect. Brian, who stood at his side fizzing what was left of his Coca-Cola, allowed Howe to grip his hand like a father, and lead him away. Bloodless but animated, just the touch of a satyr about his shining lips, Monsieur Dulac gripped one female and leaned his weight on the other. A troubled vision of life, or of time, symbolized by the feeble old man between the women, one a wife and another a mistress, for a moment spread a film over Howe's eyes as if he might weep. "Ah me!" he said aloud, relieved to have a little child there to lead him.

Entering the garden they skirted the table where the two ladies were writing postcards, one preoccupied with the writing, the other with the stamps. "I wish you wouldn't lick them," the younger one observed, but she got no reply.

Monsieur Dulac was seated at the place of honor, in a chair with arms. Frau Dulac sat on his left, Katherine on his right, with the boy between her and Howe. Spiegel sat across from Howe, with Wolfgang on the chair at the end of the table. Under the arbor the air seemed close. Or was it the wine?

As she turned to tie a napkin on the boy, Howe noticed that Katherine looked a little sunburned. That would explain Wolfgang's unhealthy glow, and the bruised rings around the eyes of Spiegel. His dark glasses were off. The thumbs of both hands he rubbed at his bloodshot eyes. Monsieur Dulac, as if the lamps might burn him, still wore the limp-brimmed panama; in its shadow he resembled a bearded crone on the edge of sleep.

A young woman with rolled sleeves, thick rather than plump, leaned over Howe to ladle soup from a tureen. Her moist breath smelled of beer, however, rather than milk. Beneath the arch of her arm Howe glanced up to catch the knowing smile of Wolfgang.

"Like old times, eh?" Wolfgang dipped his own head so that her arm would not muss his hair.

"Whatever became of Mizi?" Howe inquired.

As if a hand had jarred him awake, the old man rocked his head back, chirped, "Mizi, Mizi, yes, yes. Mizi?" A glint of moisture, no more, indicated his eyes. Having sounded the note, however, he seemed to lose the rest of the tune. "Mizi, Mizi," he repeated, and the bird-like claw plucked at the center of a slice of bread beside his plate. The name seemed to mean nothing to Frau Dulac.

"Eat, eat!" she said, and placed a spoon in his hand.

"I understand—" Wolfgang dampered his voice to deliberately heighten Katherine's attention—"she's in Ottenschlag. Married a miller to feed her brood of kinder. I hear one is tall and clever. Would it be yours?"

Howe let the steam rising from his soup veil his face. Katherine Brownell, spooning soup to the boy, pretended she had heard nothing: nothing of interest. But not the boy. He let the soup steam his face while he recorded what he had heard, the meaning superimposed on the picture he took of Howe. And Howe? He deliberately posed for it. From an album of lovers, good and bad, he selected the expression he thought suitable, but it was not the one the boy saw on his face. That was one of pity. What a pity the tall clever boy might resemble Wolfgang more than Howe.

"Tall and clever?" said Howe. "Might be Spiegel. He was there in the spring, you know, for the weekend."

"How's that?" Spiegel raised his face from the soup. Steam, like a film of oil, seemed to modify some of his features. A woman's soft, spaniel eyes glowed in his face. Howe stared: it had crossed his mind he had no idea, none, of what his friend had *once* looked like. The sheet was blank. Spiegel was as he saw him, or not at all. "Now what?" Spiegel dropped his spoon to blot his face with a napkin. It came away damp, stained with soup. "I don't tan," he said, "I just burn. Think it'll peel?"

Howe turned to stare at Wolfgang. He stopped smiling and raised a hand to his nose. "I suppose we all got something," he said. "Is it bad?" Not trusting Howe, he turned to Katherine.

"You've no idea," she said. "You've no idea what a wonderful comfort it is."

It took a moment to realize she meant her blindness.

"I'm sure you're a sight, darling," she went on, putting her hand to the boy's forehead. "If I could see I'd be just sick. Is it bad?"

"Only on my knees," he replied, and puckered his lips as he put his hand to them. But that was not all. His freckled face was spotted like a maple leaf.

"Eat! Eat!" cried Frau Dulac, slapping her hand on the table. "Do not talk so much, eat!" As if to demonstrate she dipped her spoon, blew on it, served it to Dulac. Some of the gruel stuck to his upper lip, like a runny nose.

"It's probably just me—" Howe said, and shook his head.

"Sunburnt?" said Spiegel. "Hell, we all are." He beamed around. "Look at the schnoz on old Prutscher."

Spiegel and Brian both laughed. The humor of it was lost on Wolfgang. "I've some lotion in the car," said Katherine, "if I can ever find it."

"It's nothing," said Wolfgang. "I rather like a bit of tan."

"I wasn't thinking of the sunburn—" Howe put in.

"You will soon as you have to blow it," said Spiegel. The boy's laugh was short, as if he might miss something. Was that why he had not laughed all day?

"It just crossed my mind," said Howe, "that I can't really think how anybody looked." They waited, and he said, "You know, back then."

"Allow me to congratulate you," Katherine said. The remark seemed so pat Howe was relieved that she could not see his face.

"Who you mean?" asked Spiegel. "I remember FDR better back then than I did later. Same with Lindbergh. Hell, I didn't even *know* him later. Same with Gable, Norma Shearer—" he paused there to look around— "or you mean somebody in particular?"

"I think he means *us* in particular." Wolfgang looked about him, at each of them in turn, as if to test the impression. "I can recall how you looked quite well, Warren. I think unspoiled was the word. Time has changed that some. As I recall, the girls found you attractive. Perhaps they still do."

"That may have been how I *was*," Howe replied, "but not how I looked. It's the look that escapes me." He turned to gaze at Spiegel.

"Orange juice," Spiegel said, "don't that do it? I can see you standin' there. I can see you pourin' orange juice."

Clearly, as if the slide was held before him, Howe saw the face of a man he did not remember seeing. He stood with one thumb hooked in his galluses as he tossed off his drink. Howe's head wagged.

"You don't see me?" said Spiegel. "You're lucky. It was hard on my mother to see me."

"When you said orange juice," said Howe, "I saw a face, a man's face, I never remember having seen. Farmer in his shirtsleeves. How you account for that?"

"What's so mysterious about it?" said Katherine. "It's an attic. Like rummaging in an attic. You find all the stuff you've spent your life trying to forget."

His eyes closed, Howe said, "One of those shirts without collars. My dad wore one. Stud left a green spot on his neck."

"Sure it wasn't him?" That was Spiegel.

"It's just a big wastebasket," Katherine said, "and you can find in it what you want to."

"Wouldn't a woman's purse do better?" Wolfgang smiled.

"What interests me," Howe said, "is that he was there and I didn't know it. I didn't know it."

"Don't you think unspoiled is still a good word for him?" Katherine beamed a weary smile toward Wolfgang.

"I like that," said Howe. "It means there's more life in us than we're aware of. Maybe more sense. Somebody took that snapshot when my back was turned. It isn't something I dug for, having buried. I'm not sure attic is the right word for it—"

"Talk, talk talk!" cried Frau Dulac. "Do you nothing but talk?" With her own wet spoon she pointed at their soup bowls. In the boy's a fly had given up the struggle. He fished it out.

"Use any word that pleases you—" Katherine had lowered her voice— "but give my darling a chance to eat his dinner." The boy sat there. Was he already half asleep? At the corners of his parted lips the soup dried like a sticky mucilage. His head was tipped in the manner of a child listening to grace. On what assurance did Howe feel that this ridiculous evening was being sound-taped: that the future—impersonally recorded—was being stored in this carrot-topped dome? None. It was merely a notion that pleased him.

"You know—" Wolfgang had been gazing at the boy's head—"I can recall how we looked quite well. Hungry, I think. Weren't we *always* hungry? But I just can't *imagine*—" his head shook—"what in forty years this lad will look like."

"Haven't I enough problems as it is?" Howe could sympathize with her apprehension. The growth of prodigies was not reassuring. Too much head compromised what, at its best, was a staggering problem, the harmony of parts that were not, it would seem, meant to harmonize.

"I simply can't see it, can you?"

Wolfgang had put the question to Howe. What did Howe see? A collage, more or less, of the many facets of Orson Welles, most of them indistinguishable from Citizen Kane.

"He's not gonna be a bag of bones," said Spiegel.

"Not if he's like his father." Katherine said no more. Did it help? Howe visualized a bearded giant in a soiled T shirt on which he wiped his paintbrushes. An arrogant bawdy-minded Irishman. Just the sort she would like. Stereo-fashion, as if one ear was tuned to what they thought, one to what they said, the boy sat as if he wore a pair of headphones, cut off from their talk.

As if the taste had just come to him Spiegel said, "Potato soup. We got the potatoes. Why can't we make the soup?"

Ignoring that, Katherine said, "I can't believe I'm really here. Wherever *here* is. Did anybody come for a sensible reason? My God, I hope not."

"I have given it some thought." Wolfgang peered slantwise down the table at Dulac. He had stopped eating. Floating in his soup were the rabbit-size pellets of dough he had rolled. They waited, and Wolfgang continued, "If you'll forgive me, it was not for old times' sake. Not at all. I felt some curious sense of obligation, God knows to what."

"Wolfie—" Katherine interrupted—"if you'll excuse me." Howe had never dreamed that she had called him Wolfie. It changed him. In point of fact, he sat grinning like a wolf. "You always spoil everything with your sensible obligations. I remember so many. How I admired them. Didn't you just come because you felt like it? Or wanted to see me?" Like a schoolgirl, she actually pouted. Only without her glasses would she risk that.

"I'm sorry to be so dull," he replied, "but what do we ever do merely because we want to?" The spoon Katherine had been holding slipped into her soup. She left it there, just the tip of it showing.

"Why'd I come?" Spiegel held their attention. A searching tongue puffed his lip above the gum line. "The ride. I come along for the free ride, didn't I, Howe?"

"That's how it looks from here," Howe replied.

"I don't mean to say, now I'm here, I ain't glad I come. Far from it. Like it better this time than I did the first time. Not so goddam cold." He returned to his soup.

"And you?" Wolfgang beamed at Howe.

"Warren hasn't changed," Katherine said, speaking for him. "He came along to take notes. It helps him believe it."

"Believe what?" Wolfgang tipped his head forward, his napkin trailing in his soup. Without comment, Frau

Dulac leaned forward and fished it out with her fork.

"I doubt that it matters," Katherine said. "It's all so far back I can hardly remember."

"Remember?" Wolfgang's head wagged. "Isn't it rather what we imagine? Don't we invent what we choose to remember? Isn't that it?"

"I can well believe it is for some people," Katherine leaned away from her food as if finished. It was curious how her eyes were now appropriate to her mood. Opaque. Neither opening inward nor looking out. A relief that he had missed her, not possessed her, and was free of the sentiments this would now cost him, seemed greater to Howe than the chagrin he had felt in having lost her. For this Morley, her husband, he felt a late twinge of sympathy.

"If you'll excuse me—" Wolfgang put a napkin to his lips, daubed at his forehead—"we're being *sentimentalisch*. It is not honest to grossly simplify, is it? It is your American fear of the complex. You want to be crazy, but you do not want to be *thought* crazy."

"I suppose American fear is different than Viennese fear?" cried Katherine.

Wolfgang paused to think. "I would say so. I fear loss of money simply dreadfully. Quite irrational. But it is nothing to how I fear such a thing as divorce."

That required no comment, and Katherine made none.

"I don't want to be a spoilsport," said Spiegel, "but when I'm crazy I know it. So do other people. When I turn it into money I don't mind it. How you like that?"

"Money, money, money!" Frau Dulac chanted the

word in English. "You come all this way to make money?" She held a spoonful of gruel just beyond the reach of Dulac's lips. His mouth hung open, showing what he had not swallowed.

"I didn't," said Spiegel, "but just supposin' I did? What is so bad about money? Havin' no money is the root of more evil than havin' too much."

Frau Dulac did not speak. Her expression made it clear she was beyond the reach of such twaddle. "Eat, eat!" she said to Dulac, and held the tipped spoon to his lips.

"One should be grateful for small favors," Katherine said, "and I am. I can't see a damn thing."

"That's no *small* favor," put in Spiegel. "If you know what I mean."

Wolfgang moved his plate to make room for his elbows, but the gesture was expressive.

"O-kay," said Spiegel, "money's out. You name it, we'll talk about it."

On the edge of her plate Frau Dulac rapped her spoon, placed Monsieur Dulac's bowl into her own, which was empty. The young woman who had served them stacked the bowls on her tray and put down plates of stewed meat and dumplings.

"What's wrong with old times?" said Spiegel. "They don't have to be good to talk about 'em, do they?"

A tune, popular at the time, popped into Howe's mind. A little hoarsely he sang—

> Don't know whyyyyyyy
> There's no sun up in the skyyyyy
> Stormy weaaaa-thurrr

"Your voice has changed, darling," said Katherine, "or I have."

"You come to sing—is that it?" Frau Dulac fanned the air to see them more clearly. At her side, the orange striped cat had settled down in the lap of Dulac. Did he know that? His lips were parted, his eyes closed. As he tipped slightly in her direction, she propped him up.

"I'm afraid we've all been lying," said Howe. "Didn't we come because we were invited?"

"To a funeral," said Spiegel. "Damn near forgot it."

"I haven't for one moment," said Katherine. "I'm firmly convinced that he planned it. He brought us here just to see him kill himself."

Howe winced, as if kicked under the table.

"Does anybody not know that?" Katherine cried. "Are we all crazier than he is?"

"Children, children!" Wolfgang put up his hands, the palms out, and flagged them slowly.

"I couldn't agree with you more, dear, but I don't think it's fair to Brian." Katherine slipped her arm around the boy's shoulder. Had he fallen asleep? For the first time Howe recognized in his face an accepted childish expression. One associated with sleep and thumb-sucking.

"If you'll permit me—" Wolfgang had reared up after filling their wineglasses. The new wine had the pale color of a bad soft drink. He tipped forward to tap Howe's glass, then straightened to pronounce a toast. "To Schloss Riva," he said, "and Monsieur Etienne Dulac."

Wine spilled as they turned and stretched to tap glasses.

"We got better in Napa Valley," said Spiegel. Did Frau Dulac take exception to that? The wine she had swallowed had gone to her eyes, tearful as she blinked.

"Ach Gott!" she said. "You should have seen him when young!" Seen who? It seemed a strange challenge. If she meant Dulac, when he had been young she had been a child. There was a pause while they pondered whom she meant. She turned to look, with disbelief, at the old man beside her. He had fallen asleep.

"And when was that?" Wolfgang smiled, but he was curious. Frau Dulac fingered the buttons of her dress. It seemed clear that she had slipped. Telling them *that* would be telling too much. "You knew him," Wolfgang continued, "back then?" It could not be ruled out. Not of the life of Dulac. After all, what did they know about him when young, whenever that had been?

"Know him?" Sadly the head of Frau Dulac wagged on her shoulders. An expression new and strange to her face forced a wan smile. No, no. No she had not known him. What she had said was she had *seen* him. She dropped her eyes to the bag she held in her lap. Howe thought she searched it for a piece of tissue, since her nose was running. But she found none. She continued to peer into the bag. After a moment she withdrew an oblong piece of paper. On the front of it, in an oval frame, a photograph. She passed it to Wolfgang who was obliged to tip it to the light to see it. Howe was able to read the date on the back, August 1910. "Quite a figure, I must say—" Wolfgang observed, smoothing the wrinkled lines on his forehead. Was he lost in thought? Absently he passed the print to Katherine.

"What is it?" she said. "Baby pictures? I'm sure he

must have been a gorgeous baby!"

"You like me to describe it for you?" said Howe. Frau Dulac reached for the picture but her bag filled her lap, her arm was too short.

"Please do," Katherine replied, letting Howe have it. "I have never forgotten your description of Riva. It's what I still see!" She laughed.

Howe moved to where the light seemed better. "Quite a figure indeed."

"That's very good," Katherine mocked. "Brian, darling, you listening?"

"Members of the Baron's family," said Howe, "seem to be resting after a partial ascent of Matterhorn. The peak stands at the back. A wicker basket of wine and food at the front. Two small boys, dressed like dolls in Alpine costumes, sit on a rock before a woman who appears to have no legs. Baron Dulac himself, a coil of rope around his shoulders, leans casually on an alpine pick. He stands where it makes one dizzy to look at him. His wife, the ugliest woman in Europe, has moved her head just as the picture was taken, so that one sees, in profile, her better points."

"What does he say?" Frau Dulac had her suspicions. She reached to take the snapshot from Howe, give him, in its place, a brittle newspaper clipping. The headline read

DIVA IN TRIUMPH

The dateline was Cedar Rapids, Iowa, October 9th, 1924. The photograph showed a gentleman at a piano, a woman emerging from a basket of flowers. Nothing else was clear. Framed by the handle of the basket, Madame Dulac seemed part of Alice's wonderland.

Before Howe could comment on it, Frau Dulac had plucked it from his fingers. In its place he held a portrait, the head only, the faintest tint of rose on the cheeks and lips. The silken hair lightly waved, the ears inset, the nose so well-bred it appeared to be skinless; the head seemed the model for those busts done by Houdon.

"You see! You see!" In Howe's face Frau Dulac saw it all very clearly. In his youth Monsieur Dulac had been a looker. No doubt about that.

"What now—?" said Katherine, extending her hand. Whether Frau Dulac meant to show her, or to keep it from her, was not clear. She half arose, forgetting the open bag in her lap, to take the picture from Howe. Newspaper clippings, snapshots, and even glass slides spilled around Howe's feet. He pushed back his chair and stooped to help. As if she had spilled a sack of apples she tried to scoop it all up at once. Crouched over, she had no wind for complaints. Howe fished out a clipping, several of them, and a sheet of paper that had been folded around a slide. Did she know what was on it? "No, no, no—" she cried. "Do not look, give it back!" She reached, but her lap was full of what she had picked up. "No, no, no—" she repeated, but turned back to recover what had spilled. She raked it into a pile, and hovered over it. Howe stood there, holding the paper, and the cracked glass slide repaired with tape. Was it something private? The figure on the slide was hard to see clearly. The tape repair cut across the face. The sheet of paper, however, was embossed with a coat of arms. An invitation? No, it seemed to be a menu. Elegant and sumptuous. What was there about it that seemed strange? The first, of more than a dozen courses, was Baba au Rhum. A printer's error? The second was Grands-Échezeaux and assorted cheeses. Howe ran down the list quickly to see what was last. Vichyssoise, of course. A menu, if not a meal, served in reverse order. Howe glanced up to see the faded newsprint Wolfgang was holding, illustrated with the picture of a Paris street cleaner, with his broom and his cart. Did he look familiar? Very. The man in the uniform was Monsieur Dulac, beardless, but with the gleeful smile of mischief on his lips. A bright, clever child caught with the jampot over his face.

At that moment Frau Dulac, her skirts gathered to hold the clippings, moved around the table to snatch the print from Wolfgang's hand. Not a word. Her distress was too deep for words. One might have thought it had been an early snap of herself, caught with her knees showing. If there had been a place for her to go, she would have gone. From Howe—he offered it to her— she took the menu he was holding, and folded it around the slide that had been repaired. Her hands were steady. Soberly, now, she cleaned up what she could no longer help. Did it cross any mind but Howe's that simple Frau Dulac was a force to cope with? That her hand would be steady shaking down the ashes at Buchenwald?

"You seem to forget," Wolfgang said, without his customary composure, "that we are his friends. We all know something of his life."

Frau Dulac made no comment. Did she consider the case closed? In her broad lap she put in order the life, or lives, they had disordered.

"What in heaven's name *happened?*" Katherine's

question hovered like the flies between them. "As for knowing something about his life, I don't know a thing. I'm not even sure I want to."

"He seems to have lived it upside down," said Howe. "Nuts to soup. Not a bad idea."

"You'd like that, wouldn't you, darling?"

The boy sat, Howe realized, as he had seen children sit confronting television. His hands gripping the chair. Both alert and stupefied. What had he made of the scene he had just witnessed? Nuts to soup. The upside-down grown-up world. He faced, without apparently seeing, the figure of Dulac at the end of the table, the hat concealing his drooping head. A picture tube in which the light had gone out.

"Nuts to soup ain't bad," said Spiegel, "know what I mean?" He rolled his eyes to make it clearer. "Got this cousin in St. Looey. Nice, decent sort of people. Got these three youngsters. All children. Last one is not too bright. Every time she writes she says she and Carl don't know what to think. Know why? Poor damn kid is just a little nutty. Mother knows what to think, but she don't want to think it. Nuts to soup!"

As if she still saw too much, Katherine veiled her eyes.

"Point is," said Spiegel, "what's so wrong with it? People like that got less worries. There's plain and fancy nuts, eh? He's the fancy type." He nodded his head toward Dulac. "Takes brains to be a fancy nut. More'n I got."

Katherine said, "I couldn't agree with you more, Mr. Segal."

"Spiegel," he replied. "Irish wing of the family."

"I know just what you're thinking," she said, "but I'm not!"

"I am," said Spiegel, "Semitic anti-Semite. Look what the Jews made of me, for example."

"O my God!" Katherine tried to push her chair back, but the legs caught in the dirt.

"Mine too," said Spiegel. "One God, one world, one goddam Jewish problem. Know what I think?"

"I don't, and I don't want to!"

"Know what I think?" Spiegel repeated, but the tone of his voice had changed. Calmly deliberate, even pleasant. That of a man surprised to know what he was thinking. "Know what ails *him?* Ten to one he's a Jew."

As if summoned by one of those whistles heard only by pets, Frau Dulac rose from her chair in such a manner it toppled. She let it lie. Gripping her bag, the tangle of wool, she crossed the garden to the door of the Gasthaus, the light coming on just as she stepped inside. No one spoke or rose to call her. From the pitcher of wine Wolfgang fished a fly that was drowning, lowered him, carefully, to a napkin.

"Why, she left him!" Katherine cried. "She forgot him!"

Monsieur Dulac dozed undisturbed in his chair.

"She won't go far—" began Wolfgang, but he was interrupted by the bang of a car door.

"What'd I tell you?" Who had he told? He looked around for the missing person. "She can hear what she wants to hear. She understands this lingo better than I do."

"Is there coffee?" asked Katherine. "Could I have some?"

Wolfgang tapped his wineglass to signal the waiter.

"Not me," said Spiegel. "Keeps me awake. If there's one thing I don't want to do in that barn it's lie *awake.*"

"I wouldn't think even Riva would trouble *your* sleep, Mr. Spiegel."

From her bag she fished a cigarette, put the wrong end of it to her lips. The boy, without comment, plucked it away and inserted it correctly. "What would I do without you, darling?"

"Smoke nothing but filter tips," he replied.

Spiegel was the only one to laugh. "Why not? Maybe that's the way to do it. Use the selected tobacco to filter the tip. From what people tell me couldn't taste any worse."

In the pause Katherine filled the air with a gasp of smoke. On Howe's level the smoke screened them off, but the boy sat in a clearing beneath it. Was there a meaning to that that escaped him? Howe felt there was.

"Tell you something," the voice of Spiegel said, "I never told anybody." Through the smoke Howe could see the faint eclipse at the tip of his cigar. "When I got my first job in Chicago I told the boss my name was Bushman. Walter Bushman. My ideal at the time was old Francis X." He paused, then added, "Be funny if it still was."

"Mr. Bushman," said Katherine, "why did you give it up?"

"Tell you something else," said Spiegel. "Nobody seemed to like it. Boss called me Fatso. Couldn't remember the Bushman part myself."

There was a pause.

"Know what the job was? Movie usher. Best years of my life."

"What movies did you see?" asked the boy.

"See? Hell, all I did was hear 'em. Talkies comin' in. All I seen of Al Jolson was them damn white gloves."

"Isn't it time we put some people to bed?" Katherine put her hand on the head of the boy, her eyes on Monsieur Dulac. A fly was trapped under his hat, but the buzzing did not disturb him.

"Know where I see him?" said Spiegel. "Pershing Square. Old days it was nuttier than a fruitcake. He'd a loved it. They'd a loved him. Why'd he come here?"

"I'm afraid that isn't quite the picture," said Wolfgang. "It made no sense, so he did it."

"You know," said Spiegel, "when you push that, it begins to make sense."

Perhaps the leg of her chair, as Katherine pushed it back, disturbed the outstretched leg of Monsieur Dulac. The hat still down over his face he cried, "Ada! Ada!" like a child in the dark.

"Isn't that her?" asked Katherine. "Where is she?"

The sound of her name seemed to have calmed him. His head drooped; once more he was about to doze off.

"Perhaps we'd better get him back—" said Wolfgang. "If one of you will draw out the chair." It was Howe, moving in behind, who slipped the chair away as he was lifted by Wolfgang, his left arm, free of the crutch, turned over to Katherine Brownell. Was he awake? He seemed to be accustomed to this sort of handling. The proprietor himself, with a knowing smile, tilting his head as one would an empty bottle, went ahead of them to open the door. In its light they saw the car, and in it the glint and flash of swordplay, like the mortal combat of knights in a tangled wood. Only the hands of Frau Dulac, not her face, the hands and loose tangle of wool in her lap, were visible through the windshield as they approached and she did not interrupt her knitting. "Here we are!" Wolfgang said. She let them wait.

Nine

Monsieur Dulac, the Meister of Nonsense, slept with his head on Frau Dulac's shoulder as they drove through the landscape where Howe and his Uncle Fremont, with a dozen others, those without guns serving as beaters, had hunted, by moonlight, for a rabbit known not to exist. And why not? For what *other* rabbit should one hunt? So Monsieur Dulac, his beard stiff with the drool from his nose, would have told them. What would Fremont Osborn, what would Charles Horney, what, indeed, would Warren Howe have thought of that? It occurred to Warren Howe that he had hunted such a rabbit all of his life.

No talk. Had there been more than enough? In his grandmother's lap the boy slept; on the shoulder of his wife Monsieur Dulac slept; Wolfgang dozed; Spiegel hummed as he drove. The tune? "Stormy Weather." He had picked it up from Howe. A dim, ghostly light, the moon behind clouds, the white-framed windows of Riva were like luminous road signs on a curve. No lights. In the hulk of Riva not a light.

"There's no point of your going to the trouble," said Katherine, but no one in the car seemed to be listening. Not Frau Dulac. She clasped the bag of knitting in her lap. Her expression was that of a mother who knew her child would soon be taken from her. Resigned, her mind on the child that remained. In the orchard the lights lit up the trees, the fruit hanging like Christmas baubles, insects rising from the ruts like water from a sprinkler. Monsieur Dulac's *loony bin* loomed up before them like a stranded ark. And why not? A refuge from the floods now inundating the world. A place to wait it out.

"And then it rained," Howe intoned, "for forty days, and forty nights—"

"I wouldn't care if it did," said Katherine, "if I could just go to bed and sleep."

"Kid in the block keeps a skunk," said Spiegel, "little devil just curls up and goes off. Kid calls him Shut-eye. Had him de-smelled when he was a pup."

They all spilled forward, thumping the seat back, as Spiegel slammed on the brakes. His head thumped, the boy howled.

"Good God!" Katherine cried. "Was that necessary?"

Spiegel did no more than wave his hands at the lights. Right there before them, gleaming with a new paint job, was a car. Did it look familiar? Under the new coat of white paint was the green car Katherine had driven out from Vienna. The hardware on the convertible top had been neatly touched up. No doubt about it, none whatsoever, since even Katherine could see it. "O my God," she said. The boy stopped howling to turn and look at it. "O my GOD," Katherine repeated.

"Always comes a time," said Spiegel, flicking the foot pedal, "when they carry it too far. Boy I knew in the army. Nice kid. Crazy friends he had nailed his bed to the ceiling. Poor bastard came home and saw it on the ceiling. Nuts ever since."

"We're suffocating!" Katherine cried. "Will you shut off the motor!"

Spiegel shut it off. "Temper! Temper!" he said, wagging his finger at her image in the rear-view mirror. Katherine closed her eyes. The boy sat erect, a bump on his forehead, his eyes wide and happy. Why did the zany—the really nutty—always please the kids? The kid in Howe, likewise. With some effort he controlled the impulse to laugh.

"If I don't get air," Katherine cried, "I'm going to faint!"

Howe and Wolfgang moved at the same instant, opened opposite doors. Over the top of the car they gazed like strangers pleased with each other. "Brian!" Katherine cried, but the boy scooted into the lights. He wiped his finger on the back of the car, then sniffed it.

"It's wet," he said.

Spiegel had to check on that for himself. Holding up the white tip of a finger he said, "Quality's poor, but it's paint. Nothing to do but let it dry, paint it over."

The smell of paint, turpentine, cut the sweetness of the night air.

"Do something!" Katherine cried. "Can't something be done?"

"Might help if you turn off the lights," said Spiegel.

That helped, but not very much. The car glowed with a spectral light of its own.

"They'll think I'm crazy. Absolutely crazy. They'll think I came all this way to go crazy."

There was no need to comment on that: it seemed obvious. Spiegel said, "Know what it does? Ties it in with the place." Like one of those prepared sketches supplied to children, white, and only white, had been applied to Riva. Shrilly, as if she saw something strange, Katherine laughed.

"What's so funny?" said Spiegel.

"Just me. Must be my eyes," she said. "I could just see you tied in with it too. All white. All white and sticky." She laughed.

"Christ—" said Spiegel. He turned to Howe. "Forgot *we* got a car. Think he will?"

Monsieur Dulac had been awakened by Katherine's laughter. "Light! Light!" he jibbered, sitting up, as if he had awakened and found the room dark. Frau Dulac hushed him.

"What's he think of the paint job?" said Spiegel. "Can he see it?"

If he saw it he made no comment. Wolfgang had stooped to help pry him out of the seat. The nap had done him good. He seemed almost spry. "Light! Light!" he jibbered. "Yes, yes?"

"*Moon*light," said Frau Dulac calmly, as if the other types of light had been dispensed with. Wolfgang stooped to reach her bag of wool, help her out of the car.

"What the hell do we do about the car?" said Spiegel.

"Want me to watch it?" said the boy. "Why don't I stay and watch it?"

"And have you all painted white too?" Katherine gripped the hand with the white-tipped finger.

"I have the feeling," said Wolfgang, "he may have run out of paint. I see the front of the car is unpainted."

"Some joke," said Spiegel. "Has he run out of paint, or is he just savin' it? Know what I better do? Better drive it back to Stein. Spend the night in Stein and pick you up in the morning."

"I knew you'd get out of it somehow—" said Katherine.

"Out of what!" bawled Spiegel. "You and the kid want to do it?" He took the keys out of his pocket and held them out to her. Katherine did not see them.

"She can't *see*," said the boy. "She can't see in broad daylight!"

Monsieur Dulac, Frau Dulac's arm around him, had turned to see that they were not at his heels. He thumped the leg of his crutch on the moat wall. "Come, come," he said, "come sleep, yes, yes?"

"You people run along," said Spiegel. "I'm stayin' right here. While that crackpot's on the loose, I'm stayin' right here." He ran the car window down to switch the radio on. "Nice here," he said, "what the hell."

Monsieur Dulac's metal leg rattled on the wall.

"We better humor him," said Katherine. "Isn't that it?"

"We better get him settled," said Wolfgang, "then we can decide. We can decide later."

"When you do," said Spiegel, unpeeling a cigar, "I'll be right here." He leaned into the car to turn up the volume. Twisting the dial he said, "Sinatra."

At the curve in the ramp Monsieur and Frau Dulac stood waiting for them. A single, stout, two-headed figure, the metal leg like a sword loose in its buckler. As they approached he put it aside, leaned it on the wall beside Frau Dulac, and spread his stiff leg to one side so that he could kneel. What was he up to? They could hear a cropping sound, like cattle eating. To the boy, who was the first in line, he looked up to hand a tuft of grass, or weeds, pulled up by the roots. The boy held back, but the old man reached and took one of his hands, cupped the palm, and placed the small plant in it, firmly. "Yes, yes," he jibbered, "from Riva, yes?" and stooped to pull another from the dirt of the ramp, clawing up the soil around the roots. This one he straightened to offer to Katherine, who stood back till Howe urged her forward. She took the pack of roots without a word, her palms cupped as if holding water. Howe was next: he received a plant with a prickly stem, an herb-scented flower, the earth at it roots cool in his hands. For Wolfgang a piece of sod, with several shoots of long-stemmed grass. "Yes, yes?" he jibbered. "Riva, Riva, yes, yes?"

"He likes you," said Frau Dulac. "He only does it to people he likes."

"Plan it, yes, yes. You plan it, yes? Take with you and plan it!"

They stood in the moonlight holding his offerings. Dirt fell with the sound of rain on Wolfgang's rubbers.

Snuffling, Katherine said, "What is it? Won't it die, poor thing?"

Wolfgang said, "Let me put them in the car." He

spread his hands to make room for them. With the bouquet of weeds he walked back to Spiegel.

"Know just the thing," said Spiegel. "A hubcap." They heard him prying it loose from the spare tire in the rear. "Looks like this one could use a little paint," he added.

Wolfgang came toward them, dusting his hands. Frau Dulac, with Monsieur Dulac, led the way to where the ramp entered Riva. The door stood open. Frau Dulac took a candle from the box on the wall.

"Don't you ever lock up?" asked Katherine.

Frau Dulac made a sound as if the match had burned her. Cupped in her palm, the candle sputtered. "What is there to lock up at Riva?"

"I don't think it would hurt—" Katherine paused as if to hear what she was saying—"to lock up some of the paint."

Frau Dulac merely sighed. She couldn't agree with her more. The candle she gave to Monsieur Dulac, who went ahead of them, his metal leg creaking. A pool of milky light filled the inner court. They cast no shadows as they crossed it to the stairs. Katherine put up her hand as if to ward off something.

"Bats," Wolfgang remarked. "Bats in the crypt." Howe glanced up to see one against the sky. It dropped as if shot. "Oh!" Katherine cried. A wing fanned the air on Howe's damp face. On the landing they passed two doves perched like ornaments in a window.

"Look!" said the boy, pointing. "They got white feet!"

So one had. Had the mad painter caught the bird and painted just its feet? "I think what's happened—"

Wolfgang paused to try to see a little more clearly—
"I think what's happened is he painted the perch.
Freshly painted the perch."

"Can't something be *done* about him?" Katherine
blew the nose she had been snuffling. In the door to the
stairwell Monsieur Dulac was beckoning. A cool draft
sputtered the flame of his candle; the melting wax had
made a seal of his fingers. The smell of apples was not
so fresh as the smell of paint. Frau Dulac spread her
arms, suddenly, as if to hold them back from a pit that
had opened—on the stone floor of the stairwell, and
on the stairs, were gleaming white tracks. Foot tracks.
The right foot of a large, flat, barefooted man.

"Bear trag! Bear trag!" cried the old man. "Yes,
yes?" The sight seemed to delight him. Hoisting the
candle, he peered up the stairs in the direction they led.
Without a word Frau Dulac swept to the landing, pushed
the door open. Her hands went up as a bird flew at
her, then away, departing through the open window.
Nothing but moonlight filled the room. A tarnished
mirror reflected Frau Dulac, fragments of her, as in
a damaged painting, with a candle lighting her moist,
distracted face. Two cots were made. But only the
cracked washbowl gleamed white. No bear or bear trag
crossed the stone floor.

Did Frau Dulac sigh with relief, or merely blow dust
from the saucer? She took the candle from Dulac and
passed it to Wolfgang. *"Bitte, bitte,"* she said, "place
for two, *bitte."*

"I think you're right here," said Wolfgang, turning
to Katherine, and opened the door on the upper level.
A casement window framed a view of the hills like a

painting. White as if freshly painted, a night pot sat
under the double bed. On the wall near the door a single
wire coat hanger, like an abstract bird. Wolfgang
stepped aside to let Katherine step in, the candle lighting the beamed ceiling.

"What's that?" The boy pointed at the bed. A hide,
black spots on white, served as more of an ornament
than a spread.

"Do you remember," said Wolfgang, turning to
Howe, "that buffalo hide you slept under?"

"Moose," Howe said, "think it was moose."

"Something big," replied Wolfgang. "All I recall is
the odor."

"This a leopard?" said the boy. He had moved in to
lift one corner of it.

"I can't see a thing," Katherine said, "but if it's the
hide of something, we don't want it."

"What's it a hide of?" said the boy. Poised with the
candle, Wolfgang seemed to be wondering. But it was
no leopard. No, the hair seemed a little short. Frau
Dulac moved in to turn down the covers, lift and slap
one of the pillows. A bed was a bed. She leaned on it
to creak the springs.

From the hall Monsieur Dulac said, "You like, yes,
yes? You like it, yes? The dok, yes. A fine dok, yes,
yes?"

"A *what?*" Katherine asked. She turned toward the
door. Without his candle, the figure in the hall seemed
immaterial as an apparition.

"Dok! Dok!" he replied, then in a shrill high pitch he
barked. "Woof-woof! Yes? WOOF-WOOF!"

"My God!" Katherine cried. "A dog? Take it off!"

She would have left the room but it was too dark. "Take it off. Take it out! Will you please?"

Howe came forward to take the hide from the bed. Nothing to it. A shapeless tangle of withered ends. "Out! Out!" Katherine cried. "Please take it out!"

In the hall Monsieur Dulac barked, "Woof-woof!" then a big "WOOOOF!"

"Schlafen sie wohl!" Frau Dulac said, departing.

"We'll be right here next door," Wolfgang added.

"Woof-woof!" barked Monsieur Dulac. "Woof-woof-WOOF!"

"Will somebody shut him up!" Katherine called.

The door of the room thumped Howe as he left. A moment later it slammed, the bolt snapped in the lock. The hide over his arm—he had to hold it high to keep it from sweeping the floor—Howe followed Wolfgang, who still held the candle, into their room. A draft—one that went in the direction Frau Dulac was going—puffed out Wolfgang's candle and slammed the door at their backs. Alone in the dark stairwell Monsieur Dulac barked, "Woof-woof, woof."

But that was all. Frau Dulac was back with a kerosene lamp to look for him, the smell of it reassuring, the glow like a wood fire under the door. *"Schlafen sie wohl!"* she cried, but only Wolfgang thanked her for it. The matches he struck a moment later he used to light a cigarette, not a candle. Howe folded the dog skin over the back of the chair. The excitement had stirred up one of the doves perched on the frame in the window: it cooed amorously, the neck feathers fluffed. Visible from the room was the white roof of the bell tower, an arrow pointed straight to heaven; visible in the room was the white spotted hide of the dog.

"He had a name," said Howe. "What was it?"

Wolfgang inhaled deeply before he answered. "Fido," he said. "Fido Dulac."

Ten

In this room, under the hide of a moose shot, it was said, by Monsieur Dulac himself, in this room lit up by the snow on the roofs, a fine sifting of snow in the cracks in the floor, Howe would lie, in all his clothes but his shoes, listening to the voice of Madame Dulac dug out of the grooves of her Victor gramophone with the dog in the horn. The hint of a line, no more, divided her from some sort of monster visible at a sideshow. A frog with an angel's voice. As Minnie, the barmaid, concealed by the bar, or regally enthroned on a white horse, she had thrilled music lovers in Zanesville and Cedar Rapids in Puccini's *Girl of the Golden West*. Having heard the voice Howe could believe what the clippings said. A voice *out of this world*. A voice like nothing heard before.

Nevertheless she found time, in Cedar Rapids and Palermo, to bear Monsieur Dulac two children, both sons, one fair and pretty as a schoolgirl, one dark and ugly as sin. Howe had seen them, briefly, between Christmas and New Year's, when they came home from the school in Geneva. Briefly, since the pretty one spent the day and night with his mother, the ugly one with his father, riding, skiing, or quarreling with George. With George, the ugly one had had a feud. Something to do with his ugliness, the faces George made at him seated on the roof. With his riding crop the ugly one would chase George down the long corridors, in and out of the courts, into and out of the moats, getting close enough to flick him smartly with the whip, but no more. Otherwise George, who was easily excited, and forgetful when he was playful, might have damaged him. Two, three times a day snow would fall where the ugly one would be standing, sometimes from the roof, sometimes from buckets emptied from windows, sometimes, so it seemed, out of the clear sky. The pretty one, his mouth full of chocolates, wearing a cowboy's hat and bandanna, would lean from the window to aim a real six-shooter as they crossed the court. Since the company had belonged to Monsieur Dulac, Madame Dulac had kept the costumes, a wild assortment of stuff believed by Italians to be worn by cowboys and cattle thieves. A madhouse? Not so mad in perspective. Not a bit madder, and a lot more fun, than the opera Madame had starred in. A vivid scene in the life of the girl of the Golden West.

"What about the boys?" Howe asked. "Don't the boys ever show up?"

The legs of Wolfgang's cot creaked as he moved, but he said nothing.

"Kids like it crazy," Howe went on. "I would have thought they might have loved it."

"It?" Wolfgang echoed. "They liked it, I guess, but they hated him."

"Hated?" That seemed a little strong. They might have thought him a fool, but would they hate him? "He probably scared the hell out of them," Howe went on, "but I don't see them hating—"

"They began to hate him—" Wolfgang paused as if calculating the moment— "when they knew he didn't care for anything else."

"Anything *what* else?"

The hand Wolfgang raised in the air, and slapped on the wall, was visible. "This place. Schloss Riva," as if that went without saying.

"Seems to me," Howe replied, "all he really gave a damn for was himself."

"Gives," corrected Wolfgang. Did he mean that to be funny? "But it adds up to the same thing. Dulac is Riva, Riva is Dulac."

"A lot of men feel that way about a place. Hell, my uncle Fremont feels that way about Texas. His piece of Texas, until it blew away."

"Most men," replied Wolfgang, "also feel *some*thing else."

"You don't think he did?"

"I don't think he did—or *does.*"

"Does? Does he feel much of anything?"

Was Wolfgang considering? Howe could hear his fingers tapping the wall.

"I'd say he feels about the same," said Wolfgang, "and that I never knew a man with stronger feelings."

"The same? If he's senile—"

Nothing that Wolfgang said stopped him. He had merely put up his hands as if to hold off, for a moment, an invisible object. Then he let them fall. "—if he's senile—" Howe continued.

"What if he *isn't?*" Wolfgang interrupted. It was not like him to come down hard on a word, like Katherine Brownell.

"If I remember correctly, I had your word for it. Moment I saw him. Not that I wouldn't have said so myself."

"What if we—" Wolfgang paused, moving his hand on the wall as if feeling for an opening—"what if we just *assume* that he isn't?"

"For what reason?"

As if in connection with some other matter Wolfgang said, "Reasonable? Was he ever?"

"Just what are you driving at?"

"I'm suggesting—" Wolfgang paused—"that he's as *sensible* as ever. Maybe more so."

"I think you also said that that's a moot point."

"I did, indeed. And now I take it back."

Wolfgang released a sigh that seemed to make his burden lighter. "What I'm saying is—I'm saying he's as mad as ever. Perhaps madder. He's not senile. He's *acting* senile—"

"If Spiegel were here, he'd tell you *his* joke. There's a fellow in a nuthouse who leans out to give a sensible fellow advice. 'Aren't you crazy?' the fellow asks him. 'Sure,' he replies, 'but I'm not stupid.' "

Did Wolfgang smile? His hand went up like a diver about to surface, feeling for air.

"You're asking me to believe—" Howe questioned.

The wagging of Wolfgang's head creaked the straw in his pillow. "If you don't mind, Warren, I *am* crazy, but I'm not stupid. I'm not asking you to believe. I'm telling you, this is all an act."

At what point, Howe wondered, did the mind know what it refused to admit? He swallowed dryly. He licked without moistening his dry lips.

"And when," he said, "did this occur to you?"

"Occur?" Wolfgang seemed to find the term amusing. "It probably occurred when I saw him. Until a moment ago it kept reoccurring. It occurs to me now."

"A moment ago? What happened?"

"In the wings of the scene," said Wolfgang, "an old man suddenly starts barking. Woof-woof-woof."

"So what? The kid mentioned the dog. The damn dog was always barking."

"If you will recall the scene—" Wolfgang gave him a moment to recall it. "There was one moment only to start barking. Everything pointed to it. It did not arrange itself."

It seemed to Howe a point hardly worth making. To be senile, or to merely act it. He raised on his elbow to peer out the paneless window. On the roof of the bell-tower snow appeared to have fallen. Was George up there sleeping, or painting the town white? A spectral vision of Spiegel, the watchman, painted white while he snored on duty, led Howe to suddenly snort.

"You see it?" Wolfgang sounded anxious. "It helps if you can see it."

Did he mean something out the window?

"What?" Howe inquired.

"The joke. The joke!" No, Howe had not seen it. Or had he seen too many? Which joke did he have in mind? A little wearily Wolfgang added, "It takes talent, Warren. Even to see it."

"It's a talent I would just as soon skip."

"It's not unusual to turn fact into fiction, Warren, but not many have turned fiction into fact."

"It may not be usual, but the nuthouses are full of them. Fiction's a fact to them all. In what way is he different?" Wolfgang did not answer. "Well, I'll tell you. He runs his own nuthouse. It makes a difference. When his friends come to visit him they play nutty too."

"You have a phrase—" Wolfgang's tone suggested he had not heard what Howe had been saying—"beat the game. Isn't that it? To beat the game."

"We have the phrase, but nobody beats it."

"That's the point I'm making. He did—he still does."

"In those terms, that pretty well defines a nuthouse. A place where anybody can beat the game."

"I wouldn't question some do—" Wolfgang paused as if to check his memory—"but it isn't the point I am making. Monsieur Dulac is not *in* the nuthouse—he is out of it."

"The world's a nuthouse, eh?"

"Some are of that persuasion."

"And if you want to find a nuttier place than the world, just let them persuade you. I've been there. As a matter of fact some of them are my friends. My Uncle Fremont ran a place in Texas that Dulac would have loved—for one weekend. That's the time span. One weekend before you go nutty yourself." Wolfgang was silent. "Beat the game, eh? I wouldn't put it past him.

I wouldn't put it past this character to play *dead*."

As if in passing, no more, Wolfgang said, "I was coming to that." On the wall he scratched a match that left a luminous streak of sulfur. "I was coming to that—" He paused to exhale a steam-like cloud that concealed him. "If you can play *anything*—why not play dead?"

"I wouldn't put it past him!"

"As a warm-up," continued Wolfgang, "you play senile, which is *almost* dead. But not quite. Then you print up the announcements, mail them to your friends, and when they turn up—"

Howe raised on his elbow as if he found it hard to breathe. Was it the wine he had drunk? The coarse sheet stuck like a bandage to his moist body. He threw part of it back. "Aren't you warm?" he asked.

"I don't think I have *ever* been warm," was the reply.

Lying back Howe said, "I wouldn't put it past him." Did his tone suggest that he would like to?

"It's quite an idea, you know. Once you admit it. Although he's not the first man to have it. Play dead—and then wake up immortal. Quite an idea."

"Bygod, I wouldn't put it past him—" Howe realized he had said that too often. "If it's a matter of self-confidence, he has it made."

"I think he has," said Wolfgang.

It was not the assurance that Howe wanted. "It's this goddam place. When you get away from here you won't believe a word of it."

"You forget he never got away from here. That's the point."

Once more, as if for air, Howe raised his head from the pillow; at the same moment a dull pounding sounded in the wall. Was that *him?* Was Howe, himself, nutty as a fruitcake? The pounding stopped, then started again. It centered in the wall above Wolfgang's head.

"Could that be Katherine?" Wolfgang heaved up. Muffled, but unmistakable, they heard someone yelling. The boy or Katherine? Howe was the first to get to his feet. He started off, then turned back to grope for his pants. Silent, but with the haste of panic, they dressed as if the place was burning. Wolfgang, sockless, was the first to reach the door. Howe saw his feet, little more, cross the landing, then heard him try the latch to the door.

"Katherine!" he cried. "The door. It's bolted!"

The shrieking stopped for a moment, then continued. Many hands seemed to be fumbling for the bolt. Stupidly Howe pounded on one of the panels.

As the bolt slipped, and the door swung inward, something flew into Howe's face, wings flapping. He flailed at it wildly. Half crouched, he waited for another attack. Wolfgang's luminous feet, like part of the beloved recovered in a seance, crossed the room to where an apparition seemed to beckon—then wave him off. Katherine. Unmistakably it was Katherine, a lean and awakened Lady Macbeth, poised between them and the window, the cool draft pressing her flimsy gown to her flat body, tucking it between her long legs.

"A bat!" she cried. "I can't stand bats!" Her arm raised, then dropped, like a piece of animated garden statuary, comically draped. Where was the boy? He leaned at the window, his head in the moonlight.

"A bird," said Wolfgang. "I'm sure it was a bird."

"You think I don't know bats? It flew right at me.

Only bats fly right at you!"

Both Howe and Wolfgang turned slowly, searching for bats. There seemed to be none. Nor small birds.

"It's white!" cried the boy. "It's painted white!"

Wolfgang was the first to the window. But it was moonlight, not paint, gleaming on the hood of the car. Where was Spiegel? Their yells had not disturbed him.

"If we close this window," Wolfgang suggested, "I think there'll be no more disturbance."

"No! No!" she cried. Did she think the room was dark? Shamelessly she crossed it and flung the window open. "Air! Air! We're suffocating! I would rather have the bats than no air!" Had she forgotten she stood there in her shift? Howe found the word more appropriate than nightgown. The eyes she turned on them had a madcap luster. A touch of Riva luna-cy? She seemed to see better at night.

"Suppose we leave the door ajar then." Wolfgang discreetly kept his eyes on it. "If something should get in, it might get out."

"I can see how that might appeal," she said, and raised her arms to toy with her hairpins. "I'm not sleepy at all," she said. "Who would like to take a walk?"

Did she mean as she was?

"Ten past eleven," said Howe. "Could that be right?"

"O my God, it seems like four in the morning."

"I'm afraid that's all it is," said Wolfgang. "I have seven past."

"I'd rather be taken for mad," Katherine cried, "than have some fool tell me it's ten past eleven! Darling—" she turned toward the window—"does your grand-mother look a sight?"

"Hi!" the boy said, but not in reply to Katherine. In the moonlight his head appeared to be dipped in a blue rinse.

From the ramp the voice of Spiegel: "What's new, skipper?"

"We had a bird. Katherine thought it was a bat!" A man's contempt for the female saddened his voice.

"Sounds familiar," said Spiegel. "Wasn't a *white* bat, was it?" Howe moved over to peer down at him. The face of Spiegel, smoke-wreathed, reflected the moonlight like a hubcap. With the glowing tip of his cigar he made signs on the air.

"Like me to spell you off?" Howe called.

His head shook. No, one could see that he loved it. Spiegel, the fearless night watchman. "You know what? Room here for twenty cars." He waved an arm to indicate the area. "All this place needs to get off the dime's a new management. Little ad in the *Saturday Review* would do it. *'Lookin' for a Place to Hide? We got it.'* "

"Tell him that's why your grandmother's here, darling. She saw the ad."

A hooting sound, melancholy and haunting, might have come from Spiegel whose mouth stood open. It came again, as if an owl had perched on the painted tree in the courtyard. A freshly painted owl.

"You hear that?" Spiegel asked. "What the hell?"

"Are we going to stand here?" Katherine shuddered. "I'm freezing!"

Howe and Wolfgang moved to the door. Framed in it Wolfgang said, "Would you like it left ajar?"

Did they hear her teeth chattering? Like a shawl, her long arms crossed on her front, the fingers gripping her back. "Do you want your grandmother painted white, darling? It's what they paint towns."

The boy did not reply before Wolfgang closed the door. They stood a moment in the hall, where the mournful hooting seemed to be trapped in the stairwell, one of the ghostly guests. Back in their room, their beds, Wolfgang said, "Warren, where were we?"

If Howe had not been turned to face the window Wolfgang might have noted the smile. Wide, one that might have been drawn on a snowman, sliced into a pumpkin, or sketched on a wall with a daub of white paint. Where, indeed, were they? As of twenty past eleven, visible on the wrist Wolfgang had placed on his forehead, where were they so much as in the carrot-topped, deep-freeze head of the boy? All of them, lock, stock, and barrel, part of a novel that was yet to be written, part of a canvas that was yet to be painted, objects and places so curiously grouped, so freshly, frankly, or strangely apprehended, that the last shock of recognition would be their own.

Where were they? Howe was on the point of saying that it hardly mattered, since it was out of their hands, but the sounds from Wolfgang indicated that he no longer cared. His wrist had moved to cover his eyes, and between his measured breathing, like the strokes of an oarsman, Howe could hear the tick of his watch. Time in or time out? To Howe it seemed rather time-less. In that place where he had gone order reverted to disorder, the flux out of which new order would emerge. One could not help it. Or stop it. It might be described as thy will be done. Time—such time as there was—Howe could see on the luminous dial of the watch, the sweep of the hand like an airport beacon probing the surround of darkness. A surround of darkness? Was that time enough? In the mind of Wolfgang a flickering current lit up a cavern that had been closed for the night. Time-out but not time-off. Glowworms, so they would look, loose in a multi-leveled labyrinth where the watchman, with his time clock, made his rounds. What time was it? Skull time. Such time as there was.

A veiled but orphic awareness of the time-less, like the watch without hands that George carried, induced in Howe a curious vision of time-less felicity. In the upside-down mirror of his mind the loony bin of time was right side up. Momentarily he saw things through the eyes of Monsieur Dulac. What things? Before him he saw a lean shrouded frame, horizontal as if levitated, in the nickel-plated chair of the Hereford Barber Shop. A steaming towel concealed the figure's face. The only sound was that of the brush whipping the lather, as Howe, holding a *Police Gazette,* waited for his Uncle Fremont to return to the scene from which he had just departed, his new face visible in the tarnished mirror. What time was it? The voice of time itself pronounced the word *Next!*

Was it an ocean of time on which he floated? Howe was aware it was neither the best, nor the freshest of metaphors. But that could not be helped. He heard it falling, a light drizzle, on a surface of overlapping circles, pretty as a pattern on stain-resistant linoleum. As for the ocean of time it was there on his eyelids, the curve of space. The drizzle fell in the shallow pan of his brain. Dimly, since the image had a flicker as circle overlapped circle, he saw the backside of a figure dip-

ping water from a bin on a kitchen range. He used a
long-handled dipper, the enamel chipped on the lip.
(To avoid that metallic lip Howe had learned to dip
left-handed.) A suit of underwear, oatmeal-colored, fit
him snugly except at the bottom where the flap hung
open, like the top of a flour sack. A pair of four-buckle
galoshes, unbuckled, were on his feet. The scene was
unmistakably time-past, but the effect was new. Fremont Osborn, inventor of the dustbowl, resembled something new in spacemen: the dim corner of the kitchen
the interior of a rocket to the moon. A dubbed-in voice
spoke up, saying, "Old sport, if it's old enough, it's
new," being the voice of time disguised as Seymour
Gatz. Strange as it seemed, but what could be stranger
than time?

"Spiegel!" a voice cried. "Isn't that Spiegel?"

Howe prepared himself to deny it. Open-eyed, he
tried to focus, through the overlapping circles of time,
on the figure of Wolfgang, stork-like, at the window,
his feet white on the floor. The voice of Spiegel, sugges-
tively baying, was unmistakable. It seemed to be accompanied by the nasal beat of a drum. For a moment,
like a swimmer, Howe thrashed at the surface of time
above him, his head popping whitely into the moonlight,
gasping for air. The door stood open. Wolfgang had
already gone. Calling his name (he remembered that
later) as if he feared to be abandoned, Howe groped to
the stairwell, stumbled into the adjoining room. Erect,
but staring as if asleep was the boy. At a casement the
moon no longer whitened stood his grandmother. Her
gown lapped about her like a shift of light. She gazed at
the ramp as if doubting what she saw. The voice and the

drumming came from a point where the moonlight seemed the brightest: whiter than white, Howe recognized the hood of the car. Whiter than white, to the elbow, was the arm that thrust through the window, waving, the hand that slapped on the side of the door. A drumming sound.

For a moment they stood, without movement, as if the voice behind them had cried, "*Camera!*" and a scene that had long been in preparation was being shot. Behind them, shooting it, was the boy. The drumming ceased, the voice of Spiegel hoarsely bellowed, "Stop the goddam gawking, will you? Get me out!"

Get him out? Had something locked him in? The voice of Spiegel showed considerable strain. His white arm hung limp as if it had been drumming for some time. Both the hood and the fenders had been painted, along with the rear half of one side; on the other side more of Spiegel had been painted than the car. A heavy coil of rope, looped through the handles, passed to the rear where it was tied to the bumper, sealing both doors. Of the madcap painter there was no sign. No, not even a track.

Without a word Wolfgang, followed by Howe, careened down the stairwell into the court where the moonlight glistened on the coin-like drips of white paint. It might have been a draft out of the stairwell, or one of the birds at the bedroom window, but the sound, if sound it was, led Howe to lift an arm, bent at the elbow, as if to protect his head, and with the other out before him give Wolfgang a thrust toward the passage door. "*Run!*" he blurted, to save his breath, and they both tumbled into the passage. There, in the darkness, they stood wheezing.

"May I ask—" began Wolfgang, but it was pointless. Howe knew only too well why he had panicked, but he was not fool enough to say so. That he had heard, or *thought* he heard, snow sliding from the roof. Heard the soft sibilant hiss of it across thirty years, a meaningless time vacuum. When he had put foot in the court time had picked up where it had stopped, the night the first whispering slide had buried him to the ears. He had heard George gleefully hooting on the roof as they dug him out. Snow had packed down the sleeve of the arm he had raised so that it thrust out stiff, as if in a cast of plaster. For hours it seemed a muffled alarm rang in his ears. For several days, weak on his pins, he had the sense of something indefinable, broken, or out of place. As time proved, he was right. About the neck of his bewildered sense of time a sign hung that read OUT OF ORDER. What order? The order that prevailed in the world. Henceforth, the time that he *observed* was his own.

"A match, please?" Wolfgang was not so calm as he sounded. The match Howe struck, then cupped in his hands, lit up a face all eyes and ears, like those carved in stone on the pillars in the crypt. By its light they saw the white drippings on the stone floor, a smear of white on the door bolt. Wolfgang seized it with both hands, as if to throw it open. Nothing gave. As if he thought someone actually might, Wolfgang shrieked, "Open up!" The paint-smeared palm of one hand he slapped on the door. An ineffectual sound, like a trapped bird flapping, came down the corridor. An owl hooted. The voice of Spiegel wearily bayed.

At the far end of the corridor, framed in the doorway, the white tree stood as a symbol of something. Howe's bare feet chilled as he brooded on it. Once more—or was it still?—he was a captive in Schloss Riva. Like old times, as Wolfgang would say. Just like old times. A snow-white light glowed at the cracks in the door. In a silence like this they had stood on the rim waiting for Wolfgang's nose to stop its bleeding, an empty cigarette pack stuffing his upper lip. It had been Howe who had smoked the last cigarette.

"I must say he planned it very well." The voice of Wolfgang was resigned but casual.

"Like old times, eh?" Howe put in. Wolfgang's laugh seemed a little hollow. He searched for, then crumpled, an empty pack of cigarettes. White-palmed, the hand of Wolfgang hung limp, as if awaiting further word. Spiegel's clamor, the drumming of his hand, came to them like an ovation at a political rally. The people in the valley would think they were mad. Were they right? The glow Howe saw in the darkness was not that of a match head, but Wolfgang's watch.

"Quarter to five," he said. "Isn't this Sunday? There should be several early tourists from Vienna. Look for a rescue between nine and ten o'clock."

"That's a little long for Spiegel," said Howe.

"It will give the paint time to dry," replied Wolfgang. Did he mean to be funny? Without his face Howe could not tell. The clamor died as if the speaker had ascended the platform, enjoined silence. Was the cock Howe heard crowing in the canyon or in Howe's head? "You never married?"

"What?" Howe said, although he heard it plainly.

Nor did it strike him as a curious question. They were merely picking up with a conversation interrupted by a nosebleed. "Oh, yes. Oh, yes, I married."

"You are presently married?" Howe slowly wagged his head. A moment passed before he remembered they stood in the dark.

"No, not presently," he replied. The exchange was casual but formal. It called to mind Howe's application for a post office job. He felt he had a question coming, so he said, "How about you? You still married?"

"There are no divorces in Italy," Wolfgang replied. Howe was about to challenge that when he added, "In any case, one marriage is enough."

Baying like a leashed dog, Spiegel called Howe's name, his hand thumped the door.

"You were her lover?" It might have been, Howe thought, the voice of her father. Apprehensive but resigned. Not without a faint touch of relief. A sound came out of Howe as if Wolfgang had pronounced the word exhale.

"Nope," he said. "Were you?"

"A clever woman," was Wolfgang's reply. "I miss the tooth. Isn't that strange?"

It was not strange at all, of course, since Howe also missed it. The missing link. The symbol of what might have been in the gap of what was not. The taste of it. Had it been rough or smooth to the tongue? These things, oddly enough, did not seem to pertain to the woman upstairs, flailing her arms at bats. No more than Howe pertained to the young man who did not catch her cold. Nor Wolfgang who had missed more than her tooth. Circle overlapped circle, and memory proved to be the great falsifier, a cheat to which the word experience was extraction without pain. The word time accumulation without addition. Only a madman, like Dulac, would turn time endwise, bottoms-up, letting the hourglass trickle in reverse. An illusion to displace a delusion—would he put it like that? Probably not. To put it was to give it the lie. The moment. The given-taken moment contained such time as there was. In the darkness of this corridor at Riva, pointing at the green dawn in the door frame where time—as much as Howe might have it—widened like a circle on the space, an apt word for it, known to be located between Howe's ears. In that frame, like the first man casting his humped shadow before him, the figure of George, pail in hand, appeared. What had he been up to? Painting the moon, that hung like an ornament in his white tree? Did he see their eyes glowing at the back of his cave? If so, he little cared, a shutter clattered on the wall above his head, and like Caliban, sensing trouble, he wheeled and went off.

"That's Katherine!" In his haste Wolfgang collided with Howe, his white paint-smelling hand brushing his face. Close on his heels, Howe entered the court. Had she found another bat? Her voice was both anxious and hushed. From the door to the stairwell she spoke to them as if the boy had gone to sleep.

"Good God! Where were you?"

Over her flimsy gown she had slipped her raincoat. Her breath smelled of the tobacco her fingers, with the shell-like nails, plucked from her lips.

"Yes, yes—" Wolfgang led them off as if to keep her silent. Howe peered into the room without seeing the

boy, the floor white with moonlight. A creaking floor
board led her to stop and hush at them, as if she heard
something, then lead off without comment. Wolfgang
stopped where the window slanted to the rear court.
Was it the white tree? The light, a blend of the green
dawn and the waning moon. A spectral scene, as Howe
would imagine it on a lunar-lit but verdant planet, one
of the strange inhabitants crouched munching an apple
at the foot of the tower. Beside him the paint that kept
the planet bright. With it he had freshly daubed the
moon, low in the sky. Old trees were made new. He
rested a moment before turning to paint the world white.

The head of Wolfgang wagged but he said nothing,
since Katherine had put her hand to his sleeve. The
door she pushed open had been left ajar, as if Frau
Dulac had been waiting up for them. She sat near the
window, her braids down, the tasseled ends topping the
apples in her lap. Had she been in the orchard picking
them? Her feet were bare and looked wet. Monsieur
Dulac's straw hat, on the floor at her side, served as a
container for the wormier apples; the good she kept
in her lap. She glanced up to see who entered, her scalp
gleaming at the part in her hair.

"*Bitte?*" Wolfgang said, but her head wagged, and
she extended him an apple as if to keep him quiet. So
they stood, as if waiting to be asked in. A moment
passed before Howe, at Katherine's elbow, saw the
carrot-topped head of the boy in the shadow, like a wig
that had been hung on the post of the bed. Tipped
slightly, attentive, he gazed at the figure propped in the
shadow, the tasseled nightcap back on his head. No
visible tremor. Motionless the tassel clung like a cotton

burr in his bearded face. In his lap, the palms down, the hands were placed. Not crossed, not merely idle, but as if to locate the legs beneath the covers. At the foot of the bed, up like a grave marker, was one socked foot.

Had the racket on the ramp disturbed him? No, it had not. He slept. He slept a time-less breathless sleep. Neither the clamor of Spiegel nor the talk of guests would trouble him. How did one know—since they knew—that from this sleep Monsieur Dulac would not awaken? There seemed to be, strange to say, more life in it. This was not so unusual. One felt the same about an empty house. Vacant, one sensed to what extent it was occupied. But to the ordinary something new had been added. Was Monsieur Dulac playing at death to cheat life? Did he play it so well that it was lifelike, this sleep of death? It deprived the scene of its customary shroud; like the boy they stood attentive, apprehensive, waiting for the moment that the tassel wagged and the voice shrieked *Booooo!* One couldn't put it past him. Least of all, something like that. On whose authority could this plant be said to be dead? The seed sown in the seed-box head of the boy? Katherine, moving in behind him, took the boy's hand without comment, drawing him along with her into the hall. As she did the scent of apples, firm and rotten, the smell of compost in the dark corners, was like that of a storm cave, a burial site strangely appropriate to the remains, such as they were, of Monsieur Etienne Dulac. The sound they heard was Frau Dulac using the tassel of one braid to sweep the dust from her lap.

Skull time—wouldn't that do for all of them? A form of daylight time salvage, a deep-freeze where time was stored like the mammoth in the Siberian cake of ice. In his stomach green grass, on his flanks red flesh on which time had left no marking. But even that was less timeless than Howe's non-melting pond of ice. No thaw would reach it. In the round of his skull that time had stopped.

To bear in mind—what was that but the gift of life? The sane man and the madman had it, the junkman's yen for salvage. A lock of hair, a ring, a looted ruin. What could possibly be more commonplace, or more miraculous? Monsieur Etienne Dulac, the madman who had put time in its place. What place? The madcap round of his skull. Ridiculous the waste sad time on the clock's face, on the rock's face, on the moon's face, or the timeless face of Dulac. What time was it? At any moment such time as there was was present. It came and went unbidden, as Brian Caffrey had come to Riva, and would take away with him his own time-less report. Howe would never know, nor if he knew would recognize, the image that would one day emerge, like the mammoth, from the deep-freeze between his ears. Was that why it seemed a good place to hide? What, after all, was this Riva, this apple-scented bier for a madman, but a symbol, suitably haunted, of the mind? A looted ruin crowded with ghosts. That time-cheat, Monsieur Dulac, no longer truly lay on his bier of apples, but had been borne away in Brian Caffrey's block of ice.

At the window the head of Wolfgang was that of a moonlit gargoyle. To what did he listen? On the slope below Riva a hornet-like droning. The windshield of a car played with the sky's green light. Would that be Ehrlich, or Gatz, looking for a place to hide? Was this

it? Howe wondered what he might say. How sell or
lease this dispersed piece of property? The largest active
holding freshly staked out in Brian Caffrey's mind.

"I think it's Dr. Hofer—" Wolfgang said, and
leaned far out as if to hail him. He flagged his hand,
then he removed and waved his cap. A horn tooted.
Wheels spun in the applesauce greasing the drive. Perhaps this racket awakened Spiegel: once more his hand
drummed on the car. Hoarsely he bellowed. The horn
tooted. One might have thought he had arrived too late
for the boat.

Hadn't Wolfgang once referred to it as the Ark? Was
it the sight of Wolfgang, at the porthole, waving good-
by, good-by, or did Howe feel a shudder in the ancient
timbers, the tip of the floor? Unmistakably he had the
sensation that they were drifting, departing; the Ark
of Riva was about to sail off in space. Not that it surprised him. It had always been out of this world. It
seemed only fair that Monsieur Dulac, the cheat who
had turned the clocks backwards, should cheat time just
as he had hoodwinked life. Sail off, drift away leaving
Dr. Hofer frustrated as always, with Spiegel making
the sound of a portside farewell band. This illusion
would pass—indeed it was passing even as Howe tried
to describe it—but on the time of his life it would leave
its snail-like time-less track. He, too, like the Meister
of Riva, and the countless cheats of smaller kidney, in
such a fashion toyed with the facts of life.

The flagging arm of Wolfgang stopped waving long
enough for him to glance at his watch. What time was
it? The same time always. The illusive, delusive time of
one's life. A bier of rotting apples, or a fresh compost

behind a child's green eyes. Did it make one weep or smile? On Howe's face it forced an expression that was neither one nor the other; the lines that formed were new to his face and cracked his lips. A voice below the window was calling out the name of Howe.

"He seems to know you—" Wolfgang moved aside to let Howe lean from the window. A green bug of a car had joined the two white ones on the ramp. It looked smaller than the man who stood beside it, moon-faced and hatless. He had left the motor running. The exhaust flicked the long-stemmed grass at the rear.

"Old sport—" called the voice, but in the light of dawn Howe may have looked peculiar. Ghostly even. White as if freshly painted white. Seymour Gatz stared like a man confronted with the sun's eclipse, then turned to look at Spiegel, his white arm dangling from the car. Like a simpleton, he gave the door several slaps. Over the scene, for future reference only, Gatz passed the trained eye of a tax assessor. Did this look like a place to hide? Not to Gatz. Like a genie into a bottle, he disappeared into the car. Cool, indeed, was the prospect at his side: a mask with dark glasses. Hyena fashion, Spiegel howled as they drove off. Down they went, through the compost of the orchard, along the road where the wires dipped like a clothesline, down, down to where the time of the day could be plainly read on the clocks.

"Know what?" yelled Spiegel. "He thinks we're nuts. He can hardly wait to tell 'em we're all crazy. Don't let it worry you. I'm thinkin' of buyin' the place myself."

There was a pause. The passage of the car through the streets of Muhldorf had aroused the dogs.

"Mr. Spiegel," pronounced Wolfgang, "would you drive to Stein and report an emergency to Dr. Hofer? Monsieur Dulac seems to have died in his sleep."

A simple statement of fact? Like an echo from the moat the answer came back to them, "Dead, eh? You sure?"

Wolfgang made no comment. Enough was enough. His tone had been that of a man among delinquents about to riot.

"Know what?" observed Spiegel, in a reflecting mood. "Damn if I didn't forget to tell him to undo me." It didn't seem to upset him. He was trapped in the car but he still had the keys. A match flared inside the cab. A cloud of smoke puffed out as if he had caught on fire. The sun, pointing out the strange captivity of Spiegel, glowed orange on the windshield as he backed the car around. One tire was flat. He kept that in the weedy fringe on the road. On the rear, with the last of his paint, George had sketched in the face of a pumpkin, not un-like the one that Seymour Gatz had tipped to the sky.

In the room at his back the light had brightened so that Howe could see the apples, row on row, lining the shelves just above the dead man's head. Undisturbed, Frau Dulac went on sorting the good from the bad. Nothing seemed lacking; the bearded face smiled as if he saw, through the casement window, the car with its captive driver making its way toward Stein, to report the death, as had been done so often, of Monsieur Etienne Dulac.

P1